The Day the Market Crashed

W̲e believe that present conditions are favorable for advantageous
investment in standard American
securities.

HORNBLOWER & WEEKS

ESTABLISHED 1888

42 Broadway   *731 Fifth Avenue*

NEW YORK CITY

BOSTON   NEW YORK   CHICAGO   CLEVELAND
DETROIT   PROVIDENCE   PORTLAND, ME.   PITTSBURGH

*Members of the New York, Boston, Chicago, Cleveland, Pittsburgh and Detroit
Stock Exchanges and the New York Curb Exchange*

THE DAY

THE MARKET

CRASHED

by Donald I. Rogers

ARLINGTON HOUSE

New Rochelle   *New York*

Library of Congress Catalog Card Number 71-154409

ISBN 0-87000-124-8

MANUFACTURED IN THE UNITED STATES OF AMERICA

TO MAUDE L. ROBINSON
with unending gratitude
for my
Greatest Gift

Contents

Introduction

~~~~~~

I was ten years old when the Great Market Crash of 1929 occurred. I do not recall the day, nor do I remember any of the discussions that must have taken place in my home. I do know that my father was a small investor in Wall Street (he never thought of himself as a speculator) and that many of my nearer kinfolk were also involved in the market.

I do know that all in my family who were "in the market" prior to October 24, 1929, lost their investments and that some lost even more than that. In this manner the day affected me, and this I remember. I remember its aftermath, the Great Depression.

For the next twelve years, until Pearl Harbor caused America to stop holding its breath and shift gears into industrial production and manpower mobilization, I was affected both as an adolescent and as a young man, as were millions of other Americans.

We grew up in a land where hunger was as near as your neighbor's home; where, in many towns, the unemployed outnumbered the gainful workers by a wide margin; where newspapers and kraft grocery bags were saved to make innersoles for shoes; where little more than twenty-five percent of the high school graduates could ever hope to go on to college; where aching teeth were allowed to rot to stumps because dentists were a "luxury"; where people sat on flagpoles for prizes, danced in marathons for purses, and allowed themselves to be buried alive in quest of an endurance record and a much-needed award.

We matured in a nation where life was hard but surviving was easy; where family "togetherness" was so universal it didn't have to be explained; where hope remained, but the people marked time, moving their feet in one spot, waiting for something—anything—to happen.

Millions of us grew from childhood to adulthood in a land that was stagnating, and the cause was said to be the crash.

In fifteen years of working amid the magical canyons of Wall Street, I sought in vain an answer as to why the crash took place, and more importantly, whether it could ever happen again.

I think I know the answers now. I have a better idea as to why there was a crash. I have a better understanding of the safeguards that will make another, should it ever occur, the result of man's determined folly, rather than the product of mishappenstance, as was essentially the case with the crash of '29.

We are a more sophisticated people than we were in 1929, taught to be wiser by that cruelest instructor of all, experience.

The memory of the Depression, spawn of the crash, sustains a specter that hovers over and affects American thinking two score years later, and exercises greater influence on our national planning—our projects and programs—than anything else, with the exception of military defense.

Many of the great social strides of the last forty years that are designed to alleviate man's suffering, to level off his "ups and downs" and to eliminate his peaks of well-being and valleys of want, stem from the ghosts of the Great Depression, and spring from the universal resolution vowed in the darkest days that "when the nation is on its feet again," steps would be taken to preclude forever the recurrence of such a disaster.

Never again, we said then, would we allow this to happen. This was the dream of men who were forced to grow old and die before their time; it has endured as the Great American Dream.

Or has it? Is it fading now, as we move farther away in time from that tragic end to the decade of the Roaring Twenties? Have we forgotten, in these days of new challenges, that to avoid another Depression, we must also avoid another market crash?

When I first went to Wall Street there were men still there—brokers and other professionals—who had survived the crash of '29. They spoke of it with pride and some awe, as do combat veterans, downplaying the horror and tragedy and emphasizing the glamour and excitement and the strengthening quality of travail.

There were many men in those earlier days who had weathered the Depression on Wall Street, when it was a ghost town, haunted, unwanted, avoided. They, too, related their experiences proudly, saying that people who sold securities in later years were mere "order-takers," who knew nothing of the real kind of salesmanship that was required when everyone was broke and Wall Street was a dirty name, even in the White House.

Wearing their medals, their scars, their unhealing bruises, and husbanding their memories, most have limped off to retirement or to their ultimate reward. Soon even the memories of the remembering men will disappear from Wall Street, but never the memory of the crash.

Can it happen again? Will it happen again?

No scholarly effort is made in this work to answer those questions, but perhaps the reader, living again minute by minute, hour by hour through the terrible day of October 24, 1929, will find the answers, for the mistakes that were made then are obvious to the retrospective reader. But lucidity, like beauty, is in the eye of the beholder.

In this story I have been permitted to experiment with

a new form of literary journalism, to superimpose some fictional characters against an accurately documented background occupied by real people.

Harry and Helen Weedon are not real people, nor is Eddie Gallant, nor are any of the folks you meet at Raymond & Company's stock exchange firm. Fictional, too, I'm sorry to say, are Marcy and Carrie Fitton, whom I came to admire.

All other characters and characterizations are real, many of them prominent in the history of their time. All other facts are, as near as can be determined, accurate and documented. Because of the license permitted me with some fictional characters, I have tried to be scrupulous with all other details of fact.

Oddly, there seems to be skimpy biographical material about W. C. Durant, founder and twice president of General Motors, who must surely have been one of the most spectacularly impressive men of the times. This led to suspicion that the wily Durant had contrived to keep his name out of the papers. With some digging, it was learned that he had, indeed, retained a firm to serve as a "buffer" between himself and the press.

The reason for this was explained. Mr. Durant remained highly active as a Wall Street entrepreneur almost until the day he died, and he didn't like news of his affairs to be made known to the public until he was ready to reveal it formally.

The author owes special thanks to a number of people who helped make this book possible: my publisher, Neil McCaffrey, and my editor, Martin Gross, for helping me find prodigious amounts of research and for allowing me to produce some experimental journalism, the real and the fictional blend in one puree; Gerald M. Loeb of E. F. Hutton & Co.; Thomas Britland, Jr., Fall River historian;

and some of my important teachers, from Edward C. Hansen of the *Providence Sunday Journal,* who first showed me how a board room operates, to C. Norman Stabler of the *New York Herald Tribune,* John P. Forrest of the *New York Times,* Tom Staley of Reynolds & Company, Richard A. Holman, publisher of the *Wall Street Transcript,* and Joachim Silbermann of Fiscal Information Service. To them all, my thanks.

Special thanks now and ever, to my gentlest but most persistent editor and associate, Marjorie R. Rogers, who knows what I meant when I dedicated this book to my mother-in-law, and to that very special critic, Lynn Rogers Wallrapp.

CHAPTER 1

Thursday, October 24, 1929

6:00 A.M.

~~~~~~

Dimly, through the soft shroud of sleep, Helen heard the ring of the telephone. She snuggled deeper in the blanket and instinctively edged toward Harry's nest-warmth, then remembered that he wasn't there. The phone sounded again, two long rings, then paused, and repeated the signal, two rings and pause; two rings and pause.

She swung her legs over the bed's edge and sat up, pushing her bobbed hair up from her face as her toes sought the feather-trimmed mules Harry had bought her for her birthday, saying they were from Mouse, their not-quite-black Scottie dog. Their blue-dyed Maribou feathers and satiny material matched the nightie and negligee that Harry, himself, had given her. She kicked the footwear away, deciding it would impede her.

Down in the living room the telephone continued its summons; completely awake now, she straightened and lunged toward the bedroom door, then, remembering her nakedness, snatched up the wraparound housedress from the back of the chair and buttoned it around her as she raced toward the stairs.

It must be Harry, she thought, calling from New York. Why would he call at this ungodly hour? Maybe he was sick. Or maybe he wasn't going to stay the full week and would be coming home tomorrow instead of Saturday. Maybe he was going to catch the Detroiter tonight instead of tomorrow night.

The ringing stopped as she reached the bottom stair and snagged her bare toe on the tin toy Mack truck that Rick had left there.

Cursing mildly—for she was schooling herself to cleanse her language—she made the remaining distance in two strides and snatched the receiver from its hook on the phone's left side.

"Hello?" she shouted as she picked up the speaking instrument and collapsed breathlessly into the easy chair. "Hello?" The line sounded dead.

She jiggled the hook.

"Number?" the operator asked.

"Central, was someone ringing two on this line?"

"Yes, Ma'am," the operator said, "I think it was someone on the 949 line."

"Oh, yes," Helen said, "thanks. Would you ring 949-ring-4?"

"Moment," Central said, and after a metallic click, Helen heard the imperative buzzing sounds going off across the wires to Berkley. It was not a toll call from Birmingham to Berkley, though there had been stories in the paper suggesting that the phone company might put toll zones in all of Detroit's suburbs. Harry was in favor of it, but only because he owned telephone stock and hoped the company would make more money.

Kate answered after the second ring.

"Hey," Helen greeted her sister, "did you call me?"

"Yes. I had to tell you. He's done it again."

"John?"

"Yes. He never came home at all last night. He stayed in the city for dinner, and—"

"Gee, I hope nothing's wrong," Helen said. She was reluctant to point out the obvious, that John was plastered again on bootleg booze. But there was no need to.

"Oh, Helen," Kate wailed, "he promised me. He said he wouldn't touch it again after poor Wally Hendirker went blind from it. And you know they think that's what killed Joanie Palmer. It's all from the same bootlegger—Sam what's-his-name, the one who brings it over from Canada in the farm truck."

"Well, maybe it's something else. Maybe he really got tied up or something."

"Tied up? Planning the Christmas merchandise display all night long? He could plan it for Hudson's entire store in that time. Besides, he could have called. No, I know he went down to that Veterans' Social Club on the East Side. That's where they get it, you know. And even if you're a member, it's fifteen dollars for the Canadian stuff, and that's just as poisonous as the Chicago booze by the time they get through cutting it."

"Do you want to come over here?" Helen knew that Kate would be calling with bulletins every fifteen minutes all day long, anyway.

"Well, I'll have to take the streetcar. John's got the Ford—"

"I'll come get you. A little after nine. I have to get Rick off to school first."

"That son-of-a-bitch John. He thinks he's just the cat's meow, anyway," Kate began a familiar plaint.

"Oh, he's all right, Kate. There are lots of worse husbands."

"Well, I know how to handle *him.*"

"Okay, I'll see you after nine." Helen replaced the receiver. John, she mused, was, indeed, a son-of-a-bitch, but she did know a few things about her sister that might cause a man to be tempted to go astray now and again, particularly if he got hold of some bad booze.

Pushing herself out of the too-soft seat of the over-stuffed chair, she glanced out the window in time to see the bicycling boy from the *Detroit Free-Press* toss her paper under the lilac bush and pedal off too rapidly for her to scold him about the consistent imperfection of his aim. Barefoot, she went out to the front porch and down the steps to the lilac bush, its full foliage now a dull green, as if waiting for the *coup de grâce* of the first frost which hadn't yet reached down to the Detroit area, though the papers last week had reported a heavy snowfall in the Upper Peninsula region and yesterday there had been sleet mixed with wet snow right in Birmingham.

She bent to retrieve the paper from the whiplike spears of new lilac growth and remembered too late that the short garment she wore, reaching to an inch above mid-thigh, was revealing to the awakening world that she was unencumbered by other clothing. She straightened quickly and glanced across the street.

She hoped Joe Francoeur hadn't been looking out the window. He would kid her for weeks about her "cute little ass," and she knew that Harry was getting a little upset already with Joe's overintimacies, which, Heaven knew, she had never encouraged except perhaps for that Labor Day weekend a year ago when the four families in the immediate neighborhood had made a batch of bathtub gin and had gotten smashed making orange blossoms. (She still couldn't drink orange soda pop without gagging.) She had no recollection of what might have happened at that party, anyway, though Joe had ever since treated her with an air of shared private knowledge.

She went quickly into the house, closing the door solidly behind her, and glanced at the headlines.

Senator Reed Smoot was still embroiled in big discussions about the tariff. She skimmed that. Harry said she should know about the tariff because it was going to protect their fortune, the one that was building up in their account with Raymond & Company, stockbrokers.

Helen was more interested in the news of the Washington trial of Albert Bacon Fall, who had been President Harding's Secretary of the Interior and who now was accused of having taken a bribe of $100,000 from oilman Edward L. Doheny, the man who was involved with Harry F. Sinclair in the Teapot Dome Scandal. She had begun reading about Teapot Dome because of its curiously compelling name.

In common with many Americans, Helen Weedon felt that it was cruel to allow Mr. Fall to be brought to trial.

Why, he was brought into the courtroom on a stretcher, and made to testify either from his wheelchair or from a cocoonlike nest of blankets in a morris chair that had been placed there especially for him. It was obvious to any who read the stories or looked at the newspictures in the papers, that the poor man was on his way to the grave.

In Charlotte, North Carolina, Helen read, another trial was progressing toward its close. The state was trying a group of Communists who had sought to organize the textile workers in Gastonia, but instead had set off the bloody Gastonia labor wars earlier in the year when, among many others, Police Chief Orville F. Aderholt had been shot dead.

Helen was interested because she was of two minds about the unions. Some of the stories she had read of working conditions—to say nothing of the pitiful wages paid to workers—in those Southern textile mills made her believe that the unions might be needed there. But Harry, a draftsman in the design department at Fisher Body Works and what speakers were beginning to describe as

a "white-collar worker," considered the unions anarchis-
tic, regressive, dangerous and un-American. He expressed his views on this most emphatically.

Helen began to hum "I'm Just a Vagabond Lover," as
she turned to the women's pages of her paper and noted
with pleasure that the upcoming winter fashions decreed
the matchstick profile with a beltline low on the hips
beneath a virtually straight waistline and bustline.

A closer inspection of the photographs showed the belt
to be well down on the buttocks and she reflected, smugly,
that she would do justice to the style, for she was not
bothered by "Lordosis," or the overly rounded stern that
the girdle ads warned against—in spite of Joe Francoeur's
sly remarks. As for the rest of the profile, well, up top she
had no problems at all. She was almost as flat as a boy—
flatter than Harry, by golly—even after two children. She
never wore a bra, even with the flimsiest dress, and Harry
was very proud of her modishness. "Sorority Sis," he
called her when she got dolled up, and when he put on his
porkpie and blazer she called him "Freddie Frosh." Of
course, Harry was a double-breasted suiter with starched
collar to his shirt when he really dressed up. He even
liked to wear spats in the wintertime, for he fancied that
he somewhat resembled O. O. "Odd" McIntyre, America's
best-dressed columnist.

There was the sound of pattering footsteps upstairs and
Helen knew that Debbie would soon be down with her
four-year-old's impatient appetite, demanding breakfast.
She had better light the gas ring under the oatmeal, she
thought, and get the toast ready. Helen always cooked her
oatmeal the night before, slowly steaming it in the double
boiler. She didn't really believe the ads about the good
nutritional values to be found in the new dry "Battle
Creek" cereals and she felt that a child, particularly,

needed something for breakfast that stuck to the ribs. Her two-slice toaster, bought nearly a year before, was a fine appliance, but she couldn't trust even Rick to make toast without burning his fingers when he pulled the toaster doors down to turn the slices over.

In putting the paper down she glanced at an ad for an aluminum double boiler and decided she'd get one of those for herself. She had heard that the new aluminum pots and pans were far superior to the tin, enamelware and cast-iron utensils that were in common supply. She had read stories about an industrialist named Arthur Vining Davis and a metallurgist named Chandler who had perfected and sold aluminum cookware, most successfully.

Half-rising, she folded the paper to the stock-market report and her eyes traveled quickly to the *W*s and sought out Westinghouse.

She stared in disbelief. Westinghouse had closed at 250, down 35 points? It couldn't be. It must be a typographical error. She turned back a page to read the news story of the market's activities, but couldn't find it. Tearing frantically at the paper, now, she leafed through the news section, and then, on a hunch, turned back to page one.

There it was. Wednesday, October 23, had been a bad day on Wall Street. The market had been a bit weak for the past several trading days, the story noted, but had improved on Tuesday. But a large sell-off movement had gathered force, setting off a general decline, and creating a volume of 6,374,960 shares, second greatest turnover in the history of the New York Stock Exchange.

The sleet storm that had seemed of such little consequence in the Detroit area had knocked down telephone and telegraph lines throughout the Midwest, sealing off news of the stock market from the two million "Main

Streeters and Aunt Janes" who constituted the backbone of the avid traders in the auction market.

The early news that had come out of New York had indicated some sort of distress. Then there had been no further news.

Before great numbers of lifeless ticker machines west of the Alleghenies, a large portion of the nation's investors waited apprehensively for news. As the blackout continued, doubts turned to fear, and fear to panic. Sell orders inundated brokerage branch offices throughout the nation, and were relayed by spliced-up wires in time to be recorded before the market's close, and to depress prices further.

The day before, Helen recalled, there had been some mention in the papers of a softening in stock prices on Monday that had induced brokers to call for more collateral from those who had bought on margin, but then there had been a strong rally on Tuesday. Helen had paid the stories scant heed, for with Harry in New York, conferring with the manufacturers of an automobile heater that took its warmth right from the car's radiator, she seemed to have an increased amount of work and responsibility around the house.

But thirty-five dollars—how could Westinghouse lose thirty-five points in one day? Westinghouse was a great company. She, herself, had learned quite a bit about it, at Harry's behest. Westinghouse was building radio broadcasting stations, and was also making radio sets to sell in the new market. It made air brakes for railroad cars, and turbines and generators and elevators and washing machines and other appliances. Westinghouse was a solid company, and Westinghouse was growing, progressing with America's swelling economy.

They now held nearly four hundred shares of Westinghouse, so the loss in value yesterday was close to fourteen thousand dollars, more money than Helen or Harry Weedon had ever spent for anything, except their home, in their entire lives. Their home itself, nine rooms, two baths, and a good plot of land, was worth only fourteen thousand in a good market.

Of course, Helen remembered, they actually hadn't put up all that Westinghouse money in cash. A lot of it was borrowed. They had started buying Westinghouse two years ago when it was selling for under seventy-five dollars a share. Their plan, back in the fall of 1927, was to buy fifty shares at a time, paying cash for half of it, and getting the remainder on margin. On a rising market, Harry explained, they could continue to do this until they were really rich.

Their first fifty shares had cost them $70 a share and they had used up all of their savings and had borrowed some on Harry's life insurance policy to raise the $1,750 in cash to pay for half the value of their purchase. Harry was confident that Westinghouse was going to be one of the spectacular performers, so they didn't worry. Indeed, they were cheered when, day after day, it tacked on gains, confirming Harry's analysis and prediction.

In March 1928, when the stock reached ninety, Harry bought a hundred shares. She had never fully understood the arithmetic of the transaction, though Harry explained that by margining fifty percent they bought one hundred shares at ninety but actually paid for only fifty shares, or $4,500.

On the original fifty shares, bought at $70, they had still owed $1,750, so Harry sold twenty shares at $90, netting $1,800, paid his loan with the broker, and they then owned thirty shares outright.

Since the only out-of-pocket cash they had paid was the

original $1,750, this meant that they had bought their thirty shares for about $59 a share, and the stock was now worth $90 a share (Harry had explained in March) so the profit was a little better than $30 a share, or, roughly, about $900.

To buy the hundred shares at ninety on fifty percent margin, they needed $4,500 in cash. Harry had collateralized the thirty shares that they owned, receiving $2,500 cash, and had taken out a personal loan at the bank for the remaining $2,000.

Using the same technique and procedure, Harry had bought another 100 shares when Westinghouse reached 150, another hundred when it reached 250, and a final hundred only last week at $285 per share.

They had actually bought 450 shares, but with each transaction Harry had paid off some part of the obligation by selling some shares, and had then incurred a larger debt to purchase the additional new shares at the higher price.

Helen supposed that they owned—or held—something less than 400 shares of Westinghouse, perhaps in the neighborhood of 380, and that they owed about $15,000 on their margin account and another $10,000 or $12,000 on notes at the bank—or banks, since Harry was now dealing with three different ones.

But who cared about $25,000 or so in indebtedness when their stock, right today, even after yesterday's sell-off, was worth—Helen did some mental calculations—well, it was worth about $95,000!

They could sell out tomorrow, pay off every debt, and have something like $70,000 to put into the bank.

Bank, my foot, thought Helen. Bank in a bee's knees! That money, if they sold, would go right back into the market where it belonged. Where else could you parlay

$1,750 into a $95,000 fortune in a year's time?

The sound of Debbie's thumping grew louder upstairs. Helen put the paper aside and went into the kitchen. Wall Street, she thought, as she ignited the gas ring from the pilot and prepared to cut some slices from the loaf of bread, Wall Street remained a mystery to her even after their educational visit last August.

Being a junior executive and a white-collar worker, Harry was entitled to an entire week's vacation each year, and instead of taking a cottage at the lake as they had planned, this year they had left the kids with Kate and gone to New York. They really did the town, staying at the Hotel Astor, right at Times Square. They drank champagne at Texas Guinan's, and saw several other "speaks." Each day they took a ride on the Seventh Avenue IRT subway down to Wall Street. Each day they queued up to visit a brokerage board room, and once, after a long wait in line, they attained the Visitor's Gallery in the Exchange.

Harry had been armed with a letter of introduction to someone at Raymond & Company's main office on Wall Street, but it had been unneeded. When they arrived there the first day and found Raymond & Company's office—on the twenty-fourth floor, mind you—a veritable crowd, estimated by Harry at six hundred people, was trying to jam into the board room where quotations were posted on a huge black wallboard that ran around three sides of the room. Boys racing along a platform snapped the white figures (they looked to be made of light metal) into little grooves under the symbols of the stock.

Harry waylaid a perspiring and rushing shirtsleeved man to ask him if he could see Mr. Armstrong, for whom he had a letter of introduction. The man looked right past him and to a man standing in the crowd said, "F'Chris-

sake, Marvin, howinhell am I gonna get 'ny work done
with all these yella-shoe goddam tourists around?"

"Aw, tell it to a cop," said Marvin, and turned away to
be absorbed instantly in the milling throng.

It was later, while talking to a couple from Topeka, that
Helen and Harry learned why everyone seemed so inso-
lent and grumpy around Wall Street.

It wasn't the weather. That was exceedingly fine for
August, unexpectedly cool and with low humidity. It
wasn't the market, either. The averages continued to soar
skyward to record highs.

It was the work.

The roaring market caused unceasing work. "Back
rooms" in the brokerage houses were working through
the night, with crews trying desperately, and not always
successfully, to keep abreast of the paperwork. At a time
of year when anyone with any kind of position customarily fled the hellishly heated canyons of Manhattan's nether tip and sought the mountains, lakes and
shores until after Labor Day, everyone was constrained to
stay on the job and handle the volume of work.

To add to the woes and compound the misery, tens of
thousands of investors from all parts of the nation and
many other parts of the world had decided to do exactly
what Helen and Harry had done; they spent their vacations in Wall Street, trying to see firsthand how it was
they were becoming so rich. They crowded into the narrow alleys of the financial district until, as one observer
remarked to Helen, it looked like Bourbon Street on Mardi
Gras night. Several strolling tourists, with whom Helen
and Harry had struck up conversations, revealed that
they had simply quit their jobs back home and intended
to stay right there in New York, visiting Wall Street's
board rooms daily, until they had amassed sufficient

wealth to retire, which, from the way each one said it, wouldn't be far in the future. Each seemed to have some fixed goal—$250,000, or a half-million, or sometimes only $100,000.

One man tried to interest Harry in the fact that Florida's real estate was a good buy at this time because the Big Land Boom had burst three years before and there were bargains galore, from St. Augustine down to Miami.

Mr. Morton, his name was, and his idea was that so many people would get rich in Wall Street that they'd want to retire to the perpetual sun in the land of the palm trees. He had some plat maps of the land he thought might interest Harry. It was in an undeveloped area of a new city called Coral Gables, being built south of Miami. But Harry said he couldn't turn his back on the stock market at this time and was going to keep everything in securities, at least for the present. It turned out that Mr. Morton was from a small town in Northern Ohio, an admission he made after Harry confessed they were from a small town outside Detroit, and Harry promised to look him up when he decided to invest elsewhere than in the stock market.

Eating in the Wall Street district that summer was a problem, but the enterprising New Yorkers created innumerable back-room "Private Luncheon Clubs," patterned, it was said, after the exclusive clubs where the big shots and regular denizens of the district dined daily. Mr. Morton introduced Harry to the headwaiter of one such club, who for twenty dollars signed up Harry and Helen as members. Thereafter, Harry showed his card to the headwaiter at the door, but it was never noticed, and they were admitted anyway.

It was possible to get a drink—a real drink—in the club. New York had voted "Wet" but Prohibition was still the law of the land, and it made Harry very nervous to sit in the small dining room, filled with strangers, all imbibing openly without thought as to whether revenue agents or cops might see them.

Helen learned to like martinis there, though they burned her throat a bit. The waiter called it a "commuter shot," explaining that the drink was invented at the men's bar in the Commodore Hotel and was designed to give a mighty lift to commuters going into the adjacent Grand Central Terminal. Martini, he said, was the inventor's name.

It was necessary to get to the club promptly at noon, else there would be no seats available until after two, and at noontime it was impossible to walk across the street, it was so jammed with people. It could take twenty minutes to walk the few hundred feet from William Street to Broad Street.

When trading resumed after lunch, though, it was nice to stroll through the district and feel that you were a part of it all, to put your hand into the pockmarks on the J. P. Morgan Building left by the anarchist bomb, or to stroll past Federal Hall where George Washington had been inaugurated and Alexander Hamilton had worked as Secretary of the Treasury and where, even earlier, John Peter Zenger had learned of his reprieve after serving his prison term in behalf of freedom of the press.

Helen was enchanted with Trinity Church at the head of Wall Street and was impressed that it predated the Revolution. After standing beside Alexander Hamilton's grave in Trinity churchyard, she and Harry had strolled hand in hand to the iron fence at Broadway and looked down the stubby length of Wall, that most important street in the world.

"Isn't it strange," she had said, "that Wall Street, which

holds the hopes of so much of mankind, has a graveyard at one end and a dirty river at the other."

Both slices of toast were burning. Well, she'd have to slice some more.

The doorbell sounded.

Now who could that be at this hour in the morning? The toast would have to wait.

As Harry had trained her to do, she peeked through the side curtain before opening the door. It was, she saw, a Western Union messenger boy, replete in green uniform, visor cap and leather knapsack, and with an official-looking pencil stuck behind his ear. His bike was leaning against the front steps.

"Weedon?" he asked, when she opened the door.

"Yes."

"Sign here." He handed her the small yellow envelope.

"Wait a sec," said Helen and went to the kitchen to get her pocketbook.

She gave the boy a quarter and closed the door before she thumbed open the envelope and unfolded the slip of paper, still sticky from the gumming device.

YOU ARE HEREBY NOTIFIED THAT PURSUANT TO LOAN AGREE-MENT WE ARE ISSUING A CALL AND DEMAND ON LOAN REPRE-SENTING THE MARGIN OF YOUR ACCOUNT. FULL AMOUNT OF FIF-TEEN THOUSAND, FOUR HUNDRED FIFTY-SEVEN DOLLARS AND EIGHTY-EIGHT CENTS ($15,457.88) IS HEREBY CALLED AND DE-MANDED AND MUST BE PAID AT OUR OFFICE IN DETROIT THIS DAY.

J. J. ARMSTRONG

RAYMOND & CO

NYC.

"Oh, my God!" Helen cried aloud. "I'll have to call Harry."

CHAPTER 2

Thursday, October 24, 1929

7:00 A.M.

～～～～～～～～～～～～～～～～～～～～～

The knocking at the door became more persistent and Eddie Gallant opened one eye to the semigloom of the room and grunted.

"'Eh?" he said.

"Mr. Gallant, sir. It's the bellboy. You wished to be awakened at seven."

"Oh, yeah. Thanks. Oh—ah—wait a minute. . . ."

"That's all right, sir. I'll see you later. It's Harry, sir. Number Thirty-One."

"Okay, Harry, keed. See you later. And thanks."

Eddie sat up in bed. Gawd, the room was stuffy. And dark. And it stank of that raw Woonsocket booze that the guy had said came straight down from the Vermont border. If it had, we oughtta declare war on the goddam thievin' Canadians, Eddie thought, and shuddered as his belly rumbled.

He tossed aside the covers and strode to the two windows so he could raise the shades and let in some light and some fresh air. He opened the window to the sharp clanging of a pair of argumentative streetcars that were fussing at some parked trucks and the arrogant blare of claxon horns on what must have been an expensive limousine. A smell rudely blended of raw spices, roasting coffee, slack seawater and heated industrial oil engulfed him as he gulped in the fresh air that was blowing around the corner from Weybosset Street.

Low tide in Providence, he thought, smells like the blow vents over the ovens of Hell.

Even so, he liked Providence. He was a big man in Little Ol' Rhody, and the Keith Circuit billed him as a headliner when he played at the Albee Theatre. And they liked him so much here at the Narragansett Hotel that they knocked ten percent off his bill whenever he was a guest.

He liked the Narragansett, too. It was big and old, and solid, with oversized pieces of heavy mahogany furniture, and walls paneled in thick dark walnut creating a cavernous lobby that was set agleam by myriad lights and refractions from glittering crystal chandeliers. It was modern, yet retained the richness of the good days before the war; it bespoke quiet wealth.

His meeting this morning with Sam Glanzman, head man of the Circuit in this district, was set for 9:30 in Sam's office in the Turk's Head Building, and Eddie intended to be on time and in good shape despite the ravages of that late poker game and the Woonsocket juice after the last show.

Eddie stepped back one pace, filled his lungs with air, stretched his arms to each side and in rounded stentorian tones declaimed: "Day by day, in every way, I am getting better and better!" He repeated this twice, with his eyes tightly closed.

Émile Coué, the diminutive French psychotherapist, had made his most serious impact on America's twin search for tranquility and prosperity with this exhortation two years earlier.

Then it was estimated that at least ten percent of the

population daily recited the "Day by day" credo, but Eddie had remained a devotee when others had turned to newer inspiration, and he firmly believed that the daily reassurances that his Outer Mind gave to his Inner Mind did, indeed, bring about some self-improvement. He knew—he simply *knew*—that he was becoming a better person in every respect.

In his secret mind, Eddie Gallant was a bit ashamed of his foray into Couéism. He had been reared in an orthodox Jewish family in the Bronx and he was by nature pragmatic and practical. His father had been disappointed when Eddie—whose legal name was Jeremiah Abramowitz—had resisted the long training necessary to use his good voice as a cantor, and had chosen, instead, to be, in his father's words, "an ordinary song and dance man."

His father never understood that Eddie was also a good "stand-up comic," which made him capable of carrying an act all by himself and thus becoming a headliner. Only last week Eddie had done a show from the Hi-Way Casino outside Boston and it had been carried on nineteen radio stations, among them WJZ in New York, and his mother and father and sister had heard his act. On the telephone later his mother had told him he was "absolutely marvelous," and Shirl had said he was the funniest comic she had ever heard, but his father had said, "Your voice still needs some training."

Eddie believed his future—if he wanted one—was to be found in radio.

He had read that there were more than ten million homes in America equipped with radio receivers, and he had a clipping that quoted David Sarnoff, general manager of Radio Corporation of America, biggest builder of receivers, as saying that within ten years nearly every home would have a set of some kind.

Radio Corporation of America's subsidiary, National Broadcasting Company, was being run by a former utility lawyer from Utah, Merlin H. Aylesworth, and he flatly predicted coast-to-coast networks for the near future.

Earlier in the year, William S. Paley, son of the owner of Congress Cigar Company, quit his job as sales manager of his father's firm to organize the Columbia Broadcasting System, after he had been impressed with a steep increase in cigar sales in response to some radio commercials.

There had been several stories in *Variety* since then, making note of Paley's acquisition of United Broadcasters, as well as CBS's affiliation with a large number of stations.

Eddie was keeping a file on the growth of radio, just as he was keeping notes on the demise of vaudeville. He was never sure now, whether people came to the theater to see vaudeville and his act, or the new talkies.

Playing in first-run houses in Providence at the time were *Gold Diggers of Broadway; The Pagan,* with Ramon Novarro; *Sunny Side Up;* and *Puttin' on the Ritz,* all first-class shows with Vitaphone or sound tracks, all with good reviews, and all chalking up good box-office records so far.

The competition, Eddie realized, was getting tougher. But he figured that the world would always pay well to be entertained, amused and induced to laugh, and it made little difference to the performer whether he stood on stage, sang in a studio or did his routine before a camera. Eddie could see no reason for allowing himself to follow vaudeville into oblivion.

Eddie knew that he was a good comic. He could "feel" an audience and pace himself to it, and he had perfected an instinctive sense of timing so that he could deliver a punch line just right. He liked quick lines. "Snappers," he called them.

He also liked his humor as topical as possible. He had two stories involving heavy Sunday traffic on the Post Road that were usable anywhere south of Portland and north of the Grand Concourse.

There was also a series of jokes involving President Hoover. One concerned a fishing trip; another involved the President discussing with widower Vice President Charles Curtis his troubles in getting Washington society to accept as his hostess his widowed redheaded sister, Mrs. Dolly Gann. A third concerned a meeting between the President and Bishop James Cannon, Jr., the ardent dry and crusading prohibitionist, whose financial and amorous activities had recently been in the news. A final presidential joke dealt with a confrontation between the mild, judicious, pipe-smoking Herbert Hoover and the fiery governor of Louisiana, Huey P. Long.

There was also a slightly off-color story about Primo Carnera's girl friend and the prizefighter's size. The Italian boxer stood six feet eleven and one-half inches, weighed 280 pounds, wore size twenty-one shoes and a size twenty-four collar. In the same vein he had one on Helen Wills Moody's plight when she caused a furor by playing tennis bare-legged instead of wearing the traditional white lisle stockings affected by other ladies on the courts.

Because the football season was coming up he had Zac Goldstone working up a couple of jokes about the manner in which high salaries were being paid to some of the leading stars of the college gridirons. There had also been much in the news about that. In Providence, Eddie eliminated his good little story about the flat-chested flapper from Pembroke who met the deacon on the Merchant's Limited.

For filling in time he had a lollapalooza about a sailor who got discharged in Newport and took a job as a chauffeur for one of the Newport Four Hundred Families and whose first assignment was to drive the flask-toting daughter to Vassar, but narrow-minded Sam Glanzman didn't like him to use it. Also available to him were a couple stories about his mother-in-law (Eddie wasn't married); and a couple about Model T's.

Eddie's songs ranged from such rollicking numbers as "Sweet Sue"[1] (Every star above, knows the one I love, Sweet Sue, it's you) and "You're the Cream in My Coffee"[2] (You're the salt in my stew) to the sigh-inducing ballads, "I'll Always Be in Love with You"[3] (Sweetheart, if you should stray, a million miles away, I'll always be in love with you) and "I'm Just a Vagabond Lover"[4] (in search of a sweetheart, it seems). He ended with a medley of two sprightly new ones, "Should I?"[5] (Should I reveal, exactly how I feel? Should I confess I love you?) and "S'posin' "[6] (S'posin' I should fall in love with you? Do you think that you could love me, too?).

If Eddie sensed that vaudeville was ending, he also reasoned that radio was just starting. He knew there would

1. "Sweet Sue—Just You," words by Will J. Harris, music by Victor Young. Copyright 1928, Shapiro, Bernstein & Co., Inc.
2. "You're the Cream in My Coffee," from the show, *Hold Everything!* words and music by Bud G. DeSylva, Lew Brown and Ray Henderson. Copyright 1928, DeSylva, Brown & Henderson, Inc.
3. "I'll Always Be in Love with You," words and music by Bud Green, Herman Ruby and Sam H. Stept. Copyright 1929, Green & Stept, Inc., assigned to Shapiro, Bernstein & Co., Inc.
4. "I'm Just a Vagabond Lover," words and music by Rudy Vallee and Leon Zimmerman. Copyright 1929, Leo Feist, Inc.
5. "Should I?" from the film, *Lord Byron of Broadway,* Arthur Freed; music by Nacio Herb Brown. Robbins Music Corp. Copyright 1929 by Metro-Goldwyn-Mayer Music Corp.; assigned 1929 to Robbins Music Corp.
6. "S'posin'," words by Andy Razaf, music by Paul Denniker. Copyright 1929, Triangle Music Pub. Co., Inc.

be a place for him somewhere. He wasn't worried. In fact, he felt very secure.

His sense of security came not alone from confidence in his future in the art, but also from his broker. He was getting to be quite rich, thanks to some good investments, among them Radio Corporation of America, whose stock he had bought at about $60 and which was, last time he checked, selling at about $114. His 10 shares of Commercial Solvents, purchased at $100 per share, were now worth close to $515 a share. To parlay $1,000 into $5,150 in such short time was a remarkable feat, Eddie told himself.

His broker had not been impressed with Commercial Solvents when Eddie had first suggested it, and if Eddie hadn't insisted, it probably wouldn't have been added to his portfolio. He had received the tip on Solvents from a candy butcher in the Old Howard Theatre in Boston, a man reported to be worth a quarter of a million in good securities. Inasmuch as his broker wasn't worth any quarter of a million, Eddie figured the man to listen to was the fellow who sold the nickel candy bars in the burlesque house. You didn't have to be a genius to figure that one out.

In the lobby, en route to the dining room, Eddie looked for Harry to give him his quarter tip for awakening him on schedule. He spotted him near the newsstand and Eddie held up two fingers, signaling that he wanted two newspapers. Harry knew which ones: the *Providence Journal* and the *New York Herald Tribune*.

When he read about the market, which wasn't as often as it should be, Eddie liked to read the pieces by the *Trib*'s C. Norman Stabler, and when he read about sports, which was just about daily, he favored the *Trib*'s W. O. McGeehan.

When the transaction with Harry was completed, Eddie went to his regular corner table, pushed back the center-piece of huge ruby-red dahlias, and skimmed the menu. It was an automatic gesture, for he knew what he wanted: two eggs, sunny-side up, fried johnnycakes and sausage.

Not having the johnnycakes at the Narragansett was like declining the baked beans and brown bread at Thompson's Spa in Boston. Served like pancakes with melting butter and pure Vermont maple syrup, they were a delicacy to rank with Narragansett Bay lobsters.

As the white-gloved waiter filled his cup and placed a large silver coffee pot on his table, Eddie picked up the *Herald Tribune.* His eye immediately caught the head-line. Losses in millions. Six and a quarter million shares traded.

Eddie read on. That bum, Stabler. He was hinting at a larger sell-off to come. Trying to scare the people, that's what. He had been predicting a drop in the market for some time. Now he wanted to prove himself right. Stabler was out of touch if he thought the market was too high.

Instead of enjoying the good New Englandy editorial views in the *Providence Journal,* Eddie turned right to its financial section and read with mounting alarm the wire-service story of the market's softening of the day before.

There was reference, too, to that crackpot named Roger Babson of Wellesley, Massachusetts, and the fact that he had stated repeatedly that a market crash seemed inevi-table.

Eddie sipped his coffee and spoke with his Inner Mind to his nerves and tight muscles, just as he did when he was awaiting his introduction in the wings. It would have to be one helluva crash to affect him too seriously, he reminded himself. It would have to drop right through the bottom and into a hole.

If prices had dropped so much yesterday, there would be plenty of bargains on the list today, Eddie thought, and most assuredly there were plenty of bargain hunters around to buy them. He began to relax. Even so, when he had a chance he would call someone over at G. H. Walker's as soon as the eleven o'clock prices were available.

Commercial Solvents. That was the big worry. Eddie seized the *Herald Tribune* again and turned to the list. Commercial Solvents had dropped 20 points. Well, what the hell, it had never reached $1,400 again after the high on September 3, but the 20 points—well, that wasn't bad. And let's see—Monkey Ward had opened at 92 and dropped to 83. Bad, but not too bad.

This, Eddie decided, had been the crash that everyone had been fearing. It had come.

Okay, they had had it, and it was over.

He'd check the guy at G. H. Walker, though.

Eddie decided not to worry, a decision that was buttressed by the arrival of his eggs, johnnycake and sausage.

And when he signed his check for 55 cents, he left a dime tip.

Sam Glanzman, who was not always the most cordial man in the world, waved Eddie to a chair and asked: "Whaddya think of the market?"

Eddie shrugged. "Myself, I have the feeling that we've had the crash. We had it yesterday."

"Phauggh!" Sam said, slamming a hand on the desk. "You talk like you believe we gotta have a crash. Who says? Why has there gotta be a crash?"

"I dunno," Eddie said. "Who the hell am I—"

"Look, crash, smash, bash. Who cares? You know what yesterday was for? And Monday? You know what those days were for?"

"Can't say as I do," Eddie said.

"They were for shaking out the schmucks and the gonifs. We got rid of the scared-rabbit speculators and we got rid of the cheaters. It was a good, honest shakeout, and the market needs them now and then to stay healthy, with only good, real, genuine, gutsy investors in it."

"I hope you're right," Eddie said.

"Humph," Sam replied, and opened a large ledgerlike book on his desk.

"Look, you're supposed to do a week in Framingham next week and then a week at the Poli in Hartford. Right?"

"Right."

"Now suppose I can get these dates postponed—postponed, mind it, not canceled—and you could get a two-week date in Fall River?"

"Fall River? Holy—"

"Wait. Don't holler. Fall *River* you say, like that, like it's a bad place. The city of hills, mills and porkpies, eh? Well, let me tell you, Fall River is one of the quick ways to hit radio. Eh-heh—you're surprised, eh? It's a tough audience they got there. Tough. They're spoiled. They get all the tryouts and the roadshow workouts. If you can please an audience in Fall River, you can please an audience in New York, and the radio people know it. They watch Fall River."

"Sounds great."

"It *is* great. I've been talking on the phone with Bill Canning. He may be able to move you into the headline spot in his house starting Monday.

"Now the thing is this. You've gotta get over there and show him your act this morning and try to get back here for the matinee performance. So you take the Old Colony electric cars. It's a fast ride, thirty–forty minutes. You gotta change in Warren. Then you sell yourself to Canning and get back here. You just call me from the depot and tell me what Canning says and I'll handle everything from there. Okay?"

"Okay. Geez, thanks, Sam."

Sam waved both hands. "Git, git. You gotta move fast if you wanna spend any time with Canning. Git going."

The ride was painless. East Providence, Riverside, Barrington, Warren. Then Swansea, Ocean Grove, Somerset, the Slade's Ferry Bridge across Mount Hope Bay, and finally, Fall River, spread like a toy city on the hill ahead, with the mills lining the riverbank and belching smoke through a hundred tall stacks, and on the face of the hillside ten thousand domesticated maple trees in a citified fall blaze of finery.

A quick transfer to a trolley car manned by a motorman named Mullalley, who seemed to know everyone who boarded his car and was greeted by name by most. Downtown, now, and many signs of the great fire that had swept through the city's center the previous winter, destroying the Pocasset mill and the Granite Block, but signs, too, of rebuilding, renovation and repair.

Mr. Canning was a professional. A quiet man, an observant and careful buyer of entertainment. Eddie's Inner Mind cautioned him to slip into his polite shoes and tread carefully before this guy.

"All right, Mr. Gallant," Mr. Canning said. "Here's your accompanist, Rene Marchand, and here's your stage. I'll sit down here and watch."

Eddie conferred briefly with the man at the piano, then sought the bright circle in center stage where a stationary spotlight mortised a ringed wedge out of the darkness. Once in the coned light he couldn't see the judicial stare of Mr. Canning, and Eddie relaxed. He nodded to the accompanist and his act began.

At the end, in the deafening silence that followed the last crescendo from the piano, Eddie stepped out of the glare and peered blindly into the dark cavern of the theater. He was startled when, from behind him, Mr. Canning said: "Do you think you can cut four minutes out of it?"

"Certainly I can, Mr. Canning."

"Good. I like it. I'll get in touch with Glanzman." Mr. Canning held out his hand. "I'll see you Monday morning," he said.

Just like that. That's all there is to it, Eddie thought. Next, New York. Just one season—well, maybe two seasons—in radio, and then he'd retire to one of these lovely seaside towns around here—say, Little Compton or Tiverton, or maybe Island Park or Portsmouth. He'd even learn to sing in the synagogue too, to please the old man.

When he reached the street, Eddie sought out a cigar store, got some change and called Sam Glanzman to report on the outcome of his audition. Sam made a grunting sound and said okay, he'd take it from there.

In the depot Eddie bought a copy of the *New York Times* to read the market story while waiting for his train. Though unsigned, he knew that the market lead was written by the highly respected and erudite Alexander Dana Noyes. Eddie read:

> Frightened by the decline in stock prices during the last month and a half, thousands of stockholders dumped their shares on the market yesterday afternoon in such an avalanche of selling as to bring about one of the widest declines in history. Even the best of dividend-paying shares were sold regardless of the prices they would bring, and the result was a tremendous smash in which stocks lost from a few points to as much as ninety-six.

Eddie read on, and encountered the sentence:

It might be conservatively estimated that the actual loss in market value on the New York Stock Exchange ran to about $4,000,000,000.

Farther down the column he read:

The collapse of the market in the final hour of trading seemed the more violent because of its suddenness, the mystery which surrounded it, particularly as to the identity of the sellers, and the tremendous volume of trading, which reached a total of 2,600,000 shares in the hour between 2 o'clock and 3 o'clock.

Eddie could feel his muscles and nerves tightening again. Suppose—just suppose the market had been oversold and prices were too high, much too high?

Maybe he'd be smart to get out now somewhere near the top of the heap, and keep his profits in cash for awhile until things calmed down. He wished he could talk to his broker. Well, he'd settle for a talk with *any* broker.

The man at the ticket window nodded when Eddie asked whether there was a good brokerage firm in town "Yeah, I use Bright, Sears," the man said.

Eddie looked it up in the phone book and called the number. He asked to speak to a customer's man, and getting one, inquired:

"How's the market?"

"Market? I can't tell you. The tape is way behind. I don't know how late it is. All I know is there's one hell of a lot of activity."

"Yeah, but is it up or down? Are they buying or selling? Or what?"

"What the hell do *you* think. They're selling. Je-sus Christ, are they selling." The man slammed down the receiver.

By golly, that did it. He would sell out. He was right. The

idiots were beginning to panic. Now was the time to switch to cash. Good hard cash. Nobody could touch that.

Sweating now, Eddie fished in his wallet until he found the Bowling Green number for his broker in Wall Street.

He gave it to the long-distance operator. After several minutes she informed him that she couldn't get a trunk to New York, that everything was busy.

"All right," Eddie said, "I'll hold the wire."

"No, I'm sorry, sir," she said, "the chief operator says that New York calls are being delayed between one and two hours because of the traffic."

"Allll AaaBOHad," shouted the man at trackside.

Eddie dashed for the car. He'd try again when he got to Providence. He wasn't going to let them clean him out of his retirement fund.

CHAPTER 3

Thursday, October 24, 1929

8:00 A.M.

~~~~~~~~~~~~~~~~~~~~~~~~~~~~~~~~~~~~~~

Edward dePlassance Newbord, managing partner of the brokerage firm of Raymond & Company, had spent a restless night worrying about the softness of Wednesday afternoon's market. Such a market was relatively new to him and he was frightened. He had thought out at least three good plans for getting out of the strong position his firm had taken in several stocks—two industrials, one utility and two railroads, particularly—every one of which had been assailed by selling orders.

One by one he had rejected each of his midnight schemes as impractical because in one way or another, someone would have to buy the stock from him and he knew such buyers would be hard to find, at least until the market improved.

But there were strong voices proclaiming that the economy of America—and hence its marketplace—was sound. Herbert Hoover had said so. John J. Raskob, head of the Democratic party, had said so, too, and he was not one to agree with Hoover. Every banker in town had commented on the prosperity's durability, viability or efficacy.

At four o'clock he had arisen and gone to the kitchen to

mix a solution of baking soda and water to ease a feeling of flatulence. His doctor had told him not to take the caustic drink to relieve stomach gas because Newbord presented the classical prognosis of an "ulcer candidate," and the baking-soda therapy for heartburn, the doctor said, was pure poison to the duodenum, that tiny but important tube where the ulcer was likely to occur.

Deciding that sleep was more important than almost anything else at the moment and that it had been eluding him because of the large bubble generated by the peach melba and the two bottles of champagne, at $70 each, that he and Shanty Marlowe had consumed at Leon & Eddy's earlier in the evening, he opted for the kitchen remedy that had been taught to him by his mother.

It proved to be a good decision, for he had fallen asleep almost as soon as he returned to bed, and was ready to arise when Miguel, his houseboy, awakened him at six and handed him his regular full tumbler of fresh-rendered orange juice. Against the advice of Miguel, a true gastronome, Newbord resisted the tinned tomato juice that had recently come onto the market. He knew not why, but he rejected the notion of a vegetable or the juice of a vegetable before breakfast. No one had ever told him that the garden tomato was not a vegetable, but a fruit.

At six-twenty, attired in riding breeches and boots, a belted tweed jacket and soft cap, he was at the front entrance of the apartment building where Miguel, driving the Packard from the garage on Lexington, picked him up and took him to the stables in the park. His canter through Central Park was ritualistic unless interrupted by weather, and at precisely six-thirty every morning, unless otherwise notified, the groom was waiting with the mahogany-colored gelding all saddled and bridled and anxious for mild exercise.

Newbord's enthusiasm for rich foods, as well as for a broad variety of alcoholic liquids, threatened to produce a weight problem, and it was his desire to retain his remarkably youthful figure that sent him to the park each dawn, when less-devoted leaders of the "new" Wall Street were still asleep.

He was even getting to like riding and he was virtually addicted to the fiery, tingling feeling of massive health and of luminous muscle tone that was noticeable when he finished his ride and took his hot-and-then-cold-and-then-hot shower before breakfast. Oh, indeed, every day, in every way, he was getting better and better.

He breakfasted promptly at eight on a different variety of food every morning. He left it to Miguel to make the decision about this, his one important meal of the day. There was usually some treat or surprise. This morning the added fillip was popovers, served with bacon and eggs and guava jelly. Newbord stretched the snaking extension cord of the telephone to a small, low table beside his chair, and while he drank his coffee and sniffed at the dark and veined wrapper of his first cigar of the day, he placed a call to Jules Barnish, a partner in his firm, and second in command of the operation. Second in the hierarchy, but perhaps, if the truth were admitted, first on the firing line.

Jules commuted from Manhasset and was getting ready to leave when he took the call. One reason that Jules was more informed than others in the office was that he spent an hour in the rear seat of his 1928 Hispano-Suiza Cabriolet (with his chauffeur driving on the right-hand side) reading the *Times,* the *Herald Tribune* and the *Wall Street Journal,* as well as numerous other publications. He even read technical reports on radio, automobiles, highways, construction equipment, airplanes, medicine, textiles, fashions, railroad equipment, and, incredible as it might seem, everything that *Variety* and every other publication had to say about Hollywood, the stage, vaudeville and radio. Jules was a nut. A lovable and—let's face it—a *necessary* nut. Every good firm needed a Jules.

"Jules? Ed. What d'ya think?"

"Well, I can't say that I like it. What's to like?"

"Jules, we've got to do something. We just can't sit here and let the idiots in this market ruin us. It's time to shift gears or something. We're the professionals. We have to lead. Have you been giving it some thought? My God, Jules, you stand to be washed out just as much as I do."

"Yes, I've given it some thought, Ed. I've been up almost all night with Marty Hopeman going over our books and accounts. Our margin calls, I might say, and they're horrible. Horrible. If I should tell you right now that I have an answer, Ed, I'd be lying. What's to gain by lying? From now on particularly, no crap."

"Agreed, Jules, never crap."

"Agreed."

"So?"

"If we call all our loans and if everyone pays up promptly, we'll come out clean. Not like a hound's tooth, but clean. But you know and I know that many of our customers have been carrying too much margin and have been borrowing from us too heavily. They borrow, then they borrow on what they've borrowed. Nobody knows who owns the original money anymore. You gotta research a five-dollar bill like you should research the deed to the title for a mansion. Most of these people have more debt than they can honestly handle. If we call in all of our money—and there is no doubt in my mind that we should, even though we called the riskier ones last night—let me tell you, Ed, we're not going to get our money. Not now.

Not right away. The question is: how to survive?"

"Oh, now—"

"On the other hand, if we could watch the market closely today—today, I mean, TODAY—and if we get a chance to unload our Reading or our CNE at a fair price and if we can sell out a good chunk of our American Thread and the Puget Sound Power, we'll make it easy. We'll be in business tomorrow."

"Tomorrow?" Newbord couldn't prevent his voice from ending the word in a scream. "Jee—suss, Jules, this firm has been in business for nearly forty years. I look for a great many tomorrows."

Jules was not at all unaware that Edward dePlassance Newbord, right-side-of-the-tracker and then a debonair, handsomely graying, Pershing-mustached artillery captain just-returned-from-France, had bedazzled the somewhat giddy and giggly Kathryn Raymond with his banter and superior game of lawn tennis and had, in 1920, thus married into one of the fine old brokerage firms of Wall Street, and that when Mr. Raymond had been felled by a paralytic stroke in 1925 (leaving the old man a mumbling corpse who had been kept from sight ever since) the power of command had been passed naturally and with placid confidence into the hands of the broad-shouldered and handsome son-in-law.

"All I can say, Ed, is that I, too, think there'll be many tomorrows for us [he didn't emphasize the pronoun as he might have] but we'll have to watch ourselves today. To-day's market can make all of the difference. If we're lucky and if we're careful, we won't get buxed."

"What? Buxed?"

"New word from yesterday's early margin calls. People got busted because they didn't have enough bucks. So they got buxed."

"Yeah. Well, we can't let that happen."

"Some things we can't control, Ed, like the traders and the bankers. Speaking of traders, what *about* our call money? What do *you* think?"

"I don't know, Jules. I just don't know," replied New-bord with the flat and tight note of fear distorting his voice.

Call money, once the private borrowing preserve of the professional speculators, in the last year or two had become accessible to a great many newcomers whose financial resources remained unchecked and whose financial acumen under adversity was yet to be proved.

Call money was loaned by brokers for short periods of time—seven days, fifteen days, thirty days—to finance stock purchases. With margin as low as ten percent in some instances, an investor could buy stock with only ten percent in cash and take a broker's call loan for the balance. The interest rate was twelve percent per year, which the speculator did not regard as excessive, so long as there was a rising market.

If, for instance, he bought a block of stock—100 shares —that was selling for $100 per share, he borrowed $9,000 at twelve percent. If it increased only one point during the first month to $101, his investment was worth $10,100. The $100 in profit was roughly what he owed in interest on his loan of $9,000.

It was not uncommon for a "hot" stock to gain ten points in a month, however, so that his $100 stock became worth $110 and his investment was valued at $11,000.

Then he had optional courses open to him. He could sell his stock at, say, $110, collect a total of $11,000, pay off his call note with $10,100 (the original $10,000 plus interest of $100) and pocket the profit of $900. Or he might elect to sell fifty shares at $110, receiving $5,500, with which he could pay off $5,400 of his call loan, plus $100 interest, and to take out a new loan for $4,600 to pay off the balance on the original one. Then if the stock gained another ten points during the ensuing month, moving to $120 per share, his fifty remaining shares would be worth a total of $6,000 on which he owed $4,600 plus $46 in interest.

This left him two more courses of action. He could sell his fifty shares for $6,000 and pay off his loan with $4,646, pocketing a profit of $1,354—not bad earnings in a sixty-day period in those days, considering he wasn't using his own money—or he could collateralize his $6,000 worth of stock for a long-term loan at a bank, borrow the $4,646 at six percent, and pay off his more expensive call loan.

In actual practice the speculator would have to use either ten percent or twenty percent of his own money, but the procedure was the same.

Those who had faith that the market would continue to rise—and that included almost everyone—usually chose to hypothecate their stock, that is, to pledge it without actually delivering it, and to get long-term loans from the banks.

It would have seemed natural if the speculators, as they grew richer on paper, would avoid worries by using more of their own money and smaller amounts of call money, but the contrary was true. As more speculators entered the market and as stock prices climbed ever higher, making them richer, they found they had greater amounts of credit available to them, so they used call loans to the hilt.

It was the combination of low margin and readily accessible brokers' loans that attracted speculators from every walk of American life and from all over the world.

Once a customer got fairly well established with his broker and it was demonstrated that he was running an active account with a good deal of "in and out" trading, the brokers, who made their commissions on sales, would encourage the client to engage in as much switching as possible, thus building up the commission sales.

To induce the customers to keep on trading, margin was offered to relative strangers, so long as they maintained an active account.

In the prosaic old preboom market of the early 1920s, an investor would come in with, say, $10,000 and buy 100 shares of Grey & Simpson Machine Tool Company at $100 a share (total bill $10,000) and that's all there was to it. At the end of a certain period, let's say one year, if Grey & Simpson had doubled to $200 a share, the investor had doubled his money and he had a profit of $10,000.

Now, however, in the new, enlightened Wall Street, the traders, emboldened by a steadily rising market, had reduced margin to ten or twenty percent and offered call money for the balance.

Thus the 1929 investor with $10,000 cash, instead of buying 100 shares of Grey & Simpson at $100 a share, would buy 500 shares at $100 a share, paying $10,000 on margin and borrowing $40,000 from his broker.

When the stock hit a value of $120 a share, making his holdings worth $60,000, he'd hypothecate his profit of $10,000 and buy another $500 shares, using his $10,000 as margin and borrowing $50,000. He now owned stock worth $120,000 and owed $90,000. Already he had a profit of $30,000—on paper.

If he chose to honor the call on the first $40,000 he had borrowed—and the choice was his to make because of the increased value of his collateral—he could sell off 350 shares for $42,000. This would leave him with 650 shares at $120 per share, for a total value of $78,000, on which he owed $50,000—a profit of $28,000 on a $10,000 investment. The conventional old preboom investor would have had a profit of $2,000.

When the Grey & Simpson stock hit 140, the margin speculator would repeat his performance, taking advantage of the arithmetical fact that with only twenty dollars required for each one hundred dollars' worth of stock, the value of his portfolio doubled with every advance of twenty points.

When Grey & Simpson reached 200, double the figure at which the investor started buying, he had a clear profit of $310,000—all achieved with a down-payment of $10,000.

The traditionalist who bought 100 shares at $100 and paid $10,000 cash, had doubled his money. He had a profit of $10,000.

This was call money. The brokers borrowed their money from the banks and loaned it to their customers for margin trades. The banks required collateral from the brokers and it was provided in the form of hypothecation of their own stocks in which they had taken "positions," that is, stocks that had been newly issued when they bought and stockpiled them, or other stocks that the brokers considered to be either underpriced or facing a good future at the time of purchase. Sometimes the banks would lend in hard cash up to seventy percent of the market value of a stock averaged over the preceding six-month period.

Thus, in a rapidly rising market, more and more money was made available to the brokers so they could relend it in the form of margin call loans at twelve percent interest. The interest payments to the brokers constituted a sizable portion of their business income so they constantly encouraged the use of margin and call loans. Thus, despite liberal banking practices, credit seemed always to be tight on Wall Street. Everyone was using it.

The entire structure, however, depended on the price level of the market. When prices dropped, everything else slipped with them.

Both Ed Newbord and Jules Barnish knew that if market prices continued to tumble and their collateralized stock had less value, their bank would demand cash to cover part of their loan. Also they were obliged to maintain legal cash reserves as required by the board of governors of the New York Stock Exchange.

They must get cash to survive.

They had two sources of cash: one was from commissions; the other was from calling in their brokers' loans or margin loans. If there was a panic and if investors were forced to unload stock at a loss, those loans would be hard to collect. As prices fell, commissions became smaller. On commission business alone it was doubtful they could remain in business another forty-eight hours.

They both had been thinking the same thoughts.

"Well, the weekend's coming up," Ed said.

"We've got to hang in there for two more days," Jules said.

"Two more days."

"We'll know better at the opening."

"You going to be there?"

"I've already talked to Charley Musser and he says there's a queue of people standing along Broad Street waiting to get into the Visitor's Gallery. I'll be there, of course, but if you come over, you'd better go in the main entrance at Eleven Wall and keep away from the crowds. Brokers might not be too popular—"

"Oh, come, now. I don't think—"

"Why borrow trouble? And don't wear that expensive-looking black homburg. Or your Chesterfield coat, either."

"I suppose you're right. Well, all right, Jules. I'll see you later."

That's nonsense, Newbord thought as he replaced the receiver. A broker should look and act as though he represented millions. It imparted confidence to the investor. There was that damned ticker, though; it kept tapping out the story. The crowd, he supposed, might turn ugly, at that.

He rang for Miguel and the second pot of coffee.

"Miguel," he said. "It's a nice warm day. No topcoat, please, and get out that light-gray fedora hat for me."

As he sipped coffee, Newbord placed another call to Long Island. "Peters," he greeted the butler who answered, "may I speak to Mrs. Newbord, please."

There was a dry cough before the voice said, "Hello?" and by the metallic sound of the instrument, Newbord knew that Kathryn was using the French telephone in her bedroom. He also knew that she was still in bed and that she was smoking, which meant that she had already had her juice, at least, and was preparing to face the day.

"Kay?"

"Hullo, Edward."

"Hello, Sweetheart. I'm just checking to see how things are."

"Checking on what?"

"Nothing in particular. Just wanted to chat."

"I tried to chat last night. Where were you?"

"I thought you were at the bridge at Lawrenson's."

"I was. I called you when I was the dummy."

"Oh. I was at a meeting with some of the boys in our shop and a couple of other brokers. We had a very bad day in the Street yesterday."

"Yes, I know. That's why I was calling. Did you sell my CNE? And my Bethlehem? And my Coca-Cola?"

"No. I don't think you should sell now, Kay."

"You don't? Well I do. And so does Eric."

Newbord tried to control his temper. Eric, who had married Kay's sister Margery, had inherited well over a million and had been to Wall Street only to have lunch in some of the better clubs. Yet, because he was rich, Margery was always relaying his opinions about the market, and Kay, damn it all, was always listening to her.

"Kay, I think you'd make a mistake to sell CNE in a bad market. Central New England Railroad is regarded as an adventure. It's highly speculative. You need a market that's—"

"Speculative? Vanderbilt's in it. So's Morgan."

"They can afford to speculate. The average investor doesn't look at it that way."

"Well, how about getting rid of that silly one—that Coca-Cola."

"I think it's well worth holding onto. Some analysts think it has been one of the sleepers."

"Oh, for Heaven's sake, Edward. It's a soft drink!"

"Well, Wrigley's was just gum."

"That has nothing to do with it, Edward, and you know it."

"I think it has quite a lot to do with it, particularly if we're going to have some hard times for a few months. Low-priced items will—"

"Edward, you're not going to sit there and allow me to lose my shirt, are you?"

"Don't worry, Darling, I'll be right here to take care of you."

"You'll have all you can do to take care of that floozy you see three nights a week—the one you were with last night."

As the shaft penetrated the bull's-eye, Newbord lost his

temper, something he had promised himself he'd never do again.

"If you lose your shirt," he said, "you'll still be wearing more clothes than you were at Buddy Sheaffer's beach party."

"Ohhh!" said Kay, and slammed down the phone.

After some remedial sips of coffee and some soothing puffs of the rich smoke on his Corona-Corona, Newbord placed a call to Shanty Marlowe. He *knew* that she'd be abed, but he also knew that she wouldn't mind being called, for she had the capacity of falling asleep again within moments. She could fall asleep within moments of a titanic fight, within moments of a dramatic and tear-inducing declaration of love for her, within moments of gay hilarity and within moments of one of her not-uncommon gusty and noisily threshing orgasms, which at times threatened to awaken the neighbors.

Her first and second names were improvisations on fact, remnants of her brief, unrewarding and firmly terminated stage career, which she had hoped ultimately would bring her to nightclub stardom in the manner that Libby Holman's early career had brought her to nightclub fame. Shanty could sing "My Man" in a way to make the listeners wish to cry, but, alas, not because of the beauty or the soul of the rendition.

There was something about her, though, that fascinated Ed Newbord and produced in him feverish emotions beyond anything he had ever experienced. In addition to his frantic arousal as a male, he responded to her bewitchment in the one manner that pleased her most: he lavished her with money and gifts. In return, she was lavish with her femaleness.

"Kitten," he said, when he heard her mutter sleepily into the phone.

"Purr," she said. The speed of her responses, even when emerging from deep sleep, always amused him, and now he laughed.

"Why are you calling in the middle of the night?" she asked.

"Look, I'm on my way to the office now. It's going to be a bad day. It was bad yesterday, but it's going to be worse today. And I'll have to meet with some of my staff tonight. We'll have to cancel our dinner. I'm sorry, honey, but there's plenty of trouble in Wall—"

"Did you talk to your wife about Christmas?"

"N-no. Not yet."

"Do you think you'll have to go to Palm Beach with the family for two whole weeks?"

"Look, sweet, I don't see how I can get out of that. Particularly now. I've got problems at home, too. Kay—"

"Christmas isn't that far away, lover, and we've got to make plans."

"I just don't see what I can do, Shanty."

"Holidays alone just kill me," she said.

"I know."

"Well, if you're going to be nailed in a box at Palm Beach, I think you should send me on a cruise of the Caribbean—maybe South America."

"Say, that's a splendid idea. Why don't you plan it out and let me know about it. Really, I don't see how I can—"

"All right, lover. Run along to your meetings. I'll probably go to a movie tonight."

"All right. Good-bye, Shanty."

"Mmmm. 'Bye."

He tossed his cigar into the brass tray on the table and made his way to his bedroom to check again that his tie was straight, hair properly combed and mustache and sideburns trimmed evenly, then, straightening his vest and buttoning the three front buttons on his suitcoat, he picked up the light fedora and the *Times* from the foyer table and punched the elevator button. Miguel, he knew, would be at the curb with the Packard.

His daily egress from the building where he lived was a precise military operation. The elevator man had hovered only a couple of floors away and no sooner had the button been touched than the doors slid open and the uniformed attendant snapped to attention and said, "Good morning, Mr. Newbord," just as though he hadn't seen him in riding clothes earlier.

Newbord nodded. After an express drop to the lobby floor, Newbord strode out to find that the doorman was holding the door wide. At the curb, the Packard was purring and Miguel was holding open the rear door. With brisk strides and a curt nod to both the doorman and Miguel, Newbord entered his limousine as though he were en route to a meeting with several chiefs of state.

As the vehicle pulled away and turned into Park Avenue, Newbord opened his copy of the *Times* and saw the day's problems looming ahead in the black headlines that were stretched between his hands.

On page one he read the two-column headline:

PRICES OF STOCKS CRASH
IN HEAVY LIQUIDATION,
TOTAL DROP OF BILLIONS

PAPER LOSS $4,000,000,000

2,600,000 Shares Sold in the

Final Hour in Record Decline.

MANY ACCOUNTS WIPED OUT

But No Brokerage House Is in

Difficulties, As Margins Have

Been Kept High.

ORGANIZED BACKING ABSENT

Bankers Confer on Steps to

Support Market — Highest

Break Is 96 Points.

CHAPTER 4

The Sands of Time

The age of technology had dawned in America and the need for capital to feed it was brought to Wall Street to be cultivated. It mushroomed into the auction markets of the stock exchanges and loosed the virus of a speculative fever that spread into millions of households from Eastport to San Ysidro, from Key West to Bellingham, directly affecting seventeen million U.S. citizens, and that reached across the seas to attract the hoarded wealth of regal families, the riches of Asian potentates, the fortunes of international shippers, the secret savings of poppy growers and the anonymous deposits from Swiss banks. When the fever had run its course it left the world with its most severe economic depression in history, a convalescence that required ten years and the advent of mankind's greatest and most disastrous war to bring it to an unmourned end.

Within two weeks of the crash, unemployment in America jumped from seven hundred thousand to three and one-half million.

Before many more months, twelve million American breadwinners were unemployed and without hope. Twenty-five percent of the families in the nation suffered sustained hunger and undernourishment to some degree.

In the early fall of 1929, there was no premonition of impending disaster; everyone was still convinced that the war-awakened and Prohibition-parched Junior Giant of nations had found the key to a special self-perpetuating prosperity.

The national capital was named Wall Street and it stretched from Broadway to the East River, a chunky six blocks. The nation had determined that its future was with business and trade, commerce and industry, rather than with statesmanship. Striped pants in Washington looked pretty and might even be necessary when engaging in some deals, but the real heart of the adolescent giant abided in the narrow canyon set between cloud-reaching buildings near the bottom of grimy, jangling, crowded and delightfully corrupt Manhattan.

The man in Washington's White House was a friendly, soft-spoken engineer whom everyone called "the Chief." He had taken office in March after defeating in national elections, the previous fall, Governor Alfred Emanuel Smith, of New York, a Roman Catholic and an outspoken anti-Prohibitionist, who courted disaster by admitting that he liked a tot of hard drink, in a nationwide address over the wireless which he called the "raadio," pronouncing it with a soft *a* as in radical, thus seemingly casting his lot with the Bohemians instead of the numerically superior Babbitts. That Hoover was a good and efficient engineer no one doubted. He had broken with tradition and ordered a telephone installed on a small table beside his desk right in the presidential office. His predecessors had used an adjoining room for making or receiving telephone calls.

Hoover was working on Farm Relief and had brought many great minds to Washington to consider it. He had said that much was at stake but he had neglected to reveal exactly how much.

At stake were the food-producing small farms throughout America, deserted by the youth for the more respectable, less arduous jobs in the cities' factories and offices. At stake also were hundreds, perhaps thousands, of rural banks, left holding the worthless mortgages of abandoned farms. In exceedingly prosperous America, bank failures were mounting in farm areas to a rate of two a day.

World peace seemed assured. In January the U.S. Senate had passed the Kellogg-Briand Multilateral Treaty for the Renunciation of War as an Instrument of National Policy, and every other major power had either already signed or seemed likely to do so. Naval disarmament was a Hoover hope, and it seemed likely to become a fact as soon as the navy-traditionalist British could be made to see the light. Henry L. Stimson, the cool and competent Secretary of State, had been to Geneva to patch up America's past disregard of the League of Nations.

One thing that bothered Americans about being capitalists in 1929 was the fact that they were also consumers. They made goods, but they also bought goods. They grew food, but had to buy additional foods. They thought it was proper to realize a profit on goods that were manufactured and sold and on food that was raised and sold, but there was a problem when those who worked in commerce and industry came to pay for their food, just as there was when the ones who grew produce and meat came to pay for manufactured goods and nonfarm services.

The question was: How much profit is proper?

The problem accrued from vacillating views on competition. If you raised food for a livelihood, it was natural to believe that the rich industrialists who manufactured goods or the wealthy entrepreneurs who performed services should have good, stiff competition from abroad to keep their prices in line. If you were in the trades, commerce or industry, you thought it quite proper for farmers to have some competition from foreign growers to keep food from getting too costly. After all, food was basic. You might very well do without the 1929 model of the Jordan automobile, but you couldn't get along without bread, milk, eggs, meat and some other staples.

All of this resulted in a great deal of tugging and hauling on the complex, hotly debated problem of tariffs, a problem that candidate Hoover had promised to solve.

Traditionally the Republicans, who were in power and who had controlled both Senate and House for a full decade, were in support of high protective tariffs to cut down on competition of foreign imports, especially farm produce. The Democrats, committed by tradition to speak for the nonfarm urbanites, were for sterner competition from abroad to keep prices from rising too high.

Trouble was, in 1929, too many Democrats were earlobe deep in a market where they were trading the shares of industrial corporations which, as investors, they wanted to see grow richer, from higher domestic prices, if need be.

And on the farms were soil tillers who, newly awakened to the geegaws and gimcracks of the mechanical-industrial world, wanted more manufactured items, at the lowest prices possible, made lower by foreign competition, if need be.

The traditional positions on tariffs were no longer definable, and in the White House, the Chief, acutely aware of the conflicting crosscurrents, decided to let the matter be settled by Congress.

For the entire year Congress debated tariff problems as Senator Reed Smoot of Utah, as perfect for his role as though he had been cast in Hollywood, struggled to come up with what—a full year later—was to be known as the Hawley-Smoot Tariff Act. Hardly a day passed that the newspapers did not carry complex, sometimes salty, sometimes humorous stories about tariff discussions.

The tariff was as much in the mind of the average Wall Street trader as it was in that of Reed Smoot, former president of the Provo, Utah, Commercial and Savings Bank, Apostle of the Church of Jesus Christ of Latter-Day Saints, regent of the Smithsonian Institution, ardent golfer, bird watcher and vaudeville patron, widower, father of six, rich, conservative, tight-lipped, and chairman of the Senate Finance Committee.

The difference was, Wall Streeters didn't know for sure whether they wanted tariffs to be higher or lower. Reed Smoot knew what he wanted, and he fought the good fight for protectionism for the farmers every step of the way. His ultimate effort raised the barriers to protect farmers and some others, including makers of clothing, bricks, lumber, glass, cement and roofing materials.

When in November 1929 New York's high-spending, fun-loving Democratic mayor Jimmy Walker was reelected, defeating Republican Congressman Fiorello H. LaGuardia by an eight-to-three margin, the whipped pudgy fire-eater, destined to become known as the "Little Flower," moaned: "People just don't resent graft anymore."

Perhaps he was right. There was much of it around.

Graft, corruption and violence were prevalent throughout the nation in 1929. Much of it could be blamed on the national Prohibition Act, for not only did it breed and provoke violence among purposeful lawbreakers, but the government, itself, scattered many angry bullets among the citizenry, frightening and sometimes maiming and killing innocent victims.

One of the most gruesome crimes of the century had taken place in Chicago—the St. Valentine's Day Massacre. It terminated a year-long feud between the gang of George

("Bugs") Moran, a booze peddler, and that of "Scarface" Al Capone, the nation's Number One gangster.

The scene was a liquor and beer distribution depot on North Clark Street, run by Moran and disguised as a garage belonging to the S.M.C. Cartage Company. In it were seven of Bugs Moran's leading henchmen, including his own brother-in-law and second-in-command, James Clark, and his Number One gunman, Peter Gusenberg. Six were impatiently watching a coffeepot that was slow to boil and the seventh was tinkering with a beer vat that was loaded onto a truck body. Suddenly a long, low police car, identical to those used by the Chicago Detective Bureau, slid to the curb. Out jumped four "policemen," two in uniform, carrying submachine guns, and two in plain clothes, carrying sawed-off shotguns. They ran into the garage.

The hoodlums, at once resigned to the pinch, raised their hands over their heads.

"Line up against the wall," snarled one of the policemen.

The Moranmen did as ordered. Then the same policeman said, "Give it to 'em." One hundred bullets were fired in a matter of seconds; ninety-two entered soft human flesh. With the seven bodies lying on the floor, the uniformed cops with the machine guns fired close-range volleys into each head that showed any sign of life.

The uniformed police then turned the machine guns toward the two plainclothesmen, who raised their hands over their heads. In this fashion the four walked out to the waiting car. To all observers it appeared that the police had made another quick gangland arrest. The four got into the limousine and it sped away, cutting first onto the wrong side of a streetcar, then disappearing into the thick midmorning traffic.

Bugs Moran was five minutes late that day. His tardiness saved his life. The next day, livid with incoherent rage, he sputtered to reporters, "Only Capone kills like that." Al Capone, as unconnectable with this as he was with other crimes in his domain, was at Miami Beach, soaking up some peaceful February sunshine.

In May, however, police discovered in an abandoned automobile in Spooner's Nook, a desolate lover's lane section of Hammond, Indiana, three bullet-riddled bodies. They were well known to police as John Scalisi, Albert Anselmi and Joseph Guinta, proud and professional assassins, members of the dwindling Capone mob, and three of the quartet that had mowed down the Moranmen on St. Valentine's Day.

By mid-May Chicago's gangland had rid the world of twenty of Chicago's toughest gangsters.

Carnage was not confined to the lawless. In Big Falls, Minnesota, Henry Virkula, a quiet man, liked and respected in his community as the gentle owner of a candy store, took his wife and two children for a ride in his car. They crossed the border into Canada, enjoying the scenery. It was darkish when they came back toward Big Falls on a lonely road. The two children were asleep on the back seat. Mrs. Virkula sat up front with her husband.

Suddenly two men leaped in front of the car, one holding aloft a sign that read: "STOP! U.S. CUSTOMS OFFICERS." Virkula braked his car and pulled to the side of the road, but a volley of shots crashed through the rear windows. Henry Virkula died instantly with a slug in his neck.

No liquor was found in the car or on the corpse or on the widow Virkula or on the two little Virkula children. The avenging enforcer of the law explained: "He didn't stop quick enough."

Earlier in the year when authorities in Aurora, Illinois, suspected Joseph de King, 38, of selling liquor from his home, Deputy Sheriff Roy Smith, armed with a warrant, tried to make a search. De King refused the sheriff admittance. Smith went off but returned with three more deputies who threw mustard-gas bombs into the house and smashed down the front door. De King was clubbed into submission with near-fatal blows on the head. His wife was at the telephone calling their lawyer. Smith held his shotgun—loaded with heavy slugs—against her abdomen and fired point blank. She died instantly.

The de Kings' twelve-year-old son, seeing his mother dead and his father presumably dead, found a pistol and sent a retaliatory bullet into Deputy Sheriff Smith's leg.

After the boy was beset by the deputies and subdued and disarmed, the search of the premises was finally conducted. The protectors of the public weal found nearly one gallon of weak homemade wine.

Earlier in the year oilman Harry F. Sinclair was put in jail as a result of his refusal, back in 1924, to answer Senate questions about a suspected gift of $250,000 worth of Liberty Bonds to ex-Secretary of the Interior Albert Fall in exchange for drilling rights at government-owned Teapot Dome in Wyoming.

This was somehow closer to Wall Street—many owned Sinclair stock—and it was discussed in the board rooms with renewed interest now that Fall, aging, suffering with pneumonia, was back on the witness stand in Washington.

The case of Albert Fall shared headlines with the stock-market reports in October 1929.

Much of the talk on the Street and in the coffeehouses and speakeasies uptown (there were 34,000 of the latter in New York, according to police) was of the Federal Reserve Board. Back in February it had stated that brokers had borrowed nearly five and three-quarter billion dollars to finance margin trades and warned that the practice was taking too much money out of the regular money market—cash that was needed by other businesses, and broader interests.

This set off a wave of speculation that the Fed would raise the discount rate, making it more costly for banks to borrow from the Central Bank, but weeks dragged on and nothing happened until August, when the rate was raised from five percent to six percent.

There were other warnings against overtrading and wide speculation and "gambling in the market." One such had come from respected Paul Warburg, chairman of the board of International Acceptance, which had but recently merged with the Bank of the Manhattan Company (and more recently to be merged into Chase Manhattan Bank). Mr. Warburg had been a member of the Federal Reserve Board from 1914 to 1918. He said that banks were too liberal with their loans to brokers and he also spoke out against the numerous investment trusts that were cropping up, some of them formed by respected brokerage firms. The Warburg warning did cause banks to withdraw money from the market to some extent a week later, and it was a short-lived experiment that set off a minor crash, the memory of which lingered in October.

Still in circulation in the fall of 1929 were copies of the comforting speech given in May by Edward Henry Harriman Simmons, president of the New York Stock Exchange. It was estimated that 100,000 reprints had been made. The speech, made to quell the carping of the Federal Reserve and critics like Paul Warburg, had been more than oil on troubled waters; it had been an unguent that made fears simply disappear.

The day after he delivered it, his office was inundated with more than 40,000 requests for reprints.

The increase in loans to brokers came not from banks, Simmons said, but mostly from private corporations over which the Federal Reserve Board had no control. The Federal Reserve Board itself, he said, was scaring capitalists so that instead of putting their money into stocks, it was going into brokers' call money. This, said Simmons, who had been president of the Exchange since 1924, was the "safest form of investment known in this country."

Millions of traders who worried that their margin might be raised—or worse, that their brokers' loans would be called —pointed to that portion of Simmons' speech that advised the fiscal authorities to keep hands off and warned that if the enormous masses of capital invested in stock-market loans were to be siphoned off and put into commercial businesses, it would cause runaway inflation—"A huge rise in commodity prices, inflation of inventories, and an artificial business boom." The end of all this, he forecast, would be a "colossal smash." Thus it was patriotic to be in the market with low margin and high loans. It prevented inflation and a depression.

The safe place for money, Simmons concluded, was the stock market.

And that's where it was, in October 1929—billions and billions of dollars' worth.

On Monday, October 21, there had been so many selling orders that the ticker had dropped behind. Some recovery set in before the close, and Professor Irving Fisher of Yale made a statement calling the sell-off "beneficial" because it shook out the "lunatic fringe" of speculators—a phrase that would endure in later years.

The next day, Tuesday, October 22, Charles E. Mitchell, chairman of the board of National City Bank and regarded as a foremost expert, arrived back home from a business trip to Europe and when pressed by reporters, stated categorically that he regarded the market as "sound" and he predicted that it would correct itself. He had followed trading closely on shipboard. His ship, like most liners, had a full board room with instant quotes relayed by Marconi wireless and posted just as quickly as they were in New York City.

Then came Wobbly Wednesday, when ice storms severed the telephone and telegraph lines across the country and jitters spread through the isolated Midwest, sending prices plummeting on the Exchange and occasioning an unprecedented number of margin calls.

On Thursday, October 24, 1929, only the professionals and "insiders" were really worried, and the professionals, when asked, continued to make glowing statements reflecting supreme confidence.

The talk around the Street was still redolent with baseball phrases as fans glowed over the World Series championship won the week before by the Philadelphia Athletics over the highly favored and flashy Chicago Cubs. Cub Manager Joe McCarthy had gone home disgruntled, and the A's had pocketed $6,000 apiece for making it in four straight games.

New Yorkers and visitors that fall were seeing Ziegfeld's *Show Girl*, starring a brilliant new comedy trio, Lou Clayton, Jimmy Durante and Eddie Jackson. For additional front-rank comedy there was *The Little Show*, starring Fred Allen, Clifton Webb, Libby Holman and Helen Morgan.

Before the hot weather set in, most had seen Alfred Lunt and Lynn Fontanne in the Theatre Guild's *Caprice*, hailed as the season's funniest play, and Beulah Bondi and Erin O'Brien-Moore in Elmer Rice's *Street Scene*, applauded then—as it was repeatedly—as the season's best play.

Those who were belatedly catching up with the spring booklist were reading a book called *Dodsworth*, written by a hard-bitten reporter whose lean and long nose sniffed out the drama in American people and committed it to penetrating words. Redheaded, starved-looking Sinclair Lewis had presented another portrait to Americans to show them how they looked, as he had done in *Babbitt, Arrowsmith,* and the bile-producing *Elmer Gantry.*

In midsummer, readers had discovered that the Dirty Huns who had occupied the German trenches eleven years earlier had felt hunger, pain, homesickness, love, tenderness and many other human characteristics that almost might be described as American. They had flocked to bookstores to be broadened by the work of an unforgiving German, Erich Maria Remarque, and had made a runaway bestseller of his *All Quiet on the Western Front.*

In October, only the reviewers and critics had seen copies of Ernest Hemingway's *A Farewell to Arms,* which also dealt with the destruction of human lives in the conflict of nations. It was scheduled for release in November.

CHAPTER 5

Thursday, October 24, 1929

9:00 A.M.
(7:00 A.M. MOUNTAIN STANDARD TIME)

~~~~~~

Marcy Fitton leaned against an adjacent stanchion and watched the Devries milking machine pull the few remaining ounces from old Rosie's once-heavy udder. Rosie was the only Jersey in his herd of twelve milk cows. Her purpose was to give Marcy's milk a heavier cream and butterfat reading and boost up his average price at the dairy. Rosie didn't give as much as a Holstein, but what she gave weighed up. He had always thought that Rosie was smarter than her sisters in the long, low dairy barn. Now she was rolling her big brown eye at him while she munched down a mouthful of bran and ensilage, as if to tell Marcy to pay attention to the business at hand because the machine was just about done with its work.

Marcy knew that as soon as he let the herd out to pasture in a few minutes now, Rosie would ignore her companions and make a beeline to the sweet grass at the far end of the lot, while the others would mope along, foraging in the brown and trampled foremeadow. Big producers, yes, but clods compared to Rosie. It would take some of them half the day to get to the good grass.

The grass at the end of the meadow was experimental, imported from Europe and distributed by the Love

County agent on behalf of the United States Department of Agriculture. It was supposed to withstand the hot, dry Oklahoma summers better than the native grasses did, and from what Marcy could see, it had lived up to its promise.

It was green and fresh even now near November, and it rippled in the parched and searing hot wind that blew down across the panhandle, raising cloudlets of dust. There was a low, thick haze of dust across the entire horizon, yellowing the bright early sunshine. It had a foreboding look.

Marcy intended to ask for some more of the seed so he could get it started on a portion of the rangeland in the northeastern part of the county where he ran his few head of beef steers. Marcy wasn't really a beef rancher, but the Fittons had always raised a few head ever since Great-Grandfather Amos Fitton had come out from Kansas as a Sooner.

Farmers, thought Marcy, were farmers, and that's what the Fittons were, and it's *all* that they were, as his son one day would discover.

They were farmers, not ranchers. Farmers, not oil men. Farmers, not clerks. Farmers, not merchants. Farmers. Farmers. Husbandmen, agronomists, agriculturalists, agroeconomists (to quote Harley Fantz in Tulsa)—any of those things, yes—because what those words meant was Farmers.

Marcy grew some cotton, some wheat in each season and some garden vegetables for market. He produced milk and he raised beef. It gave him a balanced living, for when prices were depressed in one thing, they usually weren't in another. For instance, farm prices on his vegetables and wheat had been declining steadily for the last year, but cotton was holding up pretty well, and the beeves, when he brought them in for fattening next spring, were likely to command respectable prices.

When he removed the vacs from Rosie's teats and lugged the machine to the steam room for sterilization, he also brought the huge tin containers of milk—he had taken nearly eighty quarts from the twelve cows—and strained the light golden liquid through cheesecloth discs into the cooling vats. Later in the morning he'd take the chilled milk with him in ten-gallon nickel cans and leave it at the pickup station on his way to Lake Texoma, where he intended to put in a day of fishing and relaxation.

Marcy was tired. He needed a day off. He had just completed the cotton picking and had taken the last load to the gin on Tuesday. In the next week or so he had to start getting in his winter wheat, and maybe, he thought, he'd have to hire a spare hand to help him. Paul, on whom he'd counted, was determined to work for that damn oil company in Ardmore. It made no sense at all for the last male Fitton to be an oil man instead of a farmer, but Paul had a will like his mother's.

Carrie was part mule, there was no doubt about it, and her son had inherited the streak, pure and unmodified. Take today, for instance. Marcy had wanted Carrie to come fishing with him. She needed a day away from the farm, too. He'd been thinking about it for several days. He was going to hire a skiff from old Billie Barney and they'd row out onto the lake and catch a few bass and some perch, and maybe even a pike or a pickerel, and at lunchtime they'd row over to that thicket grove he knew about and build a little fire and cook some fish.

Then, maybe they'd do a little nudie swimming. Carrie had never been nudie swimming with him in all the years they had been married, claiming she was too shy, but by Heaven, he'd seen times when she wasn't so shy.

Then, his plan went, maybe they would do a little mature man-and-wife frolicking in that grove, way in the deep shade, before going after some more fish. It would be a real humdinger of a day off for him, and Marcy had thought about it plenty while he was getting in the cotton and coming home so tired each night that he hardly wanted supper.

But when he'd broached it to Carrie she had said it was impossible for her to take a day off, that she had to make chili sauce on Thursday. The tomatoes were overripe, she said, and the green peppers were just right, and she had to make chili sauce and ketchup before they had a norther come and frost-kill the tomatoes. So that was that. Carrie was not one to change her mind. He'd learned that about her, if nothing else.

After the cows were let out to pasture, Marcy went to the other side of the barn and took the water pails away from the horses, then one by one backed them out of their stalls and let them out the other side of the barn to their own pasture. He stood and watched them for a moment, a fine matched pair of working draft horses and the two quarter horses that he and Paul rode on the rangeland when they worked on the steers.

The draft mare, the off-horse, needed to be shod, but Marcy had decided to put it off for another month when he'd have them both calked for winter. He watched the wind blow eddies of dust across the horses' flanks and thought it would be good for the land when winter did come.

At the front door of the barn, facing toward the house, Marcy stopped to inhale deeply of the crisp morning air, redolent of damp earth smells from the heavy fall dew of the night before. Despite the dust from the tilled land, there were sparklets of dew in the darker green grass near the house and tiny cobwebs were coated white with moisture, making them appear to be made of thick silk.

With his second deep breath, Marcy was struck by the sweet, spicy pungence of boiling chili sauce and he knew that Carrie had started the old four-burner oil stove in the summer kitchen and that a big kettle of the savory substance would simmer there most of the day, its steamy fragrance permeating the winy air around the entire farmstead, until late afternoon when she would can it in Mason jars for safekeeping.

Marcy felt the saliva begin to flood in his mouth as he sniffed great draughts of the spiced air. By Heaven, he thought, it's mouth-watering, just like they say in books.

At that moment Carrie appeared at the door.

"Marcy!" she called. "Marcy—come quick. There's a broadcast on the radio about the stock market."

The stock market? Now what the hell would anyone have to say about the stock market at this hour? Nevertheless, Marcy hurried toward the kitchen door. Marcy, in common with many folks around Love County, was in the market, and he supposed that for a farmer—and nothing but a farmer—he might be said to be in the market very deeply.

That's because he was a modern thinker.

Marcy was a believer in Samuel Insull. He thought that the exquisite little Englishman, former secretary to Thomas A. Edison, who lived on an all-electric farm reported to be worth a million dollars, was one of the greatest and smartest financiers in the world. Marcy had read everything about Insull that he could lay his hands on, and was regarded by friends at the Grange as a veritable expert on the life and times of the utilities magnate.

One basic thing was that Marcy and Samuel Insull liked the same things (such as well-run farms) and they believed that the age of electricity had only just started and had a brilliant future. Less than half of America was electrified, Marcy would point out.

One of Insull's men had spent a whole afternoon at the farm talking about the future of electricity, then had persuaded Marcy to put in a bid for a block of 200 shares of Insull Utility Investments, at 125. Though there was no way of checking at that hour the actual price of the stock that day, the man had said he thought Insull Investments was selling at better than 130. Marcy never checked, and his bid was accepted.

The purchase was achieved by paying twenty percent margin or $5,000, which just about cleaned out the Fittons' savings account plus the cash from the sale of spring lambs and the spring wheat crop. Before Marcy's loan for $20,000 was due, the stock had increased in value to 155, and then to 160, giving him a spread of at least $10,000 between what he was worth and what he owed, so he was permitted to buy fifty additional shares without putting up any money—that is, any cash.

The excitement of growing rich so rapidly had filled Marcy with daydreams more stimulating even than the sensual fantasies he had enjoyed as an adolescent. He dreamed of an all-electric farm with electrically heated and electrically cooled barns for the livestock.

He dreamed of creating his own cattle empire, and fixing his own prices on beef at the fattening pens—fair prices, of course, but extremely rewarding to the grower. He dreamed of a splendid winter home on the Gulf where he and Carrie would breakfast on the patio, looking eastward to the rising sun making diamond glints on the sparkling water, wherein, just offshore, was moored his sleek white yacht, awaiting his pleasure.

His dream wafted him deeper into the stock market.

Marcy had never played in an organized sport in his life, but he was a sports fan. He loved baseball and kept a record of the scores copied from the radio broadcasts. He thought Oklahoma had the finest football team in the nation. He read avidly the stories of golf, of tennis, of hockey in season, of basketball in the high schools—almost anything that had to do with sports.

"It won't be long," he told Carrie, "before most of the people in America—except farmers, of course—will be working a forty-eight-hour week, and with so much leisure time, sports must grow. Sports of all kinds. People are going to pay to watch games and somebody will make money on that. But do you know who will make the biggest money? A. G. Spalding, that's who. Spalding—he makes most of the official equipment that's used in any organized or professional sport."

Accordingly, in late summer, as soon as the cash crops were in, he had bought 100 shares of A. G. Spalding at $63 a share, and he had put up $1,500 from his cash receipts.

He took pleasure in pointing out to Carrie that the new golf ball, 6/100 of an inch larger and 7/100 of an ounce lighter, that had been approved by the United States Golf Association was being made by Spalding, and that when she conquered Helen Jacobs at Wimbledon, Helen Wills used a Spalding racket and served Spalding balls. At Cleveland, Babe Ruth hit his 500th homer of his American League career and the ball he autographed for the bashful kid who retrieved it was a Spalding. The Babe also gave the kid a twenty-dollar bill.

It appeared that he had bought Spalding at a high, for soon after his purchase had been acknowledged, the price had begun to soften. Marcy was convinced, however, that it was a temporary phenomenon. Surely the investing public sooner or later would come to see what he saw in Spalding's future.

He wiped his feet carefully at the kitchen door, and as he entered he banged the screen behind him to shake off the congregating flies. They, too, liked the smell of chili sauce.

Carrie raised a finger to her lips for silence and led the way into the living room where he could hear the Atwater Kent All-Electric Radio performing its task. He watched Carrie cross the portal toward the living room and remarked again, as he had so many times, that she was a better-looking woman in middle age than she was as a young girl, and she had been a darn nice-looking kid.

As firm and almost as trim as when they had married twenty years before, she was yet more feminine with slightly broader hips and a well-filled conical bust. She was no scrawny flapper and he was damn glad of it, because he was not an empty-brained Joe College Kid. Her black bobbed hair was highlighted with flashes of white —pure white. And that, Marcy thought, gave her more IT than Clara Bow.

As if sensing his wandering thoughts, Carrie gestured toward the apparatus, and turned the round speaker toward the big morris chair that she knew he would sit in.

"In England," the radio announcer's voice said, "officials of the Cunard Line announced that the next time the giant *Mauretania* is drydocked, a new device will be incorporated in the engine room that will add two and one-half knots to the speed of the ocean liner. The gadget, the spokesman said, will reuse the heat that is now escaping up the ship's funnel stacks, and divert it into energy. . . .

"Officials in this country as well as those in England, Ireland and Newfoundland, have given up all hope for the safety of Urban Dietman, Jr., the daring young pilot and Montana cattleman who took off from Newfoundland on Tuesday, bound for England in his small air-

plane. The officials now believe that Dietman and his tiny
Barling Monoplane may have gone down no more than
five hundred miles from Newfoundland's coast because
of the severe icing conditions that prevailed in that area
of the North Atlantic last Tuesday. . . .

"We will interrupt any broadcast upon receipt of any
further news of the brave young pilot. . . .

"On Wall Street, brokers and bankers this morning are
awaiting the opening gong of trading with their confidence somewhat restored overnight after yesterday's session, which produced such an avalanche of selling orders
that it set off one of the widest declines in stock-market
history. More on the stock market after this message."

"Oh, good," Carrie said, "he's going to repeat the story
about the stock market."

"I wish to hell they wouldn't tease us like that," Marcy
grumbled. "They start to give us news, then make us wait
while they advertise something."

"You wouldn't complain if you owned some Radio Corporation of America stock," Carrie said.

"I'd write the president and ask 'em to do it differently."

"In a pig's eye, you would."

There was a frying and sputtering sound on the receiver as the advertisers' message was concluded and
Marcy jumped to the set to adjust one of the four large
dials on its front.

"In a broad and general decline, yesterday," the announcer resumed, "the stock market suffered losses
across the whole list. Declines ran from a few cents to
ninety-six points for Adams Express. The actual loss in
market value has been estimated by experts at about four
billion dollars.

"On the Curb Exchange there was a similar slash in
prices, mostly in sympathy with the huge record-setting

declines on the Big Board. There the loss was estimated
at two billion dollars, so in the wake of the most hectic
selling in Wall Street's memory, it is calculated that the
nation's shareowners yesterday sustained losses of about
six billion dollars. . . .

"Turning to the sports news, the Carnegie Foundation
reveals that one out of every seven athletes engaged in
intercollegiate competition is subsidized to a point that
borders on 'professionalism' and. . . ."

Marcy switched the set off, even though it was his
beloved sports news.

"By God," he said, "losses up to ninety-six points!"

"Call him," Carrie said.

"Eh? Call who?"

"Call Samuel Insull."

"Samuel—Are you daft? *I* can't call Samuel Insull."

"Why not? You gave him all of our money. He took it
willingly enough."

"Yes, but you just don't put in a telephone call to
Samuel Insull. Why, he's one of the richest men in the
world. . . ."

"On our money."

"Oh, now, Carrie. I've tried to explain. I didn't buy that
stock from Samuel Insull. I bought it from the George P.
Wrentham Company. That's a firm of stockbrokers in
Oklahoma City. They got the stock from somebody else,
probably somebody just like me, only he wanted to sell it.
They're brokers—like real-estate brokers—and they find
someone who wants to sell a certain stock and someone
who wants to buy that same certain stock, and they bring
the two of them together—in effect—and make a deal."

"I don't care. It was Samuel Insull's man who put in the
order for you. All I know is that it's Samuel Insull's company and we own part of it, and we're entitled to know

how the company's doing. That's reasonable, isn't it?"

"What we want to know is how the market's doing."

"That's the same thing."

"No, Carrie. You don't understand. The market is something else again. It's an auction market, and it is based on what the public *thinks* Insull Utility Investments stock is worth—or is going to be worth."

"That's the same thing. The very same thing. Call Insull." Carrie never showed agitation; she merely firmed up her voice and it got fuller and just slightly louder. As she had on a few other occasions, she reminded Marcy of the First Sergeant he had served under in the Home Guard.

Marcy lunged from his chair and headed for the bedroom. He returned in a moment, scrutinizing the last quarterly report of Insull Utility Investments that had been sent to him as a registered stockholder. He was turning it over in his hands, skimming the type.

"Ah, here it is," he said. "Just as I thought. Here's the telephone number on the bottom."

The telephone was on the kitchen wall and Marcy braced the report against the windowsill while he held the receiver to his ear and turned the crank.

He asked for the toll operator and gave her the Chicago number. He glanced at his watch and turned to Carrie.

"It's already eight-thirty in Chicago. Probably he's in his office. He *should* be."

"He'd better be there—in times like these," said Carrie.

"Hello?" Marcy shouted. He knew that voices lost power over any great distance, and he believed in helping the electric juice in the telephone wires. "Hello? This is Marcy Fitton in Oklahoma calling. I'd like to speak to Mr. Samuel Insull, please."

"Mr. Samuel Insull?" the girl asked. "There is no one

here by that—Oh—Uh—*MR.* Samuel *INSULL?"*

"Yes."

"Mr. Insull doesn't have his office here, sir."

"Well, it's the number he gave me."

"No, sir. Mr. Insull can usually be reached at his apartment."

"Well, may I have that number?"

"I'm sorry, sir, but we're not allowed to give out that number."

"See here," said Marcy, "I am one of the principal owners of Insull Utility Investments, and it is very important to Mr. Insull that I talk to him as soon as possible. I'm sure he wants to talk to me."

"I see, sir. Just a minute, please, sir."

Marcy held the line for what seemed to him an incredible length of time, considering it was a toll call, and suddenly there was a whirring sound.

"Mr. Insull's apa'ht*mant.*"

"This is Marcy Fitton calling from Oklahoma. May I speak to Mr. Insull, please."

"One *mo*mant, sar."

Marcy could hear the receiver being placed carefully on something solid, probably a desk top.

From his secluded, breathtakingly beautiful penthouse overlooking the Chicago riverfront, Samuel Insull had been gazing at the flashing crystals of sunshine on the fine chop of the water while he digested the distressing financial news in the *Chicago Tribune.* He had been thinking about Oklahoma only a few minutes earlier and wondering how People's Gas and Coke might be made to profit from the new gas wells being discovered in that state. He thought of it fleetingly, from instinct. And he thought of the investigation that had been started against him. That, too, from instinct. And he thought about the

idiots who had panicked yesterday and sold off their hold-
ings. Instinct.

When the butler told him that Mr. Fitton was calling,
his information intruded on the bitter yet hopeful por-
ridge on which Mr. Insull was sipping, seeking the
remedial and restorative triumvirate of the inveterate
promoter, Cure, Steadfastness and Hope. Thus, for once
he broke his hard-and-fast rule about seclusion and his
privacy, even from the telephone, and said that he'd take
the call. He said it absentmindedly, and it may be that his
thoughts about Oklahoma had neutralized his judgment.

At his massive mahogany desk, Mr. Insull picked up his
French-type telephone.

"Ah, Mr. Fitton," he said. "Mr. Fitton of Oklahoma
Gas?"

"N-no," said Marcy, surprised and cowed by his success. "This is Marcy Fitton of Love County."

"Yes, Mr. Fitton. What can I do for you, sir?"

"Mr. Insull, I want to know how Insull Utility Investments is doing."

"I see." There was a pause.

"I mean, what is happening with the stock market and
all."

"I see." Another pause.

"C-can you tell me?"

"Mr. Fitton, are you a reporter?"

"Reporter? Reporter! Like on a newspaper? Good God,
no! I'm a stockholder, Mr. Insull. A stockholder."

"I see."

"I heard on the radio that the market was hit by the
worst selling in its history, and I want to know whether
I should sell Insull Utility Investments or hold it."

"I see."

"Well, could you tell me, Mr. Insull?"

"Mr. Fitton, I'm a little suspicious of this call. I have had others try to trap me into saying something. But let me advise you about two things. First, I think you should talk it over with your broker. Second, I think you should know that I fully intend to hold onto *my* Insull Utility Investments stock. Good-bye, Mr. Fitton."

"Thank you, Mr. Insull," shouted Marcy to the dead line.

Samuel Insull, who even then was being investigated by a brilliant young economics professor from Chicago University, one Paul C. Douglas, had just granted one of the rare unplanned, unrehearsed interviews of his entire career, and as long as he lived, he was to remain unsure and somewhat suspicious of his interviewer's identity. What fueled his suspicions was that Insull Utility Investments, perhaps because of the ice storms that severed communications, had not been severely hit by the sell-off. The ice had isolated tens of thousands of Midwestern and Western stockholders.

"What did he say?" Carrie asked.

"He says he's holding his stock, but he wants me to call my broker."

"The number's on the front of the telephone book," Carrie told her husband.

Again Marcy removed the receiver, cranked the handle and asked for the toll operator.

"Wrentham Company?" he bellowed when the number answered. "This is Marcy Fitton in Love County. Can you let me talk to Mr.—a—Mr.—," he consulted the cover of the phone book where several important notations had been penciled, "Mr.—PRITCHARD?"

"Pritchard here," said the Eastern-schooled voice of the customer's man who took the call.

"Mr. Pritchard, this is Marcy Fitton in Love County.

Can you tell me about my Insull Utility Investments stock?"

"Yes, sir, Mr. Britton, just a moment, please."

"Fitton," Marcy yelled. "FITTON!"

"Yes, sir, Mr. Fitton. Let me get your folder."

"He's got to get my folder," Marcy related to Carrie.

In three minutes Mr. Pritchard was back on the phone.

"Ah, Mr. ah, Fitton? Mr. Fitton, you're not in bad shape. Not in bad shape at all with your Insull Utility Investments. Of course you realize that the market hasn't opened back East yet and I'm quoting yesterday's prices, but yesterday you lost about ten points. Insull Utility Investments closed at 85."

"Oh, fine. Good. Good." Marcy nodded toward Carrie so she would know that everything was all right.

"But you do have Spalding, don't you, Mr. Fitton."

"Yes. How did Spalding make out?"

"Well, I'm afraid that Spalding is down to $46. You bought it at $63 and you have a loan of $4,800 on it. I'm afraid we'll have to call that loan. I'm surprised you haven't heard from us, Mr. Fitton."

"Well, sell it. Sell it. Get rid of it at 46 if you can. I'll send you the other two hundred or however much it is in cash, plus your commissions, whatever they are, but sell it."

"Very well, Mr. Fitton. I'll put in your sell order at $46."

"Well, don't make it an order to sell at $46. Make it an order to sell at market. Let's get out of it."

"I'm not sure I think that's wise, Mr. Fitton."

"Well, it's what I want to do. I can't afford to fool with it. And who knows, maybe it'll open at a higher bid and you can get more than 46 for it."

"The last asking price was 51, but there were no takers. The bid was 46."

"So offer it at market."

"All right, Mr. Fitton. I'll do that. You'll be hearing from us. By the way, could I come see you about an investment trust that has been started by one of the leading brokerage houses on Wall Street? It's a chance to spread your risks, at no extra cost to you."

"Not now," said Marcy. "God, not now."

Marcy remained scowling at the wall for a few minutes, doing some mental arithmetic.

"We're not coming out so bad," he said finally. "We're still way ahead of the game."

"Some game," said Carrie.

"Come on," he said, whacking her across the rear as she moved toward the new Universal washing machine, "let's stop worrying. Let's go fishing. Let's take the day off."

"Uh-uh," said Carrie with that absolute finality that she always managed to work into her voice. "I'm staying right here and making chili sauce and ketchup."

Marcy headed back toward the barn. His fishing rod was stowed there.

"Where are you going to get the two hundred dollars plus commissions?" Carrie called after him, through the fly-populated screen door.

"Oh—I'll sell the damn fish that I catch," Marcy shouted.

CHAPTER 6

Thursday, October 24, 1929

10:00 A.M.

~~~~~~~~~~~~~~~~~~~~~~~~~~~~~~~~~~~~~

When the high oaken door with its gilt lettering had closed behind him, Edward dePlassance Newbord permitted himself a shudder of revulsion followed by a sigh of relief. Raymond & Company's office was in turmoil and the board room had been filled with spectators, Mrs. Orlando told him, since nine o'clock.

Jules Barnish had been right about the milling throngs of people, and Newbord was pleased that he did not look particularly like a broker with his sportier-than-customary clothes. Miguel had steered the Packard through the narrow alley of Pine Street and had turned into William to drive down the hill to Wall Street but at the intersection Newbord had seen that it would be impossible to turn into Wall because of the multitude. It was stretched from building front to building front solidly across the street and it was difficult to walk even in the middle of the road, to say nothing of the sidewalk.

He had told Miguel that he would get out there and walk to the office, and instructed the driver to go on down to Hanover Square and find his way out of the financial district as quickly as he could. He also told Miguel that he would call him at least an hour before he wanted to be picked up, so there would be plenty of time for maneuvering if traffic remained as heavy at day's end as it was then.

"Don't park here," he had said, "and don't get out to open my door. I'll just slip out and you get on home as quickly as you can."

"Sure," Miguel had said, easing the gear shift into low, and had added, *"M'gung-d'ng-Abepo,"* the traditional Tagalog salutation.

"Thanks, Miguel. Good luck to you, too."

It had taken him fifteen minutes to walk the one block to his office and he had been obliged to wait numerous times while the crowd formed into immovable knots, then diffused sufficiently to allow him to squeeze through. He had time to notice, though, that it was a beautiful day, cool, in the low forties at that hour, and that wide patches of bright blue sky reflected light like inverted lakes between islands of cumulus clouds, as glimpsed through the towers of the office buildings. "October's bright blue weather, even in Wall Street," he thought, and was slightly pleased with himself for remembering the poem he had learned in grammar school.

There was another long wait at the elevator bank as hordes of people, many of them obviously out-of-towners, waited for cars. The starter, with his hand clicker making constant staccato noises like a metal cricket, had to block the elevator doors with his body to prevent the cars from being overloaded, and frequently those of slight build would squeeze under his arms and get aboard before the doors could be closed.

The corridor was filled when he got off at his floor and he had difficulty pushing his way into the front office, which even at that early hour was filled with noise, smoke and confusion.

Only two of the younger men spoke to him. No one else

even nodded "good morning" as he elbowed his way toward the corner suite where Mrs. Orlando stood, holding open the door to his office. He reached its sanctuary and with a smile and brief "morning" to his secretary, stepped inside and quickly closed the door behind him. Rugged. Real rugged.

Mrs. Orlando opened the door quickly and stepped inside and reached for his light fedora to hang it up.

"The men are getting *some* sell orders," she said, "but when it's a customer we know fairly well they are advising them to hold on."

"Well, I don't know as they should do that," Newbord said. "Better let me check with Jules about it. What time is it?"

"About five minutes to go. Some coffee?"

"No. No thanks. Any word from the other wire houses?" The three dozen or so brokerage firms that maintained private wire systems to branch offices and correspondents throughout the nation, commonly conferred on matters of major policy, particularly in relation to any advisories or statements that might be put out over all wires.

"No one has called," Mrs. Orlando said. "Oh, yes. Mrs. Newbord called and said to be sure to keep an eye on her Coca-Cola."

"Er, thanks. I will."

"And, Mr. Newbord?"

"Umh?"

"Should I sell my Johns-Manville?"

"I suppose you should. I guess you should. You're on margin aren't you?"

"Yes, twenty percent."

"Well, I guess you should get out."

"It—it's for my son, you know. John. For his education."

"We'll handle it for you, Maryanne." He rarely called

her by her first name. "We'll get you as good a price as possible."

"Thank you. I appreciate it."

"What time is it now?"

"Right on the dot."

A bell rang in the outer office, signifying that the gong had sounded at the Exchange and that trading had started.

"Bill Crawford's right on the job," he said whimsically. William H. Crawford, superintendent of the Exchange's records department, opened trading each day at ten o'-clock sharp, and closed it by smashing his gavel against the gong precisely at three o'clock in the afternoon.

By the time Newbord had clipped the end from a Corona-Corona and got it lighted, the phone was ringing. He knew it was Jules calling from the private loop phone, the direct line, from the trading floor.

"Ed? There's heavy volume over here. A big backlog of orders overnight. But believe it or not, it's steady." Much noisy confusion could be heard in the background.

"You mean prices are steady?"

"Yes. They're matching buyers with sellers."

"Even?"

"Off fractions only. It looks pretty good. So far it's big blocks. There was a block of 20,000 shares of Kennecott Copper offered at the opening gong, and it was up eleven points!"

"Well, Jules, that's hardly what I'd call merely 'steady.' That looks like some kind of recovery."

"Maybe. You can't judge it by that one sale. Kennecott lost 11¾ yesterday, if I recall, so it has just about recovered yesterday's losses."

"If everything does that, it'll be more than we can ask."

"Wait a minute. They just sold a big block of General

Motors—20,000 in the block—and it was off just a fraction."

"Still not too bad."

"And Harry just signaled me that they're offering 15,-000 shares of Sinclair."

"All right. Keep an eye on it."

"Have you been out to the board room?"

"I'm just going. It's packed out there. I didn't realize we had so many enthusiastic customers."

"You should see the Visitor's Gallery over here. No room to squeeze in. I don't know why they want to stand around and watch the kettle boil. They can't make any trades up there."

"It's *their* money."

"Like hell it is. It's *our* money. *They* borrowed it."

"Okay, Jules."

As he left his office he glanced at the Dow Jones broad tape and saw that it had already reported that the market was opening steadily, and it noted the Kennecott and General Motors transactions. "Those are good boys over there at the *Wall Street Journal*," he thought, and made a mental note to call Oliver Gingold and Eddie Kostenbater when it was all over, and congratulate them on their efficiency.

When he approached his own board room, where prices were being posted on the huge felt boards that covered three walls of the room, he heard the beginnings of a low rumble that swelled and built in volume as he approached.

Angus Felt, a customer's man, was standing near the door.

"What's happening?" Newbord demanded.

"They're selling at market," Felt said, keeping his eyes on the board. "The damn fools are selling at market—

asking no prices. They're dumping. Just plain dumping, and it's bound to knock the hell out of prices. Look—just look."

He pointed towards one of the boys who had just posted the price on Standard Brands. A block of 15,000 shares had been offered, and the price was off two points. Another boy was posting United Gas Improvement, where an offering of 12,000 shares had depressed the price by two points also.

A young man touched him on the arm.

"Would you take the phone over here, Mr. Newbord? It's Mr. Barnish." Newbord nodded and followed the boy.

"Jules?"

"I don't like it, Ed," Jules said. "There's too much coming on the market all at once. Now there's 10,000 United Corporation and 15,000 Packard Motors, and 10,000 Westinghouse and 10,000 Allegheny Corporation."

"Yes, but what are the prices?"

"That's it, Ed, the market is moving too fast. The tape hasn't reported the prices on half of these."

"Then why are you worrying if you don't know the prices?"

"I've been checking on the second sales that are coming in. There are losses of a point, two points, sometimes as much as five points between sales. I don't know how much of it is real or how much is caused by the fact that they can't match the buy orders with the sell orders."

"You sure about the losses?"

"Of course I'm sure. Oh, damn. Just listen to that. Listen to it, Ed—I'm going to hold this receiver out toward the floor."

Newbord heard the roar, like the hurricane surf he had heard in the Florida keys.

"Can you hear what they're shouting?" Jules bellowed

into the mouthpiece. "They're saying, '*Sell at the market!
Sell at market!*'"

"Yeah, I hear 'em."

"And you heard about Steel?"

"No. What about it?"

"Off two points at the last sale."

Ed Newbord glanced at his own board. The Big X—
United States Steel Corporation—didn't show any sales
whatsoever. The quotation was yesterday's closing price
of 204. But as he watched, the boy posted a new figure—
205½.

Big Steel had lost eight and a quarter points on Wednesday and everyone was watching it gingerly, praying that
it wouldn't sag below the 200 level—"the magic 200"—
because that would set off a psychological grenade that
could shatter the rest of the market.

Newbord turned from the board and shouted into the
phone.

"What do you mean it lost two points? It just gained a
point and a half. It's two-oh-five-and-a-half."

"It is like hell," Jules said. "That's what it was ten minutes ago. And now it's lost another point. It's down to
202½!"

"What's wrong with this tape?"

"Late, Ed. It's very late. I don't know how you can keep
up with this."

"Where's Harry? Is he down on the floor?"

"He's down here somewhere. Everybody who owns a
badge is down here."

"Well, get him over to Post Two as soon as possible to
let us know what's going on. We've got to start calling in
loans."

Post Two was the trading home of Steel, the Big X, and
Jules glanced across the floor.

"Good Lord," he said, "it looks as though there's a fight at Post Two. Look, Ed, I'll call you back."

The clock said ten-thirty. Newbord glanced around his noisy board room. The half-dozen boys who posted figures were scurrying back and forth across their raised platform as the tickertape recorded symbols and figures at a constant high speed and they relayed them to the boards so all the spectators could see them.

Angus Felt pushed his way through the packed room, holding a six-inch-wide sheet of paper, and reached across some shoulders to hand it to Newbord.

It was the Dow Jones tape. The blue capital letters had been printing an earnings report when someone had typed—"BUST IT! BUST IT!"—and then had followed with the message that made Newbord lose all color:

AT 10:30 A.M. THE NEW YORK STOCK EXCHANGE TICKERTAPE WAS RUNNING FIFTEEN MINUTES BEHIND. THE CURB EXCHANGE TICKERTAPE AT THE SAME HOUR WAS RUNNING SIXTEEN MINUTES BEHIND.

DJ 10:33 EST.

Newbord signaled Felt.

"I'm going to my office," he shouted.

He had no sooner reached the door than Felt was behind him and crowding into his office with him.

"Harry is on the loop phone," he said. "There's a big row at Post Two and the last Steel price was 201½. Nothing on the tape."

"Oh, God," Newbord said as if beginning a prayer, and sank into his chair, feeling total frustration at the lack of communication.

"Just keep everything coming to me, Angus. Every bit of information that you can get. Get 'em organized so that

I know what's going on just as soon as anyone hears about anything."

"Yessir, I'll do that. We'll get it routed in here."

Suddenly Newbord wanted a drink. He wanted a drink so much he could almost smell the misty char aroma of Scotch. But he never kept it in his office.

Instead he stared at the gleaming surface of his immaculately clean desk and wondered what on earth could be the matter with those fools around Post Two.

Harry Hoerner, Raymond & Company's trader, knew what the trouble was at Post Two. There were people trying to support the price of Steel, but just not enough of them to absorb all of the orders to sell "at market." Those who were selling knew that the support would soon dry up and were eager to make their sales before the price dropped still lower. Those at the back of the crowd around the post sought to get to the center to make the trade, and those who were closest tried, as politely as possible, to prevent them.

Harry had to leave. He received a signal that he had sold his 500 shares of Johns-Manville. He had been able to get 175. Off five points in the first three-quarters of an hour. He had put in an asking price of 180, the figure for yesterday's close. He knew it was for Maryanne Orlando and he hoped she wasn't taking too much of a licking.

At that moment there was a great roar from the crowd around Post Two, and the word spread like lightning across the cavernous trading floor.

"Steel broke 200! She's down to 199!"

Harry got on the loop phone again to report it to Newbord.

The latest quote from the ticker had just been placed on Newbord's desk. Steel was quoted at 202⅜.

It meant that buyers and sellers of U.S. Steel Corporation stocks throughout the world were sending orders to their brokers and their brokers were relaying them to Post Two—orders that couldn't possibly be matched up. Even orders to buy had to be ignored.

The specialists—those who keep the books and are responsible for maintaining an orderly market even if they must use their own money to do so—simply couldn't match up the orders to buy at certain prices with orders to sell at certain prices. For every buyer there must be a seller and vice versa, and in an auction market, a supervisor, the specialist, must bring together the bidders and the askers, else there is no orderliness to the market and firm prices cannot prevail.

No sooner had Harry finished his call than the loop phone sounded again and it was Jules.

"There are losses up to ten points between sales," Jules reported, "and the ticker is much later now. You won't have information on what's happening right this minute until a half-hour from now."

"Well how the hell are we going to handle our orders?" Newbord shouted as he eyed a memo that Angus Felt had placed on his desk. "We are getting a lot of sell orders now and we're calling for a lot more to cover loans."

"We'll just have to sell at market. Just keep 'em coming."

"We are. We're literally pouring orders at you."

"Wait a minute, Ed—hold the phone. . . ."

Jules conferred with someone at his side and Newbord could hear him saying, "Why, yes, so it is. Sure, that's him."

"Ed," Jules resumed, "there's a bunch of brass up there in the Visitor's Gallery. They've got Winston Churchill with them. You know, the round-faced fellow with the long cigars, who used to be chancellor of the exchequer of Great Britain."

"Yeah. I know him."

"Well, he's here. In the Visitor's Gallery."

"He should be on the phone, getting some of that British money to support the market."

"Here's another quote, Ed. Auburn Motors, off 25 points!"

"Auburn? That's impossible. Not 25 points."

"That's the latest sale. Anything's possible today."

"God help us."

"Yeah."

Winston Leonard Spencer Churchill, who had been ousted from his post in the exchequer by the victory of the Labourite government of James Ramsay MacDonald in June, held an unlighted cigar in his hand as he stood beside Richard Whitney, vice president of the Exchange, and from the high gallery overlooked the pandemonium that was to presage the icy Depression that gripped his island empire and all of Europe as well as his mother's homeland of America during the entirety of the next decade. Perhaps his role of leadership in the days to come was being formed amid the shouts, cries, waving arms, stamping feet and bitter oaths, two floors below. So far as is known, he was noncommittal as he beheld the historic spectacle, and left a few moments later to keep a luncheon date. A severe critic of America's reparations program toward Germany, Churchill was visiting the country as a political observer to keep an eye on the conference, earlier in the month, between Prime Minister MacDonald and President Hoover, who had tentatively agreed to naval disarmament.

"Steel 197!" read the note that Mrs. Orlando placed on Newbord's desk.

She returned a minute later with another note. "Don't forget Mrs. Newbord's Coca-Cola," it read.

"Oh, yes," he said. "Get me the quote on that, please."

As she left, Angus Felt entered with still another note:

WHEAT OPENED OFF TWO TO THREE CENTS IN CHICAGO.

"Thanks," Newbord said. "Keep it coming."

"Coca-Cola quoted at 47," Mrs. Orlando said from the doorway. "Shall I tell them to sell?"

"No. No. Wait a minute. It closed at 46½ yesterday and had lost only half a point. No. It has recovered. This is good news. We'll hold it."

"I'll call her and tell her."

"Good, you do that."

"Maybe we should check on her Bethlehem first."

"Good idea."

While she was gone he flipped open his *Times* to check yesterday's close on Bethlehem. Right, just as he thought, it closed at 101 for a loss of ⅜ of a point. He had been right to tell her to hold it.

"Bethlehem is at 97½," Mrs. Orlando reported from the doorway.

"Well, I guess we'll still hold it. Call her, please, and give her the quotes."

Newbord noticed that he was sweating. God, dealing with Kay even secondhand these days made him tense. He left his desk to open the two corner windows of his office. He glanced down at the street and was transfixed by the scene. Broad Street, on the side of the New York Stock Exchange where visitors were admitted, was a solid jam of humanity. The crowd backed up to the Sub-Treasury Building on Wall Street.

He opened wide the windows and looked out, and then

the noise assailed him. It rose in billows, an angry roar
with mournful undertones. There were undulations in
the crowd, as if people were swaying to and fro as they
moaned, and from so many floors above it seemed like a
restless sea of heads and hats.

He made a quick assessment and decided that the
crowd was not far from violence; it could become a mob
at any moment.

Behind him a phone was ringing.

"It's Jules, Ed. Montgomery Ward is off 20 points. Auburn Motors is down more than 40. There's no way we can
get exact prices unless we're right at the post. The ticker
here is thirty-five or forty minutes behind."

"It's awful. Well, I don't know what to tell you to do,
Jules. You'll have to do what you think best."

"I suppose so. Have you heard the rumors about the
suicides?"

"Suicide? Whose suicide?" A chill tensed Newbord and
the perspiration streaking down his sides felt icy.

"Suicides. With an *s*. Plural. There's a rumor that four
speculators have already committed suicide by jumping
out of buildings."

"How horrible."

"Yes. But it'll get worse."

"Nobody could commit suicide out here. He'd jump
onto a solid mass of humanity. The street is filled with
people. You should see how it is on Broad—packed solid."

"I know. Mike Moss just went down to get a drink at
Eberlin's and he was telling me about it. He says you can
hear the noise of the trading floor out on the sidewalk on
Broad Street."

"Jules, where the hell is Harry Simmons? He should be
doing something about this. Somebody's got to do something. Muster the bankers, or something."

"Harry? Our dear president? Have you forgotten? He's in Hawaii on his honeymoon. Look, we're lucky to have Whitney here. Yesterday, when things were almost as bad as they are today, our beloved vice president was over in Far Hills, New Jersey, serving as a presiding steward at the racing program for the Essex Fox Hounds."

"Yoicks," said Newbord bitterly, and Jules knew that the pressure was beginning to get to him, for he rarely attempted humor.

"I'll keep you posted," Jules said, and hung up.

Mrs. Orlando was slipping a note on Newbord's desk:

REPORT SAYS SIX PEOPLE HAVE COMMITTED SUICIDE IN WALL STREET DISTRICT. THIS IS A RUMOR.

M.O.

Angus Felt had entered the office bearing a sheaf of quotations, and Newbord handed Mrs. Orlando's note to him.

He read it and laughed. "I heard it was seven," he said. "The rumor factory has them leaping out of windows like grasshoppers. You expect to see them fill the air like confetti."

"I hope it *is* just rumors."

"The cops had to come and break up a big crowd over at Bankers Trust building just a little while ago," Angus related. "A man was up near one of the top floors, innocently working on some masonry or copper flashing, and someone hollered, 'Look, he's going to jump,' and thousands of people gathered to watch him do it."

"That's awful. Macabre."

"Well, I suppose to the crowd, he seemed to be someone who had more problems than they had."

The phone was ringing again.

"It's your wife," Mrs. Orlando said.

"Hello, Kay?"

"Edward, what in hell is the matter with you? I told you to sell that damn Coca-Cola."

"It seems to be holding firm, Kay. I think you'd be smart to hold it."

"Well, it's *my* stock."

"Of course. But unless you need the cash for something, I'd recommend that you hold it. Coke is going to do all right."

"How about Bethlehem. I just talked to the board room and it's down to 95. I *want* to sell that, Edward."

"All right, Kay. But I still advise against it."

"No. I want to sell. And sell that Coca-Cola, too."

"Okay, I'll put it through."

"Both of them."

"Yes, both of them."

"All right. Good-bye."

All the grace and charm of a barracuda, Edward thought, as he replaced the receiver.

Suddenly the office seemed to crowd in on him. Both phones were ringing. Mrs. Orlando was approaching with some kind of memo. Behind her was Angus Felt, carrying some other papers. Outside the window, noise from the street rose like a threatening wind.

"JEE-ZUS!" he shouted, and immediately felt better.

Mrs. Orlando had a message:

COL. JOHN W. PRENTISS OF HORNBLOWER & WEEKS HAS CALLED A MEETING OF ALL HEADS OF WIRE HOUSES FOR AS SOON AS POSSIBLE AFTER THE CLOSE OF THE MARKET, TO BE HELD IN HIS OFFICE AT 42 BROADWAY.

"Tell him I'll be there," Newbord said.

Angus handed him a clip from the broad tape:

CHICAGO WHEAT OFF 12½ CENTS.

During the next forty-five minutes, Newbord sat glued to his desk, receiving and assimilating information in increasing abundance from all parts of the financial world, much like a commanding general in his headquarters.

There was one difference. No order that Newbord could give would stem the losses or in any way affect the terrible news that was flowing toward him, piling up around his desk, and threatening to inundate him.

At 11:30 he learned that the New York Stock Exchange ticker was forty-eight minutes behind the trading, and that the Curb Exchange ticker was lagging by forty-seven minutes.

Over six billion dollars had been lost by American investors by that hour alone.

Raymond & Company had called the loans on a vast majority of its customers and their securities were being dumped into the market's vortex, seeking, questing, beseeching buyers—that were nonexistent.

United States Steel plunged to 194½.

General Electric went from 319¾ to 302¼.

Johns-Manville lost forty points—from 180 to 140.

Montgomery Ward dropped seventy points—from 260 to 190.

National Biscuit went from 209 to 193½.

Atcheson slithered from 264½ to 253¼ in just a few trades.

New York Central, subjected to big block sales, plummeted from 213⅞ to 197.

Word came that Senator Carter Glass of Virginia had

risen in the Senate to demand an immediate curb on credit, and also a special federal excise tax on securities to dampen speculation.

"Well, if nothing else kicks the bottom out of the market, that ought to do it," Newbord had roared when he read the item.

Harry called to say that Vice President Whitney had paused briefly on the trading floor to announce that the Visitor's Gallery would be closed to the public at twelve-thirty.

The rumors intensified. It was reported now that eleven speculators had plunged to their deaths from Wall Street buildings.

It was also said that the Buffalo Exchange was closed and that the Chicago Exchange would close at noon, Eastern time.

Panic reigned.

Panic was headquartered on the trading floor and its contagion billowed up to the Visitor's Gallery and seeped down the elevator shafts and stairwells to Broad Street and spread up Wall Street to Pine and Maiden Lane and Liberty and Broadway; it reached the wires and telephones and radios and spread, in seconds, throughout the civilized world. It reached ships at sea, many equipped with their own board rooms. It reached outposts near Antarctica.

The crowds in the street stood motionless and totally silent as quotations were shouted from one segment to another by self-appointed criers. Some had devised hand-signal systems so that collaborators in the board rooms with access to the freshest figures (they were nearly fifty minutes late) could relay them to participating watchers on the street.

The bedlam on the trading floor of the stock exchange

could be heard clearly on Broad Street and it frightened the mob into immobility.

When a man fainted, no ambulance could get through and he had to be carried three blocks uphill to Broadway to the waiting vehicle. Police had to move him. Speculators wouldn't leave the scene.

Overhead the sun shone brightly on the solid stone, steel and concrete towers. The temperature rose slowly toward sixty.

Stripped now to shirtsleeves and with his tie off, Newbord received what must have been his twentieth call of the morning from Jules Barnish.

"Ed," he said abruptly. "I've got news."

"Well, that's really some surprise," said Newbord. Sarcasm provided some enjoyable release from pressure.

"This may be good news."

"This I doubt."

"Whitney isn't in the Exchange. There's a report that he has gone over to J. P. Morgan's."

"So?"

"J. P. Morgan's, Ed. Think about it."

"I am."

"There's a rumor that Thomas Lamont is going to call a meeting of the big-shot bankers to get them to support the market."

"Oh?"

"Yes, and the rumor is getting around, and already, I think, prices are beginning to firm up. Just beginning, mind you. But the rumor is getting out and I think some firm bids are coming in."

"I pray to God that you're right," Newbord said.

At the other end of the line, at the stock exchange, Jules Barnish bowed his head.

"Amen," he said, reverently. "Amen."

CHAPTER 7

The Meeting at 23 Wall Street

~~~~~~

John Pierpont Morgan, head of America's largest and richest private investment bank, was in Europe, and the acting chief executive of the influential House of Morgan in Wall Street was the silver-haired, pince-nezed partner and second-in-command, Thomas W. Lamont. Aristocratic and scholarly, ensconced in an enormous office thickly carpeted and furnished with rich mahogany desks, tables, chairs and glassfront bookcases, it is likely that even had the publicity-shy J. P. Morgan been present, Thomas Lamont, caricature of the old European banker, would have conducted any dealings with the public or the press, for this was customarily his duty when occasion demanded.

Not that J. P. Morgan and Company spent much time explaining its activities, its thinking or its policies to press or public, but when it was inclined rarely to do so, the institution spoke with the voice of Thomas W. Lamont. On such occasions, other bankers awaited his word with the same intensity as the most responsible financial reporter who was granted the most favored corner chair in Mr. Lamont's office. There was also no question that on most occasions when Thomas W. Lamont spoke, he could number among his most interested attendants, awaiting a word of what he said, President Herbert Hoover, Treasury Secretary Andrew Mellon and the presidents of both the New York Stock Exchange and the Curb Exchange, to say nothing of the financial officials of most countries and the heads of many states.

Lamont usually spoke as from a financial Sinai.

Late in the forenoon of October 24, 1929, Thomas W. Lamont spoke.

The exact time was not recorded accurately, but most observers who recollect the event say it was "just before noon" or "shortly before twelve" or "at the height of the panic," which would place it at five or ten minutes before the hour.

What Lamont said at that hour is not known, either. What is known is that he placed five telephone calls, personally. As a result of those calls, four of Wall Street's most powerful bankers met shortly thereafter in Lamont's office.

A recipient of one of the calls and also believed to have been present, or at least hovering nearby, was Richard F. Whitney, vice president of the New York Stock Exchange, brother of Morgan partner George Whitney, senior partner in the commission house bearing his own name, and the floor trader for J. P. Morgan and Company at the Exchange. It was Richard Whitney who did the buying and selling for the Morgan account.

Six-footer Dick Whitney was a man's man in a man's world. Broad of shoulder, muscle-necked in a size eighteen collar, he exuded the air of the well-connected, well-informed Man-on-His-Way-to-the-Top-in-Wall-Street. He was affable, universally liked, generally had time to listen to or to tell the latest story making the rounds, and was usually seen standing in the midst of a group of admirers wherever he paused, whether it was in the financial district or elsewhere.

On this day he was suffering from a slight case of sunburn, memento of his chore of the preceding day when he judged the horse show in Far Hills, New Jersey.

On this day Richard Whitney was to become a national hero of unprecedented stature, acclaimed in headlines from coast to coast. For a week at least he was to rank with Charles A. Lindbergh and possibly even with George Washington and Nathan Hale as a hero of unduplicable proportions.

This he did not know, though, as he responded to that imperative summons from Thomas W. Lamont.

Ever the center for intrigue and rumor, Wall Street on this day seethed with stories and reports. Many of them were well based in truth, for every registered official having anything at all to do with the Exchange, provided he could afford to leave his desk, was on the trading floor or in the Visitor's Gallery or crammed in with the crowd on Broad and Wall Streets.

The old professionals who were jammed elbow-to-rib with the tourists, the amateurs and the venal all around the Exchange building knew the identity of those who came and went—those of any prominence or significance, that is —and could speculate with fair accuracy on their destinies and missions.

When Richard Whitney left the Exchange by the Broad Street side and made his way across the V-shaped courtyardlike street, at least a thousand pairs of eyes lighted with recognition and followed his progress as he turned at an abrupt angle down Wall and addressed the great bronze door marked Twenty-Three, right at the financial crossroads of the world, at the corner of Broad and Wall.

Within moments word had spread far beyond the immediate area: "Richard Whitney has gone to a meeting at J. P. Morgan's!"

Reaction to the news was varied at first.

"Jee-sus, we really must be in trouble in there" (meaning on the trading floor), one man is recorded as saying.

"Thank God—now we're saved!" another shouted.

The latter's point of view soon prevailed.

Because Whitney's visitation to the office of the investment banking firm seemed to presage a savior in the making, many in the crowd kept a keener-than-usual watch on the Morgan mansion's massive front door.

At about twenty past twelve there appeared Charles E. Mitchell, chairman of the board of directors of National City Bank, hatted, briefcased, intent, as he elbowed his way through the throng and into the premises at Twenty-Three Wall Street.

A murmur ran through the crowd.

On Tuesday Mitchell had returned from an extended trip through Europe and had granted an immediate interview to reporters, striking a strong position that thrust him far out on a limb. He had told the press, Wednesday's papers had reported, that the market was solid and sound and that it would "correct itself." But on Wednesday the market had turned in a contrary, Mitchell-defying performance that had pushed averages back to their early June levels.

Mitchell, however, was an important man. In a matter of moments brokerage houses throughout the district were abuzz with conjecture. Was Mitchell meeting with Lamont? What were they discussing? It was estimated later that Mitchell's appearance probably set off at least five thousand telephone calls.

Hardly had the speculation about Mitchell gained headway when someone identified the average-looking, pleasant-faced man cutting across Wall Street as Albert H. Wiggin, chairman of the board of directors of Chase National Bank. He was walking to Morgan's from his office, only a block to the north. Wiggin was less formal. He was hatless for one thing, suggesting that he was merely popping into a neighbor's office for a few moments before leaving for a more important luncheon date. He, too, entered the Morgan domain and disappeared behind the door.

Wiggin's appearance was momentous news, and the crowd turned as one man to direct full attention to the House of Morgan, and symbolically, ten thousand backs were turned on the New York Stock Exchange, even though the roar of the trading floor was still audible as far as the center of Broad Street.

Hard behind Wiggin came William C. Potter, president of the Guaranty Trust Company, a cool, efficient, friendly-looking man who also appeared merely to be taking a noontime stroll. He had neglected to observe the Columbus Day fashion dictum and was wearing his now-unseasonal summertime straw hat, perhaps in an unconscious gesture illuminating his conservatism and prudence.

Someone shouted, "Hey Bill, where'd you get that hat?" but Potter, unaware that he was being addressed, also passed through the portals of power and into the secretive interior of the great stone edifice marked Morgan.

Then hurrying, shouldering his way through the dense crowd, acting as though he were late for an important meeting—which, indeed, he was—came Seward Prosser, chairman of the board of directors of Bankers Trust Company, oblivious to the fact that the eyes of a multitude were watching his every step.

As Prosser entered through the bronze door, a cheer began on the Wall Street side of the square. It was picked up by onlookers in front of the Bache office across the canyon and spread simultaneously to the observers jammed in front of the Sub-Treasury Building to the north, and thence southward among the packed mass of humanity on Broad Street.

It was one single cheer, lasting perhaps thirty seconds. It was wafted up the sheer sides of the towering buildings and driven as by force through the narrow streets from India House and Hanover Square, westward to Broadway.

"They're going to support the market!" people cried, and neighbor turned to neighbor to relay this thought as though it were solid information that had been given out by Thomas W. Lamont, himself.

At this time threescore telephones were ringing angrily, sounding an imperative summons sixty times over into the general din of the district as threescore financial editors, city editors, wire editors and managing editors tried to reach their men on the scene to relay some vital information that had just been wired and phoned to all city desks, bureaus and wire services from an employee of J. P. Morgan and Company.

The information was: Thomas W. Lamont was calling a press conference, immediately.

Minutes after the door closed behind Seward Prosser, newsmen began to arrive. They were greeted at the door, were asked to identify themselves, and then were ushered into the building and placed in a ground-floor waiting room near the elevators.

They were not, as so many accounts related, taken to Mr. Lamont's splendid office suite. They waited below.

Outside in the steets, a feeling of excitement began to spread through the throng as ten thousand pairs of eyes stared in expectation at the mute edifice. Inside that one building were assembled the most powerful bankers in America. Together they represented wealth almost beyond calculation.

Actually the four bankers and Lamont represented directly and personally more than six billion dollars in bank resources.

The crowd watched the Gibraltarlike granite building as though expecting some sign, and those nearby reached out once again to touch the scars in the stone where an anarchist had set off an infernal machine, a blockbusting bomb, which was intended to destroy the House of Morgan, but which had succeeded mostly in making interesting and historic chips in the impenetrable facade.

It was reassuring to look at the healed wounds in the building now and to realize that when the mighty blast occurred, only an occasional picture frame was knocked askew in the executives' offices inside Fortress Morgan.

A bank that could withstand that blast—the scars seemed to say to those who felt them—could certainly weather a mere selling panic in the marketplace.

The news of the Morgan meeting had reached the trading floor of the stock exchange before the late-arriving Prosser had reached Lamont's office. It had also reached a hundred nearby brokerage offices, and orders were being flashed back and forth from floor traders to senior partners, and from front offices to the commission men and customers' men.

As a result, even before the meeting began, the prices of some stocks were beginning to firm up in response to a belief that the market would be supported by the resources of the very richest Americans. Floor traders began to notice fewer losses between trades. They began to "feel" a freshness in the marketplace as it became possible to sell a block of stock for the same price or almost the same price as that offered for the preceding sale.

Could it be that the panic was over?

No, some prices were still falling off. Steel, for instance. Some motors, also.

But utilities were firming; a good sign.

So were some rails.

What could a broker say to a client, though? What could he tell a client in Chicago or Spokane or Boston or Hartford? Or, in fact, what could he say to even a nearby client in Brooklyn or Manhasset or Oyster Bay or Far Hills?

Could he advise someone to buy back into the market now?

Could he, personally, be sure that the biggest sell-off in market history was ended? What if it wasn't? Who would believe him tomorrow?

If the panic was ending, surely there were magnificent bargains abounding in the list, now.

But who to call? Who was left? Millions of accounts had been sold out and closed as margin calls had been made and were not honored.

The paperwork was so far behind that no one knew just how many Americans had been wiped out between ten o'-clock in the morning and twelve-thirty in the afternoon, the most significant two and one-half hours in financial history.

The prevalent estimate was that something like twelve million accounts had been liquidated. This meant that twelve million Americans were broke or nearly broke, and that their life savings had evaporated in the clatter of a faltering tickertape now, at twelve-thirty, at least 100 minutes late in recording and posting the ever-changing quotations.

Could a broker in good conscience call anyone, no matter what his circumstances, and recommend that he buy into this market?

The record shows that not many brokers made such calls. They dealt with the orders at hand, and gave advice only if it was requested by a client, and they adhered, generally, to a code of ethics that was really nonexistent, because nothing had ever been transcribed into writing, and to which no broker had ever been asked to subscribe.

In the face of the greatest catastrophe of financial, economic and monetary history, the self-governing members of
the New York Stock Exchange were acquitting themselves
well on that remarkable day of October 24, 1929. In days
to come, when in the bitterness of the Depression they
would be accused of many things, only the professionals
and the insiders would remember the steadfastness and
responsibility of the reputable member firms during the har-
rowing hours of that trading day.

They stood up, individually and one and all, to the fiery
blast of the panic and did the chores that had to be done,
permitting the free auction market to pass its severest test
and weather its most thunderous storm. Many brokers
joined their clients in being wiped out and ruined as their
own margin calls were received, their own accounts liquidated and their own stocks tossed with the others into that
consuming maw of the flaming panic, to be sold "at market"
for whatever price would be bid.

The meeting in Thomas Lamont's office lasted exactly
twenty minutes.

An elevator slid to the ground floor of the chandelier-
illuminated lobby of J. P. Morgan and Company. The door
opened on the five bankers who stared out at the assembled members of the press and beheld what generally
seemed to be an array of inexpensive suits, frayed cuffs,
poorly matched neckties and a formation of improvised
notepads over which were suspended yellow copy pencils
in varied stages of disrepair, clutched by a half-hundred
nicotine-stained forefingers supported by an equal number
of thumbs reflecting a dozen states of cleanliness.

Heightened in character, status and importance by their
impeccability, the bankers, in the presence of such a jarring
gathering, permitted themselves to radiate the fact that they

were aware that they controlled resources of six billion dollars and that they could influence many billions more.

More than anything, they looked unafraid. An aura of confidence billowed from the confines of the elevator.

The reporters surged forward and the five bankers stopped before the Otis elevators and faced the press. Richard Whitney was not in their midst, and none noted his absence. There were only the bankers, Lamont, Mitchell, Wiggin, Potter and Prosser.

Lamont, ever frosty, permitted his guests a winter's smile. He cleared his throat imperceptibly, then addressed the press with an utterance that must be logged as the most surprising official statement in the history of Wall Street.

"There has been a little distress selling on the stock exchange," Mr. Lamont said, waving the pince-nez that depended from a black ribbon around his neck, "and we have held a meeting of the heads of several financial institutions to discuss the situation."

One of the reporters sniggered. Lamont chose to ignore what should have been regarded as an editorial comment. He plunged ahead. The statement went into history, unchanged.

"We have found that there are no ·brokerage· houses in difficulty and reports from brokers indicate that margins are being maintained satisfactorily," he said.

His concern was not for the millions who had lost their savings, but for the brokers who arranged for the event. The important thing about the margins was not that millions had been wiped out but that the forced sale of their stocks had agreeably covered the brokers' loans, and that as a result the banks, J. P. Morgan among them, would be intact and should not lose much.

But Lamont was addressing the financial press, which then, as now, was involved more with the welfare of the purveyors of stock and all who contribute to its distribution, than with the individual purchasers of securities.

He made his statement; then there was silence. The reporters waited with pencils poised over their trifolded sheaves of copy paper. The room smelled of lead paint and heated iron because the Morgan boilers had been fired the night before in deference to the early-morning chill that for a week past had crept in at midnight from the Atlantic-cold waters of the Battery, only a few blocks away.

From the door someone said, "The movie cameras and press photographers are set up on the steps of the Sub-Treasury Building," and a reporter for City News Service, who filed for the increasingly aware radio stations, muttered, " 'T'hell with 'em."

The silence persisted. Then Mr. Lamont added, almost as an afterthought, "It is the consensus of the group that many of the quotations on the stock exchange do not fairly represent the situation."

Again silence. The reporters waited. He said no more.

The reporters had been as respectful for as long a period as their own rules permitted. They surged forward toward the elevator and filled the air with questions.

What did he mean by saying that the quotations didn't represent the situation.

By this, Mr. Lamont said, he meant that the prices of many stocks, many important issues, had been carried down below the levels at which they might fairly be expected to sell. Mr. Lamont was careful not to split infinitives.

Well, what had caused the crash?

The prices of many issues, he replied, had been depressed because of a technical condition in the market rather than from any fundamental cause.

"What?" cried many reporters. He repeated the statement.

Then he talked of "air holes" in the list, which occurred, he said, when all buying interest in a particular stock vanished or dried up momentarily, creating a spread sometimes points apart between previous sales and succeeding offers.

That this was a profound commentary on the obvious, no one seemed to note. He might well have said that generally it is wet when it rains, or that customarily birds flap their wings when they fly.

Did Mr. Lamont mean to imply, a reporter asked, that the general decline that had been going on since September was a "technical condition"?

Oh, no. He referred only to yesterday's market and this morning's.

And then came the key question:

"Is this banking group going to go in and support the market?"

That, said Mr. Lamont, was a question he could not answer.

"Why not?"

Well, how could he speak for other banks? he parried.

Someone interrupted: How about the future of the market, Mr. Lamont? Will prices go back up?

It was an unfortunate break. Lamont might have been faced down about the plans of the Big Five Bankers. He answered his latest inquisitor.

Predictions about the market, Lamont said, should be the last thing in which a prudent banker should indulge. Then, seeming to relent a bit, he conceded that it was the opinion of the banking group gathered there that the stock market was "susceptible of betterment."

It was at this point that some reporters said that Lamont made a statement about the Federal Reserve Board.

Some said he did not.

In a later interview, Lamont, himself, denied that he had said anything about the Federal Reserve Board.

Word was soon out and it spread, that Mr. Lamont had said he expected the Federal Reserve Board at its meeting that day to take some action on the stock market situation.

When this reached the news tickers a few minutes later, it was widely interpreted that Lamont, speaking for the nation's leading bankers, was revealing that the way had been cleared for a reduction in the rediscount rate charged by the Federal Reserve Bank of New York.

Heads of commission houses were in general accord with this interpretation and they began immediately to buy stocks for their own accounts. This activity served to help firm up stock prices that were already, at noontime, firming up on the strength of other unfounded rumors.

Whether Lamont was completely guileless in this, will probably never be known. The few snow-haired reporters around today who were at the meeting are as incapable of agreement as they were then. It is possible, some historians suggest, that Lamont was trying deliberately to pressure the Federal Reserve Board—which was in session in Washington at the time—into authorizing the New York Federal Reserve Bank to lower its discount rate, thus freeing billions in credit to help Wall Street out of its mounting problems.

(Later in the day when the Fed adjourned in Washington without having taken any specific action, the five bankers huddled again in Lamont's office, in a meeting lasting until after six o'clock, and at its conclusion Lamont denied ever having said anything about the Federal Reserve meeting, pointing out that he would hardly be in a position, even if he should care to do so, to forecast any action by the Federal Reserve Board.)

The question remains: Where did a half-dozen reputable reporters get the idea that he said he expected the Federal

Reserve to take some favorable action?

As it was, however, Lamont was ready to terminate his noontime interview. He indicated completion of the session by replacing his glasses on the bridge of his nose, adjusting the pinch and nodding to the members of his banking consortium.

Gravely, they nodded back and, with barely a spoken word, turned to the door and the waiting cameras and flashes of manganese powder.

As an attendant opened the door, each banker smiled and braced his shoulders.

The newsmen, flowing out behind them and thrusting through the crowds to reach waiting telephones, spread the good news, the turnabout news, the news that the world had been awaiting: "THE BIG BANKS ARE GOING TO SUPPORT THE MAR-KET!"

Lamont had said no such thing.

Nor had any other banker in the group.

Still unnoted was the absence of Richard Whitney.

As the big door closed behind the last scrabbling reporter, Thomas W. Lamont punched the button in the elevator and the door sealed him from further view. The story, whatever it was, had been told to the newsmen, and news of it was outside, en route to the hands of Fate.

The fate awaiting two of the bankers was disgrace.

At later congressional hearings in Washington, it was disclosed that Albert H. Wiggin, Chase Bank's chairman, had owned half a dozen private holding companies, three of which had been incorporated in Canada for, he testified, tax purposes. One of Wiggin's companies was named Shermar Corporation in honor of his daughter. It dealt in the stock of Chase National Bank. Wiggin headed Chase National Bank at a salary of $275,000 a year.

Shermar Corporation, under Wiggin's direction, sold

short 42,500 shares of Chase stock between late September and early November 1929, for recorded profits of more than four million dollars. During that time, Wiggin was participating in the Lamont-Morgan bankers' pool that was formed to rescue the stock market. Its rescue might have enhanced the value of Chase stock and thus have cut into the profits of Shermar Corporation.

Charles E. Mitchell, National City Bank's board chairman, was arrested in 1933 by the crusading young United States district attorney Thomas E. Dewey. He was charged with income-tax evasion.

Mitchell's income for the first half—the "good" half—of 1929 was calculated at something in excess of a million dollars, at least $175,000 a month, or, put another way, at least $40,000 a week.

Then Mitchell had invested in some banking deals that had lost him some money. On top of that came the break in the stock market, costing him heavily. At year's end he was without the cash to pay the tax on the money he had earned in the earlier part of the year. He found himself heavily in debt to J. P. Morgan and Company.

He sold 18,300 shares of National City Bank stock to his wife at a loss to himself of $2,872,000, thus wiping out the tax liability he had incurred with his high income at the year's outset.

Following a headline-garnering trial in New York City, Mitchell was acquitted.

An even harsher and sterner fate awaited Richard Whitney—but that's another part of our story.

CHAPTER 8

Thursday, October 24, 1929

12:00, NOON

~~~~~~~~~~~~~~~~~~~~~~~~~~~~~~

As the sun reached its zenith in an azure sky and the thermometer pushed above sixty degrees, the sexton at Trinity Church watched the sweep second hand on his pocket watch and clutched the clapper cord, the small handline that hung beside the thick tolling rope, and as all three indicators on his timepiece converged on the numeral twelve, he gave the cord the yank that struck the first echoing note of the noon hour. Two trading hours had passed in that vital financial nerve center two blocks away, and three remained.

The bronze peal reverberated in the vintage October air and spiraled out over the financial district, wasted. The ancient call to midday worship and prayer went unheeded by most in that area, though a few high-church Anglicans were seen to bless themselves.

The stock-market panic was at its peak. Men shouted and wept and raised clenched, frustrated fists in the air. Cries of anguish that vied with the sound of the clarion failed to stanch the spreading flow of rumors—rumors of suicides, of bankruptcies, of collapsing empires.

On the trading floor of the stock exchange, a scant three hundred paces from Trinity Church, it was technically impossible to match sell orders with buy orders.

In bedlam bordering on mass mania, traders continued to function as best they could, hoping, praying, that the bottom would soon be reached and a turnabout recorded.

It was an exercise in desperation, for stocks that had lost twenty, forty, as high as seventy points in the last two hours, could find no immediate buyers as they were offered at historic sacrifice prices.

Huge and perspiring groups clustered around the posts where the most important and most pivotal key issues were traded, Motors at Post Four and Steels at Post Two being the most anxiously watched. Those who still clung to shreds of hope thought that if United States Steel or General Motors should show an improvement in prices, it would restore confidence, yea, even inspiration, to the gasping market.

The noise was deafening. The great, high-vaulted chamber smelled of sweat and stale air. The more than one thousand traders who were jammed onto the floor were ink-smeared and graphite-grimed, and a high percentage had torn their once-starched shirt collars in futile efforts to widen the area where their building body heat might escape into the fetid air.

Despite their shouts, now hoarse and tinged with fear, many minutes would elapse and many competing offers would arrive before one sale could be consummated in a specific stock, any stock.

As the church tower clock began to chime the hour, Mrs. Orlando placed a nearly square brown paper bag on Mr. Edward Newbord's desk. It contained two corned-beef sandwiches on rye bread, four quartered slices of a large Kosher dill pickle, a folder of mustard and a knife-shaped piece of cardboard.

"Here is Mr. Barnish's lunch," she said. "You mentioned that you might like to take it over to him."

Newbord nodded, his ear glued to the phone. He was listening to Jules who was giving him quotations on stock prices that ranged to fifteen points below those being quoted on the tickertape.

"I've got your lunch here, Jules, and I'll bring it over in a few minutes."

"You'd do me a greater favor by bringing that bottle of Canadian Club from my upper left-hand drawer."

"If I got my hands on it, it wouldn't last until I got there."

"I have a date with that bottle at about 3:15."

"You'll need it."

"Ed—have you any idea how we're doing?"

"None."

"Are we anywhere near solvent?"

"There's no way to tell."

"You'd better try getting your hands on some more money—or a bigger credit line somewhere, just in case."

"I've been doing that. We're not in the clear, but I've been given a little bit of encouragement by the bank. Hal Bunnell said to call him about one-thirty or two o'clock and he'd let me know if he could extend our line of credit."

"Ah. That means something. He's waiting for the Fed to act on the discount rate."

"Maybe."

"Well, what the hell else would he wait for? Otherwise he'd simply give you a flat 'no' and tell you that you couldn't have any more credit. Bunnell is the kind of creep who delights in turning down an applicant for credit. He'd say 'no' unless he was waiting for a break from the Fed."

"Well, I've been thinking about something, Jules. You

said that there's a report that Dick Whitney is going over to J. P. Morgan's?"

"It's no longer a report. He went. He's over there now. I've had it confirmed."

"Well, I'll tell you what I think, Jules. I think Morgan and Lamont and the other big bankers are going to get together to pool up some money to guarantee—to underwrite—quick loans to the responsible commission houses. That includes us."

"It would be the smart thing to do, Ed, but when have bankers ever been smart?"

"It's the only thing to do. Somebody has to come to the aid of the responsible brokers. After all, we're not companies or corporations. We're partnerships and our personal money has to back these brokerage businesses. We can't all just sit here and be wiped out."

"Oh, yes we can. I'll admit it has never happened before, but, Ed, believe me, it can happen."

"What bothers me most is that at this point I don't know how much money we own. If someone began buying—if a lot of buy orders began to come into this office and into our branches—I don't know what we'd use for money to execute the orders."

"It's a nice problem to have. Let's tackle that one firsthand."

"Yes, but don't forget, even if they discover a year from now when they're making an audit that we didn't have sufficient reserve, it's automatic suspension—and pfft— we go out of business."

"One way or the other, it may be our destiny."

"Well, maybe the Federal Reserve Board will come to the rescue."

"Yeah, and maybe Herbert Hoover *can* walk on water. Ed, I've got to go. Bring over my sandwich when you feel like it."

"Okay, Jules. Let me know right away if you think it's turning around."

"I will. G'bye."

In Washington the Federal Reserve Board sat in closed executive session. It never revealed what transpired at that meeting. What is known is that Treasury Secretary Andrew Mellon did attend and he did acknowledge that the break in the stock market had been discussed.

He said they also discussed the open-market policy— the flexible program for supporting government bonds in the marketplace. When prices of government obligations sag, the Federal Reserve steps in and buys bonds to support the price. When prices for those bonds get too high, the Fed sells, forcing prices lower. However, the Federal Reserve Bank did not repurchase any of the government bonds that day. Prices were fairly stable. There was no need to support them.

The first meeting (of two that day) of the Federal Reserve Board began at ten forty-five, by which time a full-scale disaster was under way on the trading floor of the New York Stock Exchange. It is known that officials of the board were in constant communication with numerous persons in the financial district, including members of the New York Federal Reserve Bank, several private banks, some commercial bankers and some brokers.

Who the individuals were, has never been revealed.

No member of the Federal Reserve Board would ever admit whether there had been discussion of the rediscount rate at that morning session.

The rediscount rate—the rate of interest at which the Federal Reserve Board advances money to the commercial banks—stood at six percent for the New York Federal Reserve Bank. The rate for the eleven other banks in the Federal Reserve System was five percent. Since commer-

cial banks in New York could borrow from the Federal
Reserve Bank only in relationship to their cash reserves
and escrows for interest, the difference of one percentage
point in the rediscount rate had the effect of freezing
several billions of dollars that otherwise might have been
loaned to the faltering brokers.

The Federal Reserve Board in Washington continued to
meet through the noon hour. It issued no statements
whatsoever.

At noon in her Detroit suburb, Helen Weedon sat beside
her telephone, trying desperately to reach her husband in
New York. For the last hour she had been told at five-
minute intervals that the toll lines to New York were tied
up.

Tears streaked her smooth cheeks.

She had talked to Mr. Marcus in Raymond & Company's Detroit office and learned that she and Harry had
been sold out.

Westinghouse, just before noon, had dropped to $160 a
share and, according to Mr. Marcus, she would be lucky
if she managed to get anything near that price.

There had been no confirmation of the sale the last time
she had checked with Mr. Marcus.

She knew that they owed about $16,000 to Raymond &
Company and she had also received phone calls from two
banks where, apparently, Harry had loans amounting to
at least another $15,000, secured by stock that he no
longer owned.

Helen's bubbling imagination caused pictures to flash
on and off in her mind like the magic-lantern slide shows
she had seen at church and school events when she was
a child. She saw herself in ragged clothes standing outside the Book-Cadillac Hotel holding forth a tin cup, seek-

ing alms. She saw Harry, lying pale and pained in a white hospital bed, felled by a heart attack from the overwork caused by trying to repay their debts. In another flash she saw Harry being led from the witness stand in handcuffs, en route to jail for swindling two powerful banks and a nationwide brokerage firm out of so much money. She envisioned herself engaged in the act of prostitution in their little bedroom upstairs while the children whimpered outside the closed door and that awful Joe Francoeur had his way with her.

The entire forenoon had been a series of calamities for Helen. She had fed Rick and Debbie and then had dressed Debbie, who somehow had lost a shoe between bedtime and breakfast. She found fifteen cents for Rick's lunch money and sent him running, for he was late for school.

Betimes she had received another phone call from her sister Kate, with further complaints about the missing John.

At nine o'clock promptly—obviously it was just as soon as the office had opened—the bank had called asking for Harry, and the man had alarmed her by stating that it was "urgent and imperative" that Mr. Weedon get in touch with him right away.

She had tried to reach Harry at the hotel in New York again and was heartened, momentarily, when the call went through. But no one answered in Harry's room. In her frustration she had neglected to leave word with the hotel operator to have Harry call her, and when she tried to call back to leave a message, she couldn't get a line.

As soon as the breakfast dishes were done she had called Kate and told her she would drive over to pick her up. The Model T Ford sometimes bucked and jerked when she shifted gears with the foot pedals and it had done it again this morning just as she was being passed by a man in a big Overland touring car who gave her a "Hee-Haw," and shouted, "Sell it and buy a horse!" Helen simply hated such public displays.

Then there had been the scene at Kate's. When she got there she found that John had arrived home a few minutes earlier, sick and green and still weaving with drunkenness. Kate was screaming at him, which made him sicker, a diatribe that intensified until finally he vomited on the kitchen floor. Helen seized that opportunity to depart, leaving her sister to decry her martyrdom and to pursue, alone, the olympian task of John's reformation.

She had returned home to the ringing of the telephone bell and, thinking it might be Harry, had rushed, panting, into the house and snatched the receiver from the hook. It was the second bank, requesting an immediate call from Harry.

In the security of her home, Helen poured herself another cup of coffee and sank down in the chair beside the kitchen table, trying to analyze the frightening sense of impending doom that goaded a feeling of panic. If only she could have the reassurance of Harry's call. Surely Harry must know by now that the market was in trouble. He would call her soon.

The next two phone calls were from the banks, however, the first informing her that they were calling for a loan for $9,000-plus, and the second serving notice that they wanted immediate repayment of a loan of something over $6,000. Both loans had been secured by hypothecated shares of Westinghouse Electric.

Belatedly, at twelve-fifteen she remembered the twelve-o'clock news and rushed to the radio to turn it on, but when the set warmed up and she adjusted the several dials, the time had passed and a farm program was in progress. That told of falling prices on commodities, but she didn't understand it. Because there was nothing else to do she sought out some more distant stations, thinking that one might be carrying some stock-market news. She tried for WTAM in Cleveland, then KDKA in Pittsburgh and WGY in Schenectady, but when she tuned them in, waveringly, they were broadcasting nonnews programs.

Helen went into the living room and in silence sat beside the phone and waited. Debbie played alone in the sandbox in the back yard.

In the Narragansett Hotel in Providence, Rhode Island, Eddie Gallant treated himself to a noontime showerbath. He was hot and sweaty from his quick trip to Fall River and excited at the prospects it offered. He was sweating, too, because he was exceedingly nervous. He was nervous because he couldn't reach his broker in New York. He had tried again as soon as he entered his room.

He was toweling himself in the white-tiled bathroom when his phone rang. It was the operator, and she reported that she had succeeded in placing his call to New York.

"Hello? Max? Max, this is Eddie Gallant. What's the market doing?"

"Eddie, you call me to ask a stupid question like that? How's it doing? It's doing bad. Real bad. That's how."

"Well, I wanted to check on my Radio Corporation of America stock."

"Eddie, you ain't got much Radio Corporation of America stock. We had to sell you out. It's now down to forty-eight. Forty-eight! Can you imagine that? We didn't know where to reach you. The hotel said you were out. We called your bank and asked for money to cover your margin loan but they said you didn't have this kind of discretionary account. We had to sell you. I don't know yet what we got for it."

"My God, Max, that's my life's savings."

"It's more than that, Eddie. You'll still be owing us, I'm afraid."

"How about my Commercial Solvents?"

"Commercial Solvents you've still got. It's down a little —oh, maybe twenty points—but we haven't had to call your margin loan on it. Yet. I repeat, Eddie, *yet.*"

"Well sell some, Max. Sell enough to cover the loan. Leave me something, for Heaven's sake."

"Sell? Sell? Eddie, to whom?"

"Come on, Max. There's a market there someplace. Get rid of some of my Solvents to pay off my loan and let me ride out the market with what's left."

"Okay, Eddie, I'll do my best."

"Max, believe me, it's for your own good. It's the only way you'll ever get paid what I owe you."

"Oh, don't worry, Eddie. With a career like yours, you got no real worries."

"I got reason to worry, Max."

"Ech. It's a waste of time. You don't seem to realize it, but you're another Jolson."

"I'd rather be rich."

"Be rich."

Eddie was sitting on his bed and realized as he replaced the receiver that he had created a dark semicircle of dampness on the bedspread. As he resumed toweling himself he became aware of the fact that he was dripping wet, not with shower water, but with nervous sweat.

And his hands were shaking.

Curtain time was an hour and twenty minutes away. He'd better compose himself and be damn good. It looked as though he would need the job.

It was turning into a hot day in Love County, Oklahoma, hot and dry. Marcy Fitton backed the Model T flivver out of the barn. Into the small truck body that he had built in the trunk area of the car's frame, he placed his two fishing rods, his homemade tackle box, a can of worms, a can of scrabblers, his lunchpail and a paper sack containing three quart bottles of home-brew beer and a knit bag that would hold the beer bottles when he placed them in the water to chill and would later hold the fish that he would bring home.

The smell of chili sauce filled the morning air, and Marcy knew it was useless to ask Carrie again to come with him. She had her program all arranged. Well, so had he. He glanced at his watch. A few minutes after ten. Excellent. He had a full day's fishing ahead of him. Marcy cranked up the machine and climbed aboard his quivering vehicle.

In Hillview, Illinois, the manager of the Hartwell Land Trust Company prepared to attend an early lunch with an engineer from the Hartwell Drainage and Levee District to discuss some topographical questions that had been raised at the last directors' meeting. The manager's name was Emil Schram, who from 1941 to 1951 would serve as president of the New York Stock Exchange.

At Trinity College in Hartford, Connecticut, the class in English Literature I ended promptly at twelve, noon, and the lean, lanky freshman from Iowa who strolled out to seek lunch was G. Keith Funston, who would serve as the Exchange's president from 1951 to 1967.

A short time after the noon chimes had stopped ringing, Jules Barnish received word from Harry Hoerner that the market was about 105 minutes ahead of the tape. Trades made that instant wouldn't be reported to the general public—or even to the brokers—until more than an hour and a half had elapsed. Not until one-thirty or one forty-five could anyone on the outside learn what trade had been made in a specific stock at noontime.

This intelligence, more than anything else, heightened his sense of despair. There was no way that general support could be rallied beneath the market if the public couldn't be kept aware of the developments. Brokers, good solid professionals out around the country, might still be selling when smart and informed traders on the floor were convinced there was reason to buy.

It's like a forest fire, Jules thought. You may stamp it out here where it started, but it rages on in the distance, far beyond your area of control, causing increasing damage as it burns, and growing wider and wider and more destructive with each passing minute.

There is no reason why we, at least, can't have a better idea of where the market stands, he thought, and hailed a clerk to ask him to bring him a legal-size yellow pad. He would jot down some of the more significant "true" quotations—the prices for the latest trades. He'd have a list ready for Newbord when he arrived with his sandwich.

At some point between twelve noon and twelve-thirty, Jules Barnish wrote down some of the more important current quotations. They are official for that hour.

Jules looked over his hastily compiled list.

"And to think," he said aloud, "that there was a big sell-off yesterday, and the whole list has been retreating since September!"

He shook his head, sadly.

Here is the list he had ready to show his senior partners:

	Wednesday's Closing Price	Noon Price	Change
Air Reduction	195½	176⅛	−19⅜
Allis Chalmers	56⅛	44	−12⅛
American Banknote	127	115	−12
American & Foreign Power	112	88	−24
American Home Products	59¾	49¾	−10
American International	65¾	54	−11¾
American Mach & Fdry	240¼	219	−21¼
American Rolling Mills	115½	106¼	− 9¼
American Tel & Tel	272	245	−27
American Water Works	120¼	93	−27¼
Anaconda Copper	102	92	−10
Auburn Motors	260	190	−70
Baldwin Locomotive	35	15	−20
Bendix Aviation	51	40	−11
Bethlehem Steel	101¾	92½	− 9¼
Bohr Aluminum	73	50	−23
Burroughs Adding Machine	84¼	59	−25¼
Byers (A.M.) Company	121¼	76	−45¼
Canada Dry Ginger Ale	80½	60	−20½
Chesapeake & Ohio RR	257½	231	−26½
Columbia Carbon	255	210	−45
Commercial Credit 1st pfd 6½'s	91	70	−21
Commercial Solvents	448	425	−23
General Electric	314	283	−31
General Motors	57⅜	49	− 8⅜
Hocking Valley	540	515	−25
International Abbott	113	99	−14
International Business Mach.	231⅜	201	−30⅜
International Tel & Tel	110¾	79	−31¾
Johns-Manville	180	140	−40
Ludlum Steel	70½	50	−20½
Montgomery Ward	83¼	50	−33¼
National Supply	124	110	−14
Pittsburgh Coal	74½	65	− 9½
Radio Corporation of America	68½	44½	−24
Republic Steel	105¾	90	−15¾
U.S. Industrial Alcohol	201¼	169	−32¼
U.S. Steel Corp.	204	193½	−10½
Western Union	235	220	−15

CHAPTER 9

Thursday, October 24, 1929

1:00 P.M.

~~~~~~~~~~~~~~~~~~~~~~~~~~~~~~~~~~~~

Stock-exchange vice president Richard F. Whitney did not leave the J. P. Morgan office when the bankers departed. He had not appeared for what the newspapers referred to as the "impromptu press conference," though it was neither impromptu, because a Morgan aide had alerted all city desks and requested that reporters be dispatched, nor much of a press conference, since its value was more in what the newsmen *imagined* than in what they had been told.

His activities during that vital noon hour are still a matter of presumption and speculation and the details were never made clear in the brief literary postmortems of Black Thursday. Events crowded in on the historians, and with the Depression taking shape shortly after the first of the New Year, such matters as Whitney's whereabouts were ignored as being too picayune and thus soon forgotten.

It is presumed that when the bankers were being interviewed by the press, Dick Whitney conferred with his brother, George Whitney, a partner in the J. P. Morgan bank.

It is presumed also that after Thomas W. Lamont left

the newsmen, he and Whitney sat down to map out specific plans for supporting the stock market. Such plans must have been agreed upon tentatively by the bankers' consortium.

If they had not, Whitney must have indeed been given enormous and broad powers, as disclosed by subsequent events.

It is assuméd that he ate a quick lunch with either Lamont or brother George, for when he left later he went directly to the trading floor of the stock exchange. He might have foregone the noon meal, however. Many did in Wall Street that day.

What is known for certain is only what was seen and recorded. Whitney was seen to enter the J. P. Morgan and Company bank at 23 Wall Street several minutes before the four bankers made their separate appearances.

That was a few minutes before noon.

He was seen to leave the Morgan bank building at about one-fifteen and thread his way through the crowd on Broad Street and use the Broad Street entrance of the stock-exchange building. He could have used his fullback's shoulders to bulldoze a way through the packed humanity—and such was his urgent mission that it would have been excused—but several observers made the point that he moved very gingerly and asked people to move aside with what was, one is given to understand, typical gentlemanliness.

Having gained the sanctuary of the stock exchange's inner stairs, he made his way directly to the trading floor and its Hadean tumult.

Fully a half-hour had passed since word had reached the trading floor that the Big Five Bankers had created a pool with which to support market prices, and even in the absence of any evidence whatsoever, a perceptible turn-around in bidding was evident. Gains were being posted on some prices.

This might have seemed surprising to a nonprofessional observer, for there was plenty of stock "up for sale" in almost every issue. It would seem that the normal forces of supply and demand would continue to depress prices (since supply exceeded demand) until the supply was exhausted and the bidding had to be sweetened in order to induce holders to sell.

During that thirty- or forty-minute period, however, the stock-exchange specialists, the true unsung heroes of the day, had been performing their vital functions as market stabilizers.

The specialist is charged with responsibility for maintaining an orderly market in a particular stock in which he "specializes." Using his own money if necessary, he must buy for his own account when too much of "his" stock floods the trading post, yet he cannot interfere with the normal "bid-and-asked" auction process.

He must support a market when it is declining, and have stock available for sale when it is rising, placing himself always in a viable but profitless position and managing his affairs with lightning speed and incredible precision so that his "book," that is, his record of transactions, comes out even at the end of the trading session.

He's like the differential gear in a transmission, absorbing unexpected speed on one side and unexpected drag on the other, frequently simultaneously.

One misstep and he can be wiped out financially. Worse, he might cause financial loss to others. Though there are, today, safeguards to preclude mischance at the hands of the specialist, he is still the most important functionary in maintaining an orderly market, and in times of a big sell-off, such as in May 1970, he performs heroically at peril or expense to his own financial welfare.

With prices cascading all the forenoon of Black Thursday, the specialists had been trying desperately to buy stock at each level to keep the market from being flooded with offers to sell, and had been allowing only sufficient amounts to reach auction at any one time to truly reflect the descending market price. However, as it became known that huge blocks were being tossed into the market to "sell at market" as millions of accounts were liquidated for their margin loans, the prices had tumbled by unprecedented declines, despite the best efforts of the specialists.

At noon hour the specialists were loaded with sufficient stock to be able to withstand selling pressures right to the closing hour of three o'clock.

By one o'clock, however, many specialists were heard to be saying, "I'm selling on the uptick."

To the trader this meant that the stock was being proffered by the specialist at one-eighth of a point *higher* than the previous bid.

Within moments trades were being recorded on the uptick in several stocks.

Here was manifest the true value of the specialist. There was no depressing flood of offers to sell at the moment when encouraging news reached the trading floor. Specialists had been keeping an orderly check on the flow of offers to sell.

The turnabout took place in relative secrecy, for the tickertape (ironically called the *"high-speed tape"*) was running well over one hundred minutes behind transactions at the time.

The din on the trading floor did not subside. If anything, it intensified. A new kind of excitement grew amongst small groups closest to the trading posts, then within seconds spread in widening circles across the packed floor.

Traders began to match up sell orders for stocks "offered at market" with bids that were one-eighth of a point higher; then a quarter of a point. Occasionally an order was executed a half point above the previous price.

There was no cheering. There was merely louder noise, a quickening of the trading pace.

The experts were too seasoned to be tricked by a small buying spree. There had been a couple of small rallies earlier in the day but they hadn't lasted.

Those who participated in the turnabout in price trends knew that the new spirit was based solely on a rumor, a report. They wouldn't let their desire for a recovery turn into premature optimism. A fractional gain was a different matter.

They were being neither skeptical nor cynical. They were being practical. If prudence must be the key word in the handling of the funds of others, practicality is the word that governs specialists when they risk their own millions each day in a mercurial marketplace.

A good report, one that is verified, is good for a certain number of points, depending, of course, on the stock. It is worth that and no more. This is the professional trader's "edge," and he uses it whenever he can in an unstable market.

It permits him to buy or sell on a rumor or a report or a predicted important decision or an anticipated act that is expected to affect the market. He is in position to analyze the rumor, report, decision or act before the general public does, and he's there to execute his stock transaction accordingly. He risks a few points of his own money on his own judgment.

Knowing how the professional traders will respond,

specialists hedge against good rumors or reports by buying some stock to support a new trend if it develops.

On Thursday, October 24, 1929, Black Thursday, the specialists had started buying shortly after twelve-thirty, offering fractions above previous prices.

By one o'clock, floor brokers were placing orders to buy at prices that were slightly higher than those recorded in preceding sales.

Specialists then began to sell to the traders the stocks they had bought a few minutes earlier.

If the traders were right, orders would soon come from their brokerage offices to buy at prices higher than the ones they were paying to the specialists.

Therein reposed some profit, and knowing this, everyone on the floor was probably more tense, nerve-racked and fuse-primed than at any previous point in that hectic day when big, burly, ruddy, much-liked Richard F. Whitney, still politely making his way, came onto the floor and headed toward that vital focal point, Post Two, the position where the steels were traded.

Part of Dick Whitney's charm—aside from the natural likability of the man—may have been his subtle manner of defying the mores that nettled others. He believed in elitism and he was of the elite, thus he made his own rules. His one concession was to display, whenever possible, his gold Porcellian pig from Harvard on his watch chain.

If stockbrokers and investment bankers were supposed to dress in dark-blue business suits and affect somber colors, how much darker and how much more somber should be the raiment of the vice president and acting chief executive officer of the New York Stock Exchange?

Whitney, that day, was wearing a tan tweed suit. It looked to be very expensive, but it was still tan. Most of the time Dick Whitney affected extremely formal and handsome attire, but when he felt like it, he ignored such minor rules. He had in the past caused raised eyebrows by wearing brighter, tradition-defying suits to such funereal events as cocktail parties at the Waldorf and to such sobering occasions as new underwriting celebrations at Texas Guinan's.

Since fashion decreed that no male could wear anything but black or dark blue after six o'clock, and since many Wall Streeters had no time to change, most left their apartments and homes in the morning dressed as though they were en route to dinner and the theater.

With a reincarnated late-autumn sunburn that day, Dick Whitney had decided he'd feel more comfortable in his tan tweed.

As he picked his way across the massed trading floor, gently touching shoulders and elbows and murmuring dozens of "I'm sorry's," "Excuse me's" and "Pardon me's," a man at Post Two spotted him and, facing the crowd, raised his arm and pointed his finger at Whitney. Heads turned, and then, as if by high decree, as though he were Moses addressing the waters of the Red Sea, the crowd parted before him, opening a clear but paper-strewn alleyway to the trading post for steels.

It was exactly one-thirty.

Dick Whitney strode forward, and as he did, every head in the enormous room—it is estimated there were between one thousand and eleven hundred persons there—turned to watch him.

A vibrant stillness descended and the current trades that were being made were transacted in murmurs.

There came a sibilant sound as friend hailed friend to repeat the name, "Whitney. It's Dick Whitney."

All eyes watched as Dick Whitney stepped to Post Two

and jauntily, but in a loud and carrying voice, placed an order. It was for 10,000 shares of United States Steel Corporation at 205!

Steel, at the time, was trading at 193.

Whitney was buying at twelve points above the market!

Instantly the deed became—and still remains—the most celebrated single order in stock-exchange history.

In his first trade Whitney received only 200 shares at the new price.

He appeared unsurprised at the paucity of offers—he knew how the specialist worked—and said he would allow his order to stand. He wanted ninety-eight hundred additional shares, he said, and he was offering two-oh-five, two hundred and five dollars per share. He repeated the figure very clearly.

One trader in the dense crowd shouted, "Yeaaaa!"

No others joined him.

Another began to applaud, but in the absence of support, he stopped.

In near silence, Whitney stepped to the next post and placed a large order for General Motors at 57⅜, the opening price for the day and more than eight points above the preceding trade.

Calmly, then, he proceeded from post to post placing huge orders for the stocks of key corporations, and in almost every instance he offered to pay Wednesday's closing price. He bought Montgomery Ward at 74; it was selling at 50.

It was as though Black Thursday had never occurred, as though, to Whitney, the great losses of the day were nonexistent.

By the time he had completed his tour of the trading floor, Whitney had placed orders for blue-chip stocks totaling more than twenty million dollars.

Behind him, as he left one post and proceeded to another, trading resumed. In filling Whitney's orders, sales were being made at prices that hadn't existed since the opening gong.

The prices of other stocks, those not affected by direct orders from Whitney, began to move upward, a point, two points.

The noise began again. The shouting picked up around the trading posts and spread quickly to all corners of the huge room. Soon it was noisier than it had been earlier, as trading intensified at the new levels.

On Broad Street the crowd had become apprehensive during the period of silence. What had caused it? What was going on in there? The mood began to blacken.

Then word came out. A messenger told the story to a friend at the door. The friend turned and shouted the news.

"Whitney is supporting the market! The bankers are supporting the market! It has turned around! Prices are going up!"

Bedlam broke over the entire financial district. Ten thousand voices were raised in a thunderous roar.

Big, bronzed Dick Whitney became an instant hero.

Newsmen in the press room on the eighth floor were alerted to Whitney's activities by messengers who had been sent with the news by Exchange officials. Some, indeed, had been watching the drama from the vacated Visitor's Gallery.

City News Bureau filed immediately, thus alerting all city desks in town, and fortunately, the news desks in the radio stations.

Radio on that day played a major role in getting the news out to the rest of the country while there remained an hour and a half for trading.

Bulletins were issued almost immediately. Uptown, in the radio news room, reporters who didn't know a stock from a bail bondsman were pressed into service to rewrite and interpret the events being recorded on the direct wire from the stock exchange.

In all, they handled the assignment well. The news was flashed out to the world. This was good, for radio provided the only means of getting the news to the public while the market was still in session.

Without radio, brokerage offices around the country would have been uninformed of events until ten thousand telephone calls had been placed. Facilities had been overtaxed as it was, since early morning.

At the time Whitney was placing his order for U.S. Steel, the tickertape was running one hundred and twenty minutes late. In brokerage offices throughout the nation at one-thirty Eastern time, the ticker was printing price quotations of transactions that had taken place at eleven-thirty that morning, when prices were reaching toward their most depressed point.

Those lagging quotations, taken from the ticker, were then relayed by Marconi telegraph to ships at sea and to brokers and exchanges in other parts of the world. Thus information received outside the country was one hundred and thirty to one hundred and forty minutes late.

New York's afternoon newspapers, replating amid pandemonium, would be unable to get the news to the streets before two-thirty and then only in the immediate vicinity of the Wall Street area, and twenty minutes later in the Times Square, Herald Square and Grand Central districts. All papers were scheduling extra editions to be printed sometime after six o'clock under the accurate assumption that thousands of New York workers would be commuting home late that night. Street sales of afternoon newspapers increased an average of thirty percent that day. In Wall Street 50,000 clerical workers labored through the night without a break.

Radio was projected permanently into a position of primary importance in the communications field if only because it was the sole means of spreading important news about the nation's most vital economic nerve center. Around the country only the newspapers in the biggest cities were equipped to get out extra editions, so that even as the news traveled westward and gained an hour in each time zone, newspapers alone could not handle the assignment of getting the information out before the market's close.

By two o'clock, a half-hour after he had placed his first order, Whitney's role as an American hero was assured and his name was being spoken from coast to coast.

Thousands of Americans, upon hearing the news, responded by calling their brokers who were also relying on radio to inform themselves. As a result, orders began to flow toward New York from various parts of the nation, and with the renewed load on telephone, telegraph and private lines, the nation's entire communications system came perilously close to breaking down.

Whitney was heading for his office and was passing the president's office on the sixth floor when through the open window he heard the crowd in the street cheering and calling his name.

He smiled. He knew he had effected a miraculous coup. As the floor trader for the House of Morgan, his buying would have been significant. But as the Morgan trader who was also backed by an additional six billion dollars in resources from the four other banks, he was impressive beyond measure. The market simply had to respond.

He felt certain that the twenty million dollars' worth of

orders he had just placed would be well secured by the stocks he had bought and that in a few days those shares could be fed back into the rising market and the cash would be recovered at no loss to the bankers.

Perhaps, he mused, there might even be a profit in the deal.

Dick Whitney was pleased with himself. Most figured that he deserved to be.

As Whitney repaired to his office to confer by phone with the Morgan partners, his immediate superior was just sitting down to breakfast six thousand miles to the west. E. H. H. (Harry) Simmons, president of the New York Stock Exchange, was on his honeymoon in Honolulu. He and his bride were just beginning a day whose schedule included lunch with friends and a round of golf. It would be a while yet before he learned the awful truth of what had happened on this day in New York during his absence.

At that same time, a few blocks away from the New York Stock Exchange, a man who was destined to become a national villain, a scapegoat, wore a smile of success.

His name was Ben Smith, a rambunctious Irishman who disbelieved the statements of high officials about the strength of the nation's economy and the durability of its prosperity. Since September he had been selling the market short. On this day he had made a financial killing.

At about the time Whitney was placing his orders, Smith pushed into the crowded board room of the brokerage house where he maintained an office, and observing the selling pressure, shouted over the din: "Sell 'em all! They're not worth a thing!"

Smith was to be castigated in days to come by newspapers that blamed him for depressing the market with his enormous short sales, and he was to be held up as a selfish scoundrel who put his personal profit above his country's welfare, as many Americans forgot that for every seller there must be a buyer, and vice versa. In time the public became so angered at him that his house had to be surrounded by guards and his daughters protected by bodyguards.

But he made his reputation and gained his enduring sobriquet on Black Thursday. To the day he died, because of his spontaneous shout in the board room, he was to be universally known as "Sell 'em" Ben Smith.

At one forty-five Jules Barnish, munching on his now-hardening sandwich, was apprising his senior partner of the improvement in prices. They were standing on a stair landing outside the trading floor.

"You don't seem to be as cheered by this as I thought you might be," Newbord observed.

"No, I'm not," the trader admitted. "I just can't see this making any great difference. It's happening too late. Too late in the session, too late in the day. It should have been done yesterday to do any good."

"Aw, but prices are turning around, Jules. You have just been quoting some remarkable improvements."

"So I have, Ed, but let's not kid ourselves about these rising prices."

"What do you mean? How could we be kidding ourselves?"

"In the first place, Whitney has put an artificial prop under some of the leading stocks. It looks good, but it really doesn't mean much. It's just a gesture."

"Some gesture—twenty million dollars."

"No matter the cost, it's still a drop-in-the-bucket gesture and we have no evidence to show that others will go along with an artificially propped-up price. Question, Ed, why should anyone want to buy U.S. Steel at 205 if he can get it at 195? When Whitney jacked the price up to 205, don't you think that most people said, 'Let's wait until it gets down near its genuine low before we buy it'?"

"Maybe some will, but some won't, too."

"That's another point. Who's left? Who is going to do this buying? At least half of our customers have been sold out—their margin loans have been called and they've been sold out and their accounts are closed. Before I buy any stock in there somebody has to place an order for it, and we just haven't got many customers left. Not many houses have."

"We've got some left, Jules. People won't stay out of a good market. Not if prices are rising."

"Too many people have been forced out, Ed. As of right now you have a stock market with only half the customers it had yesterday—maybe fewer. As for prices being propped up by Whitney, forget it. It doesn't mean anything. The investment trusts have poured hundreds of millions into the market since ten-thirty this morning and it hasn't stopped the downslide one little bit."

It was true. The investment trusts, relative newcomers to Wall Street, and ancestors of the mutual funds, had put in their heaviest day of trading. Convinced of the soundness of their theory of "dollar cost averaging," the trusts had placed standing "scale orders" with their brokers, ranging from ten points to fifty points below the day's opening prices.

In its simplest form, the theory of dollar cost averaging is this: If you buy one hundred shares of stock that sells for $100 per share and the price drops to fifty, you can now buy twice as many shares for the same price, or two hundred shares for the price you paid originally for one hundred shares. If you do so, you now own three hundred shares with an average cost of $66 2/3 per share. Thus, for you, the market has to regain only 33 1/3 points to put your portfolio into the black.

In placing their scale orders, the trusts would leave standing orders to buy large blocks, up to 10,000 shares, in specific stocks when the price dropped ten points below the opening price. These were placed on a descending scale down to, in some cases, fifty points below the opening market prices.

When the decline had been steepest, between eleven-thirty and twelve-thirty that day, the scale orders of the trusts had served as a minor cushion to slow the descent of the falling prices. But they could not stop the downward spiral.

During the one-hour period, scale buying orders were "caught" (that is, became valid) by the hundreds and were executed automatically, and the trusts literally placed hundreds of millions of dollars' worth of orders. Some of the more successful trust operations of the day were made by portfolio managers who kept in constant touch with their floor brokers by phone and shouted their purchase orders as prices tumbled.

The point that Jules Barnish wanted to make to his senior partner was that in spite of these extensive—one might call them spectacular—purchases, prices had continued to fall.

When hundreds of millions of dollars' worth of actual technical support had failed, he just couldn't see where twenty million, used to prop up prices artifically, could succeed.

There were many seasoned veterans around the trading floor who agreed with him, but they also thought that it was the public, not the professionals, that decided the market's course.

The word was out. Whitney was a hero. Sounds of jubilation could be heard from Broad and Wall Streets and, one presumed, throughout the land.

CHAPTER 10

"The Market Will Correct Itself"

"The business of America," said Calvin Coolidge, "is business."

As he left the White House in the spring of 1929, it was Big Business.

Fifteen years earlier, America's industries had tooled up to help fight a war in Europe. This production intensified when in 1917 the nation angrily mobilized an embryonic expeditionary force and became involved in its first major foreign conflict.

In 1929, eleven years after the end of hostilities, the land basked in a benevolent industrial prosperity that was unparalleled in human experience. There had been inflation, a stock-market panic and a recession in the economy shortly after the war, but they left no scars.

The Congress of the United States had launched the twenties with two remarkable pieces of legislation. One denied citizens the right to possess alcoholic beverages. The other granted women the right to vote. After ten years of increasing sophistication citizens wondered, as the decade drew to its close, how Prohibition could possibly have been seriously considered, and why in modern times, women's basic rights had to be legislated.

Graphically, it illustrated the giant step that had been taken in human attitudes and in the national thought during the Roaring Twenties. After a lingering adolescence, America showed signs that it might grow up.

Consumer advertising had come of age. Radios, magazines, newspapers and billboards along the new highways exhorted people to buy, buy and improve their lives. Mass circulation and "Big Market" media were at their peak, and few Americans could elude the messages of the advertisers.

Instant snobbery mushroomed in the ranks of consumers. The boy with a King-of-the-Hill sled instead of a Flexible Flyer was made to feel inadequate, just as his mother was caused to feel unloved if she didn't have a new electric refrigerator in her kitchen. A house with a sign in the window that said "ICE" was not a good home, and its master was presumed to be a poor provider. The "electric icebox" manufacturers either invented or encouraged raw jokes about icemen and housewives to help husbands in making up their minds to buy.

A house that did not display a proper and oftentimes complicated "aerial," parent of the antenna, was recognized as a place without a radio, and hence was considered to be occupied by a rather shabby, if unfortunate, family.

Technology had come to the land. So had chain stores and mass distribution. New methods for making new products and new systems for selling them required huge capital outlays. Big city banks grew bigger. Underwriting and offering new securities of corporations became a major industry. Wall Street commanded as much public attention as sports or Hollywood.

To some extent, a man was measured by the bootlegger he patronized, but the real manifestation of his position in the social order was in the material possessions that showed. A fellow who had a heart of gold and not much else was pitied if not scorned, for he couldn't trade it for a new Stutz Bearcat.

The mood of America disturbed the gentler folk in the smaller towns, those who clung to prewar values, for they feared there was too little God and too much mammon in the land and they worried about its future.

They comforted themselves with knowledge that Harry Emerson Fosdick was packing the Park Avenue Baptist Church in Manhattan, that Evangelist Billy Sunday was preaching to thousands, that the unordained, vivacious Aimee Semple MacPherson was drawing tens of thousands to her Hollywood temple, and that Methodist Bishop James Cannon, Jr., father of the Prohibition Amendment, was out there slugging it out with sin. That both Miss MacPherson and Bishop Cannon would be exposed, one as a fraud, and both as venal hypocrites, had not yet been revealed.

Said Coolidge in his last message to Congress: "There was never a more pleasing prospect than that which appears at the present time."

Herbert Hoover agreed, for when he was campaigning in the autumn of 1928, he said he could see no valid reason why there should not be two chickens in every pot and two cars in every garage.

The industrial machine, enlarging rapidly, was producing new wealth for those who owned the tools.

It was also producing good jobs and what appeared to be wealth for those who bought shares in the corporations formed and managed by those who owned the tools. (The day of the trained corporate manager had not yet arrived for most companies.)

There were children working in textile mills, however, for as little as three dollars a week, and others in those and similar plants were subjected to indignities. A mature and seasoned worker often had to seek permission to go to the men's room, and it was sometimes denied. A veteran worker who was absent too long because of sickness, might return to find his job filled by another. On marginal farms in New England, in the Appalachians and in the Middle West, whole families were undernourished and inadequately clothed. In parts of America there were tens of thousands of people who had never seen a newspaper, magazine, catalog or book, had never heard of electricity or even steam power, and wouldn't have known what a privy was for.

In the big industrial cities there were grumblings among some production workers, and here and there at meetings intellectuals began to speak about exploitation of the working classes and about control of the "means of production." The names of Marx and Lenin were heard, and on college campuses and in union headquarters the descriptive "Red" came into use.

In 1929, those who were not directly oppressed by poverty believed they were living amidst unprecedented prosperity, and indeed they were. Most Americans thought they were better off than their parents had been at the same age. Many measured life in town against life on a farm, or against life in a foreign country. They called themselves lucky.

Women regarded their neat and clean gas stoves and remembered their mother's hot and dirty wood-burning kitchen stoves; they contemplated their electric washing machines and recalled their mother's scrub board and washtub; they put on sheer silk hose and thought of the lisle stockings of the preceding generation.

Oh, yes. They were fortunate, all right. They thanked Heaven for America's prosperity.

The menfolk, puffing on clean, even, ready-made cigarettes and hosing down their cars, all of which now had self-starters and many of which were equipped with balloon tires, were often heard to ask, smugly, "I just wonder what grandpa would say if he could return now and see what the world is like? Boy! Would he be surprised!"

In Russia the Soviet doctors worked on perfecting a birth-control pill, and dictator Joseph Stalin celebrated his fiftieth birthday.

In Manhattan the American Birth Control League moved out into the open from its furtive underground, with a meeting attended by Mrs. Eleanor Roosevelt, wife of New York's governor Franklin D. Roosevelt, Dr. Harry Emerson Fosdick and Morgan partner Thomas W. Lamont.

As the final year of the decade started, Secretary of the Treasury Andrew Mellon, scion of the Pittsburgh and New York Mellons, ran his business-oriented and practiced eye over the statistics and announced that everything looked fine to him and that business was going forward in fine shape. Throughout the year, both before and after Black Thursday, men in high places repeated such reassurances on numerous occasions.

The precisioned and oiled wheels of industry spun at increasing speed throughout the year. The shelves of commerce were filled, then emptied by consumers, then filled again. . . . and again. Cash registers jingled merrily, and almost every town in America began to spruce up and tried to look as prosperous as it felt. Service clubs abetted this campaign.

New buildings went up. New theaters were opened, many of them made necessary by the advent of Vitaphone and the talkies. New bridges were built and side streets were paved, some with macadam, a new, more durable tar substance named for its developer MacAdam.

On Saturday afternoons in the smaller towns and cities, men with arm garters on their sleeves scythed, trimmed and raked the tall grasses and weeds along the arteries that led into their communities, and at country-club parties that night were praised by their bobbed-haired, cigarette-puffing, stocking-rolled wives for having done their duty as good citizens.

The towns began to appear as smart as their citizens, unless, of course, one looked "across the river," or on the "other side of the tracks," where industrial workers lived, or coal miners dwelt, or newly arrived foreigners resided or nonwhites eked out their lives.

There the towns were not so pretty. There good money was not "wasted" on new buildings, especially public buildings like schools or hospitals or libraries. The new edifices that were built on the wrong side of the towns were houses of worship. The poor needed God, and sought him, and created His temples with their own painfully salvaged dimes, nickels and pennies. The spires soared higher than most other buildings in most towns.

Such was not the case in New York City, of course, where towering buildings were common due to the fact that a square foot of land in the financial district cost more than a hundred acres in many parts of the country. In 1929, Walter P. Chrysler, enthused by the success of his new car, the DeSoto, and the broad acceptance of the Plymouth he had introduced the year before, announced he would build the world's tallest skyscraper at Forty-Second and Lexington, across from Grand Central. It had nothing to do with Chrysler Motors, he said, but was a special project.

Prosperity, after all, was not measured by the height of the nation's buildings.

The sole measurement was the height of stock averages. The most important gauge was the Dow-Jones Industrial Average.

The stock market was considered by almost everyone to be a barometric measurement of the nation's economy. When it rose the economy was deemed to be healthy and prosperity laved the shores, swathed the cities and swaddled the mountains.

Stock prices had begun to rise in 1924 and the chartlines climbed steadily, with only slight dips, right through the New Year of 1929.

Oh, there had been scares. There was a big sell-off in 1926, but not much damage was caused because not so many speculators and many fewer amateurs were in the market then.

The most frightening setback had come on June 12, 1928, when, in a sudden collapse of the market, losses as great as 23½ points hit the blue chips, and drops of as much as 150 points were recorded in over-the-counter securities. Analysts said the sudden decision to sell was made by many investors and speculators when they learned that the Republican National Convention had accepted Calvin Coolidge's curt refusal to run for reelection. As the crowned author-sponsor-patron of the nation's prosperity, people feared that his withdrawal would damage the economy.

Apparently there were second thoughts about that within a few days, for the market moved forward and upward even more precipitously than before, and by August was 20 percent above the June low and was half-again as high by mid-November.

One of the differences that caused greater reaction in 1928 than had been experienced two years earlier was the presence of so many more nonprofessionals—pure speculators—in the market. A speculative fever had grown and gripped the entire nation. Stock-market players came from every station, every walk of life.

To a large extent this was encouraged by the big New York banks, which borrowed money from the Federal Reserve Bank at five percent interest and loaned it out to brokers at rates ranging from nine to fourteen percent. Brokers reloaned it to their customers in the form of margin loans, or "call money."

Using borrowed money, the millions of "little" speculators were actually betting on prices. They "bet" the price would go up or go down within a specific period of time. Most of them had but scant knowledge about the company whose stock they bought; they would not have known how to read its annual report if they had received it.

Press reporters of every description swelled the population of New York's financial district. Some were trained in the intricacies of finance; most were not. Some were good "diggers" and could ferret out special facts; some were smooth writers who captured the excitement of the times; but most were basically the essential instruments for conveying the words of the high and mighty to the little speculators of the country. They reported on what they were told.

Newspapers from almost all foreign capitals sent special correspondents to Wall Street, too, and wire services from around the globe were filing directly from the Street.

The words of the regulars and the professionals and the insiders, broadcast and disseminated to every corner of the country, were then scrutinized, weighed and analyzed by millions of people who a year earlier wouldn't have known what the terms meant.

An example, repeated many times by many spokesmen: One afternoon John J. Raskob made an optimistic comment to the press about the automobile industry, and in the next two days General Motors gained twelve points.

A favorite place to garner significant statements from the greats of the financial community was on shipboard. Brokers and bankers found much to do in Europe in 1928 and 1929 and the giant liners were equipped with Marconi-serviced board rooms with special facilities for sending rapid cables to brokers back in the States.

There was something about being on shipboard that loosened tongues, even when the liner was tied up at berth in the East River. Under such circumstances, aboard ship the night before it was to sail, even a Morgan partner—Thomas Corcoran—told a reporter he thought General Motors would gain a hundred points in the next year. The temperature of the financial fever of the nation rose several points; so did General Motors stock.

When he was Secretary of Commerce, Herbert Hoover had fretted about the conflagration of speculation and had urged both his bosses, first Harding and then Coolidge, to do something about it. When they declined, he felt powerless to act, so shelved his apprehensions.

Coolidge not only declined to do anything to dampen the speculation, but also said, as the upthrust of the market gained power in the spring of 1928, he did not consider the rise "significant enough to cause unfavorable comment." This was interpreted as being White House sanction and approval.

At the time, the public had no way of knowing Hoover's fears about the high degree of speculation in the market, so after his election, a new wave of buying pushed prices and averages higher.

In this, the Chief may have read a political message, for he did nothing after entering the White House to discourage the wild buying that occurred between March 4, when he was inaugurated, and the beginning of the slide in September. Indeed, his only comments on the subject were intended to bolster confidence in the market.

In May, the Hoover Economic Survey, which he had organized back in 1921, fanned the flames of speculation even more.

The Economic Survey issued a report showing that there

were seventeen million Americans engaged in "playing" the stock market, and described most of them as novices, unwealthy and totally uninformed on the subject. The report frowned slightly on the stock market's absorption of credit through the device of call loans. But the real meat in the document was the conclusion that the economy was sounder than ever and that there was absolutely no visible limit to the ability of the consumer to consume whatever was produced.

Here was an official green light.

Though Hoover had long since disassociated himself from the survey that bore his name, its release, two and a half months after he assumed the Presidency, had the effect of giving White House encouragement to Wall Street's activities and seemed to give official confirmation to the notion that it would all never end.

The lone cry of dissent came from the Federal Reserve Board, but it was regarded throughout the boom as a grumpy and stuffy old relative that sourly frowned whenever the kids were having any fun.

Back at the beginning of the year the Fed had started grumbling about the stock market. In February it took a look at the five and a quarter billion dollars' worth of brokers loans outstanding and objected that so much money was being absorbed by the stock market that it caused others to pay too much for the money they borrowed.

The economy as a whole, the Federal Reserve Board said, was suffering from the diversion of funds to brokers and speculators. In the wake of this appraisal, the trading community expected a rise in the discount rate, but it didn't come.

Instead there were more harmless rumblings from the Fed in the form of statements issued to the press.

In the absence of restrictive orders from the Fed, the more

conservative monetary experts looked to the banks to draw
the line somewhere, but the profitable loans to brokers may
have restrained them.

In March, however, a leading and powerful banker, emi-
nently qualified to speak, lashed out at the Federal Reserve
Board, the stock exchange, the investment trusts and the
bankers.

The aggravated banker was Paul Warburg, chairman of
the board of International Acceptance, which had recently
merged with the Bank of the Manhattan Company (now, but
not then, a part of Chase Manhattan Bank). Mr. Warburg had
been a member of the Federal Reserve Board from its incep-
tion in 1914 through the troublesome wartime years to
1919.

The Federal Reserve Board had lost control of the situation, Mr. Warburg said, because it had not taken decisive
action to control inflation before it got out of hand. The
Federal Reserve, he said, suffered from structural defects,
and he pointed out that "prompt and decisive action" could
not be expected when it required the concurrence of one
hundred and twenty men in twelve separate banks on
twelve separate boards of directors, who must also work
with a central bank board of eight men.

The recently organized investment trusts (launched by
some of the most respected bankers, including J. P. Morgan) Mr. Warburg flayed as "incorporated stock pools."

It was this Warburg blast that prompted stock-exchange
president Simmons to make his much-publicized (and
widely reprinted and distributed) speech in May, in which
he claimed that almost the entire increase in brokers loans
came from private corporations, not banks, and he described call money as the "safest form of investment in the
country."

It was all just so many words to those who were playing
the market.

The boom continued throughout the hot summer, and vacations were forgotten by bankers, brokers, investors and the millions of speculators. Wall Street was jammed all summer long.

Officials announced that the steel industry, which had been operating at ninety-five percent of capacity in the third quarter, would be humming at one hundred percent of capacity in the final quarter of 1929.

In fields in the South, black men with their wives and children harvested a bumper cotton crop. In the New England textile mills, Lancashire-accented loomfixers demanded long hours and constant production of the laboring women and children of French-Canadian, Irish-English, Portuguese and Polish husbands, men who were working or seeking work elsewhere where they wouldn't have to compete in the labor market with their own wives and children. It was a good year for wheat and corn, and farmers of the breadbasket states could look forward to declining prices from a future market glut.

The New York Federal Reserve Bank, acting alone, raised its discount rate from five to six percent, but it occasioned little response or notice in a preoccupied and sweltering Wall Street.

Among big attractions for the speculators were the new investment trusts—Allegheny, Shenandoah, United, Blue Ridge and scores more. J. P. Morgan and Company had sponsored Allegheny and United. United came out in January at 25 and in August was up in the 70s. Allegheny came out in February at an offering price of 20 and was, in August, passing 55 and heading toward 60.

Four railroad stocks were flirting with the magic 300 mark.

No one seemed to notice that a large part of the stock list had remained depressed throughout 1929, or if not depressed, lethargic. The spectacular gainers had been those stocks figuring prominently in the Dow-Jones averages, the "representative stocks."

August that year had enough dog days to fill a city pound, and as it dragged toward its close, *Times* financial editor Noyes worried about the condition of the market and published his fears. *Herald Tribune* financial editor Stabler, equally worried, wrote that he foresaw an end to the bull market and possibly even to the economic boom.

Wall Street took its traditional break for the Labor Day weekend. Only those who had planned in advance could climb aboard any of the jam-packed trains or any of the half-dozen excursion boats or get onto the Ford Tri-Motor to Boston, for reservations had been booked solid weeks earlier. It was impossible to get to Bar Harbor or Newport unless you drove.

On Tuesday, September 3, the day after Labor Day and the traditional start of Wall Street's "New Year," one of the hottest and most humid days of a hot and sultry summer, the vacationers trooped back to town and ordered stocks in such volume as to send the averages to all-time highs that were not to be equaled for a quarter of a century.

Champagne flowed like near beer in the midtown bistros that night as Wall Streeters by the hundreds of thousands toasted the new season that was off to such an auspicious start. Truly, the gloom-gatherers were off their trolleys. Everything was fine.

Next day there was some selling, and averages dipped.

And the next. Prices seemed to start off in the forenoon, with a slow and steady decline.

Not many people paid much heed.

Roger Babson, a not-too-popular bouncy analyst from Wellesley, Massachusetts, noticed. That day, Thursday, September 5, he addressed a financial analysts luncheon in Boston and said, "I repeat what I said at this time last year, that sooner or later a crash is coming."

The Dow-Jones news tape—the broad tape—carried his statement, and before the analysts luncheon was ended in Boston, the story had appeared in board rooms throughout the nation. Immediately orders to sell began to pour in and the sell-off was forever after to be known as the "Babson Break."

Then, September 24 there was another substantial break. This time it could not be blamed on Babson or anyone else.

The more seasoned veterans around Wall Street began to wear worried looks. Some went back into the lists and noted that on September 3, when the averages hit an all-time high, a great many well-regarded stocks, especially in textiles and allied fields, sold off sharply.

The speculators, most of whom regarded it as one big numbers game—a "pool" organized especially for this kind of betting—were not bothered by these minor signs.

Rumors began to be whispered, particularly among the professionals, that huge bear pools were being formed by the "insiders" so they could sell short.

Sell short—in this market?

Ominously, brokers' loans showed an increase, but there was no corresponding upsurge or support in sales to indicate that the ordinary speculators were buying on margin.

Somebody—one of the reporters—accused Jesse Livermore of coming in on the short side, but he hotly denied it.

On October 15, Charles Mitchell, speaking from shipboard in Hamburg, Germany, as he was about to embark for New York, stilled a growing number of fears when he told the world's press: "The markets generally are now in a healthy condition."

When his liner arrived in New York on Tuesday, October 22, Mitchell, having noted the softening of prices during his crossing, issued another statement to the press: "The market is sound. It will correct itself."

The next day, Wednesday, October 23, the market suffered the biggest decline in its history, with losses ranging from a point to ninety-six points. A total of four billion dollars in values was wiped out.

It set the stage for Black Thursday.

CHAPTER 11

Thursday, October 24, 1929

3:00 P.M.

〰〰〰〰〰〰〰〰〰〰〰〰〰

In the final half-hour of business, sheer madness gripped the broiling trading floor of the New York Stock Exchange. Twenty-two hundred men, sweating, shouting, gesticulating, milled and thronged around the octagonal sides of the trading posts and the din mushroomed upward to the domed ceiling and cascaded through the cathedrallike windows to wash over the crowded streets outside. In the last few minutes of trading, witnesses said later, the noise could be heard as far away as William Street, a block and a half distant.

The market had lost all direction. Some prices were rising, particularly in those stocks that had been supported by Richard Whitney or in allied issues. Some rose for no apparent reason, baffling the experts who were processing the improving bids as they came in over the telephones. Other stocks continued to fall in the absence of any visible support, bringing some companion issues down with them in sympathy.

More than ever, it was impossible for any trader to know what the last bid on a specific stock might have been. More than ever, the share owners on the outside remained in absolute ignorance of what was happening to the prices of their stocks.

It was impossible to tell how "late" the tape was running, though it was known to be more than four hours behind the orders executed on the trading floor, and there was no way it could catch up.

Twice more during the final hour Whitney came to the pit to see how prices were doing, though he did not place any additional bids. Presumably he looked at the stocks he had supported. All or most of them were doing well. If he had looked at the rest of the list he might have been disappointed. Sell orders continued to pour in and could not be matched with bids, causing skidding prices in spots, while the supported issues gained.

"It's insane," Jules Barnish told Ed Newbord over the Raymond & Company loop phone. "I simply can't tell what's happening. We have a market crash going on at the same time that some stocks are gaining good support."

"I told you that the public would be waiting if we gave them a chance to buy these good bargains."

"Ed, you persist in forgetting that a lot of the trading public is out of business. Yesterday morning we had seventeen million stockholders in America. I'll bet you my year-end bonus that there aren't three million left right now. I'll ask you the same question I asked this noon. Who's to buy?"

"There are plenty of people who want to come back into this kind of market. Here's where you get a chance to make some good profits."

"Not when you've foreclosed on their accounts, sold them out at losses and left them with debts that many of them will never be able to pay off."

"Somebody's buying in your market right now, Jules."

"These are the professionals. They're buying for their own accounts. Hell, *we're* buying, too, but that doesn't mean we'll be able to sell any of these stocks at a profit."

"Well, I'm not such a pessimist, Jules. I think there are customers out around the country who can recognize good bargains when they see them. Some of the prices on the list right now are the lowest they've been in two years."

"Longer than that, for some."

"All right. Sensible people will be buying. We're feeding the late prices that you give us out to our branch offices and correspondent houses, because the tape is so late. We're keeping the circuits open for them."

"That's a good idea. Keep them posted by phone. Just don't expect too much, Ed."

"What an absolute pessimist. You're worse than Babson."

"Yeah, but it turned out that Babson was right."

"Keep the latest quotations coming to us, Jules." Newbord was suddenly curt.

"Right."

On Broad Street the crowd was restive. All day long, since before ten o'clock in the morning, the panic of the selling had been confined to the Exchange itself and had not spread to a panic on the street, but as legs grew tired, arches ached and the midafternoon humidity mounted, tempers began to flare. In two separate and isolated spots, fights broke out. Policemen, who had been shepherding the crowd since it formed, tried in vain to get to the sites of the disturbances, but couldn't get through the solid wall of human bodies. Neighbors separated the contending pugilists.

Shortly after two-thirty a spectator from the street entered the stock-exchange building and made his way onto the trading floor where, unnoticed by the guards, he stepped into the melee and began to scream and wave his arms.

Because of the noise and confusion he wasn't noticed for several minutes. Finally two guards led him off the floor and up to the main entrance of the stock-exchange office building on Wall Street where he was turned over to two city patrolmen. Their practiced eyes enabled them to diagnose his problem as hysteria and he was hustled off to Bellevue Hospital in a cab that was commandeered on Broadway.

So far as can be determined, this was the only disturbance caused by outsiders throughout that hectic day.

At about five minutes before three o'clock, William H. Crawford, superintendent of the Reporting Department of the New York Stock Exchange, opened a locked stairwell door that admitted him to a small balcony overlooking the trading floor.

A few clock-watching brokers glancing up and seeing him knew that trading time was running out, and they intensified their activities—and their noise. Crawford, a short, slim man, hunched forward in his chair and stared at the huge clock dominating the wall.

The noise from the frantic trading welled up around him almost visibly, an unceasing roar blended of groans, moans, shouted bids and offers, and confirming replies topped with a curious admixture of hopeful utterances compounded from the improving prices that had sprung up in Whitney's wake.

About two minutes later Whitney, himself, stepped onto the trading floor; remaining silent, he stared first at the clock and then at the fury on the trading floor.

Jules Barnish did not look up. He was busy compiling a "house list" of selected closing prices for his own use, knowing that it would be hours before the tape could reveal the accurate figures.

Here and there faces were lifted as men made note of the time. The weird roar mounted in ascending decibels as eleven hundred brokers and an equal number of helpers sought to squeeze the last allowable second out of the legal trading day. The voice of Wall Street rose with the climbing minute hand of the stock exchange's official clock.

As the big hand crawled higher Bill Crawford stood up in his aerielike balcony and reached to a small shelf to pick up a mahogany gavel. He held it loosely by his side as the hand crept past the one-minute marker.

At two fifty-nine the tumult from the trading floor was deafening to the lone man in the balcony. It sounded like one loud cry, and Crawford shook his head slightly as though his ears bothered him.

Gazing fixedly at the clock's hand, Crawford tensed. He was pale and the overhead lights glistened on tiny beads of perspiration. It was obvious that Crawford knew well that he was about to signal the close of the most momentous day in stock-exchange history and that his heretofore anonymous role would forevermore be a prestigious post.

At the precise moment that the minute hand touched the hour marker, Crawford brought the mallet down with a sharp blow to the big brass gong.

The long, quavering note clanged and echoed through the great chamber, warning that business must cease.

Twice more, at about thirty-second intervals, Mr. Crawford struck the gong.

Trading was ended.

The day that was to go into the history books as "Black Thursday" had come to its official close as far as buying

or selling in the precise auction market of the New York
Stock Exchange was concerned. Trading had ended at the
same second also at the Curb Exchange a few blocks
away, the other side of the church and graveyard, at
Trinity Place.

There was a moment of silence during which the clack-
ing of the news machines and telegraph keys could be
heard for the first time that day. Then there was a great
outcry.

Men jumped in the air and shouted. Some clapped
neighbors on the back. There were some cheers and some
boos and many old-fashioned rebel yells. There were loud
groans and many laugh-tinged sighs of relief.

It was the final chorus, shrill, weird, cacophonous, an
eerie requiem to the nation's greatest financial disaster.
Men shed tears, some in relief, some in sorrow, and they
coursed down cheeks already aglisten with sweat. Some
stood transfixed, dazed, their hands clutching sheaves of
orders that would never be executed.

The "high-speed" tickertape clattered on. At the time of
the close it was printing quotations of prices that were
recorded at 11:52 that morning. It was to print its last
quotation at 7:08½ that night, four hours, eight and one-
half minutes late.

A total of 12,894,650 shares had been traded in the five-
hour session, the largest volume in stock-market history.

Happiest of all to see the end of trading were the squads
of telephone operators located at their switchboards behind the rails on the north and south sides of the trading
pit. Literally swamped with telephoned sell orders all day
long, they had virtually lost control over the annunciator
call boards, which they operate to post the numbers of
brokers, thereby notifying them to pick up a telephone
and receive an order. Many brokers had not been off the
phone all day.

Also relieved that trading was over, but still apprehensive, were the New York City policemen. On ordinary days a total of thirty uniformed men patrolled the vicinity of the stock exchange, but when the crowd began to form on Broad Street, an officer went to a call box and described the scene to Captain Edward Quinn in the Old Slip Station, and Quinn immediately sent reinforcements. He dispatched ten additional foot patrolmen, twenty mounted men and a special squad of twenty additional detectives, among them experts on "dip artists" or pickpockets, and a handful of burly "crowd controllers," who were generously equipped by benevolent nature to quell almost any disturbance as soon as it started.

Earlier in the day the police had tried to clear an area on Broad Street between the Exchange and the J. P. Morgan Building, but when it was determined that all that the people wished to do was to stare in fascination at the Morgan edifice where the meeting was progressing inside, the order was changed to allow the spectators to gather. Outside the area, barricades were erected, at Wall and Broadway, at Pine and at Liberty Streets.

Once during the day the police had had to form a phalanx in front of a score of motion-picture cameramen who had taken up operating positions at the best vantage point in the area, on the steps of the Sub-Treasury Building. Some of those who had come to watch the crowd thought they should have a turn on the steps. Arguments ensued. Police took their positions. The cameramen remained, shouting, "Get your head down," or, "Look out, there, fella," throughout the day, as young assistants braced tripod legs to keep the equipment from slipping off the worn and smoothed steps.

On the trading floor of the Exchange, Jules Barnish stood fast on a small island of floor in the midst of the still-milling and noisy crowd. He was emptying his pock-

ets of scribbled notes he had made during the day and
was assembling them on his clipboard.

Actually, he had not had a chance to analyze or ap-
praise the situation with any degree of thoughtfulness
since all hell had broken loose at about eleven o'clock that
morning, shortly after Steel fell through the 200 mark
and crashed down to 194½.

He put the slips of paper in order on his clipboard and
read the dramatic story.

General Electric broke from 319¾ to 302¼.

American Telephone and Telegraph dropped from
274¾ to 265.

Johns-Manville skidded from 180 to 140.

Montgomery Ward tumbled from 84 to 50.

Auburn Motors plunged from 260 to 190.

National Biscuit lost from 209 to 193½.

Atcheson dropped from 264½ to 253¼.

New York Central plummeted from 213⅞ to 197.

From his hip pocket Jules extracted the list he had compiled shortly after noon (see Chapter 8). He spread it out
on his clipboard and looked in horror at the erosion of
prices displayed there.

Then he realized that most of them had posted gains—
some of them quite handsome gains—during the last
hour, after Richard Whitney's boy-at-the-dike buying
support.

Knowing that it would be six or seven o'clock, at least,
before the final prices reached the tickertape, he added
two more columns of figures to the right side of his list—
the recovery from the low, and the net change after the
recovery.

It was nothing to cause wild cheering, he thought, but
the figures certainly showed marked improvement over
the noontime performance.

He had just finished making his computations when Ed
Newbord arrived, puffing slightly.

"Come on," he said. "We've got to hurry. There's a meeting of the senior partners of all of the wire houses at
Hornblower & Weeks' office. Then after we attend that
we've got to get back to our own office to put out a statement for our customers. We've got to tell 'em it's not as
bad as it looks."

Jules said nothing, but handed him the revised list.
It now looked like this:

	Wed. Close	Thurs. Low	Noon Loss	P.M. Re- covery	Net Change
Air Reduction	195½	176⅛	−19⅜	15¾	− 3⅝
Allis Chalmers	53	44	− 9	5	− 4
American Banknote	127	115	−12	2	−10
American & Foreign Power	112	88	−24	9½	−14½
American Home Products	59¾	49¾	−10	——	−10
American International	65¾	54	−11¾	4	− 7¾
American Mach & Fdry	240¼	219	−21¼	11	−10¼
American Rolling Mills	115½	106¼	− 9¼	2¾	− 6½
American Tel & Tel	272	245	−27	24	− 3
American Water Works	120¼	93	−27¼	10¾	−16½
Anaconda Copper	102	92	−10	10	——
Auburn Motors	260	190	−70	45	−25
Baldwin Locomotive	35	15	−20	18	− 2
Bendix Aviation	51	40	−11	3	− 8
Bethlehem Steel	101¾	92½	− 9¼	9	−¼
Bohr Aluminum	73	50	−23	15	− 8
Burroughs Adding Machine	84¼	59	−25¼	6	−19¼
Byers (A.M.) Company	121¼	76	−45¼	35	−10¼
Canada Dry Gin Ale	80½	60	−20½	9	−11½
Chesapeake & Ohio RR	257½	231	−26½	11	−15½
Columbia Carbon	255	210	−45	21	−24
Commercial Credit 1st pfd 6½'s	91	70	−21	——	−21

	Wed. Close	Thurs. Low	Noon Loss	P.M. Re- covery	Net Change
Commercial Solvents	448	425	−23	——	−23
General Electric	314	283	−31	25	− 6
General Motors	57⅜	49	− 8⅜	4½	− 3⅞
Hocking Valley	540	515	−25	25	——
International Abbott	113	99	−14	11	− 3
International Business Mach.	231⅜	201	−30⅜	5	−25⅜
International Tel & Tel	110¾	79	−31¾	27	− 4¾
Johns-Manville	180	140	−40	30	−10
Ludlum Steel	70½	50	−20½	12½	− 8
Montgomery Ward	83¼	50	−33¼	24	− 9¼
National Supply	124	110	−14	2	−12
Pittsburgh Coal	74½	65	− 9½	——	− 9½
Radio Corporation of America	68½	44½	−24	13¾	−10¼
Republic Steel	105¾	90	−15¾	5	−10¾
U.S. Industrial Alcohol	201¼	169	−32¼	7	−25¼
U.S. Steel Corp.	204	193½	−10½	12½	+ 2
Western Union	235	220	−15	23	+ 8

The meeting of the senior partners of the wire houses was held in the Hornblower & Weeks office at 42 Broadway, down the hill from Wall Street, toward the Battery. It had been called by Hornblower's senior partner, Colonel John W. Prentiss, for "as soon after the close of the market as possible."

The purpose, he had stated on the telephone, was to agree on a statement to be issued to allay the fears of the customers out and around the country. The statement, or variations of it that were to be individualized by each member firm, was to go out on the wires that evening.

About one hundred men, the top brass of the city's leading brokerage houses—about thirty-five firms—gathered in the Hornblower & Weeks offices for more than an hour. The press and public were barred. Collectively, the men represented firms that did about seventy percent of the business on the stock exchange.

Exactly what was said and decided at the meeting was

not recorded, nor was it repeated to the press except for its substance. Colonel Prentiss requested the press not to quote him directly. Other brokers, when they left the meeting and were accosted by reporters, would speak only in general terms of what decisions had been reached. They would not allow themselves to be quoted.

It was the "sense" of the meeting, Colonel Prentiss told newsmen, that the selling of the day had been overdone and that the market fundamentally was sound. "Important interests," it was said, had done buying of a substantial nature during the afternoon hours.

Whether this was an obvious reference to the J. P. Morgan–Richard Whitney episode or pertained to some other buying activity that had come to light during the meeting, was not learned then, or later.

The worst of the selling had been done, the brokers said they believed, and a recovery was not only under way, it would continue.

Each broker attending the meeting had expressed his view of the market, and none, it was said, could report on any particular disturbing element in the current situation to justify the selling. The uneasiness that had induced the selling of the last few days had been caused by *needless* selling, it was stated. Some of the brokers had said they regarded it as a form of hysteria. (The implication made it clear that it was the skittish amateurs, not the professionals, who had panicked.)

A note of optimism would be struck in the circulars and advisories that would go out that night, it was said. Many of these would advise customers to buy stock at current prices, and all would caution against "frightened liquidation."

Colonel Prentiss then announced that Hornblower & Weeks had ordered republished in eighty-five newspapers for Friday morning and afternoon an ad that had run in June 1926. It read:

"We believe that present conditions are favorable for advantageous investment in standard American securities."

The Hornblower & Weeks market letter, prepared for dissemination late Thursday afternoon so it could be received by many customers before the opening of Friday's market, stated,

> Commencing with today's [Friday's] trading, the market should start laying the foundation for the constructive advance which we believe will characterize 1930.
>
> We believe yesterday's wide-open collapse will prove as excessive on the down-side as mid-summer speculation did on the up-side.
>
> The market prices of leading stocks have been so adjusted in relation to their real buying power, the traces of inflation have disappeared and, in view of the country's maintained prosperity, we do not believe that the current attractive investment levels can long obtain.

The firm of Merrill, Lynch & Co., ancestor of today's Merrill, Lynch, Pierce, Fenner & Smith, Inc., sent a message to its customers asking them to keep accounts well margined without waiting for a request, and advised that investors "with available funds should take advantage of this break to buy good securities."

As they left the Hornblower & Weeks office, Ed Newbord turned to his partner and said, "I think this is so important that we should handle it ourselves. You and I, together, will write an advisory to go out to our customers."

"And tell them to buy?"

"Tell them to buy bargains. Not everything on the list is a bargain."

"I hope you're not thinking of being specific."

"Jules, you continue to be the world's worst pessimist. There wasn't one man in that meeting who could find any justification for this wild selling."

"Unless prices had been too high."

"Well, they're not too high now."

Thus Raymond & Company joined the majority of the other wire houses in sending special-delivery advisories to its clients and telegrams to its corresponding firms, informing them that in the expert opinion of Raymond's analysts and technicians, the market appeared sound and offered advantageous purchases to those capable of buying wisely.

There can be no doubt that the brokers acted out of sincere conviction that the market had reached bottom, though subsequent events soon were to prove them wrong —terribly wrong.

Market technicians, looking at the prices of October 24, 1929, some four decades later, state that there was no way to know that the level would continue to drop well into the next year.

Looking back, they say that the floor reached on Black Thursday should have held, that the prices of many corporate stocks were, indeed, bargains, for they did not represent what was then regarded as fair value in relation to sales, earnings, liquidation value of assets, and market potential.

But there remained the question: Who's to buy? Bargains are of value only to customers who can snap them up.

The brokers left their meeting feeling confident, and they were prepared to tell the world how they felt.

Word of it flashed out on the news wires.

Treasury Secretary Andrew Mellon informed President

Hoover that the wire-house brokers were confident.

The portent of what the brokers had decided to say was seized upon by analysts, both professional and amateur, and interpreted and elaborated upon for the masses of investors and speculators who, throughout the nation, were to remain in board rooms, watching the lagging prices being posted, until well into the night.

The airwaves were filled, throughout the evening hours, with radio announcements about the brokers' statements of hope.

Yet to come were the "second thoughts" of the country's leading spokesmen. Soon they, too, would be filed on the jammed news wires.

CHAPTER 12

Thursday, October 24, 1929

4:00 P.M.

~~~~~~

The influence of the New York Stock Exchange over other trading markets had never been stronger than on Black Thursday.

The Curb Exchange underwent its most severe selling in history and cash and paper profits melted to the same degree that they did on the Big Board. Losses ranged from ten to seventy-five points throughout the day, but began to show signs of recovery in the final hour and a half, a pickup that coincided with the massive purchases by Richard Whitney at the New York Stock Exchange on behalf of the bank syndicate.

Utilities on the Curb were severely hit, as were the investment trusts, including Commonwealth Edison among the former and Insull Utility Investments among the latter.

Volume on the Curb was 6,337,400 shares, highest in the history of the marketplace. The Curb's high-speed ticker closed two hours and fifty-four minutes late, and was to continue punching out quotes until six minutes before six that evening.

Trading in the wheat pit of the Chicago Board of Trade was frantic throughout the day and prices closed 4⅝ to

5⅛ cents a bushel lower than Wednesday's closing prices —which had dropped four cents during the day. It set a record in losses for any peacetime trading.

Wheat traders seemed ill-prepared for the crisis.

Chaos ruled their market throughout the day. Shortly after the opening of the wheat pit, prices fell by eleven cents, a record. Both in Chicago and in Winnipeg wheat dropped seven cents in seven minutes shortly before noon. December wheat in Chicago broke from $1.24¾ per bushel to $1.13¾. An afternoon rally, probably inspired by Whitney, restored eight cents. In Winnipeg, December futures in wheat broke from $1.37½ to $1.25, but the rally in Chicago sent it back to $1.32.

Severe losses were suffered at the Chicago Stock Exchange, among the leaders being Insull Utility Investments, which lost twenty dollars and did not respond to the late rejuvenating rally. Turnover of stocks on the Chicago exchange was 1,200,000, an all-time record, and, indeed, the first time that more than a million shares had ever been traded on that exchange in one day.

Cord Corporation, which lost $6 a share in the morning in Chicago, recovered all but $1. Commonwealth Edison lost 22½ and touched a low of 333, but it closed at 336. Among other substantial losers in Chicago were Cities Service, E. L. Bruce, Borg-Warner and Bendix Aviation.

Throughout the nation and throughout the world, the reaction was the same, compounding and multiplying the losses suffered on the New York Stock Exchange.

• The Philadelphia Stock Exchange set a record with a turnover of 423,029 shares, and thirty-five stocks traded there reached new lows. Losers included Budd Wheel, United Gas Improvement and United Corporation.

• The Boston Stock Exchange also set a record of 209,-330 shares, eroding prices rapidly for American Founders, Massachusetts Utility Associates, United Founders and Public Utility Holding Company.

• In Los Angeles both the stock exchange and the Curb Exchange recorded severe losses, and shares valued at $8.7 million changed hands.

• A new record for volume was established in San Francisco when the stock exchange recorded transfer of 439,-036 shares. Thirty-three new lows were established on the San Francisco exchange and twenty on the Curb.

• The Cincinnati Stock Exchange recorded extremely heavy losses, with price drops ranging, at the close, from a point to more than ten.

• The Baltimore Stock Exchange showed losses in Baltimore Trust and Union Trust, Maryland Casualty, Consolidated Gas & Electric, Arundel and Eastern Rolling Mill.

• The Cleveland Stock Exchange recorded losses up to sixteen points among industrial stocks and from ten to forty points in the savagely hit bank stocks.

Pandemonium broke out in the London Street Market just before its close at four o'clock (11:00 A.M., New York time) when word of the Wall Street debacle was bulletined on tickertapes. Popular Anglo-American securities broke sharply, causing panicky selling of other issues.

British-held American securities were dumped in wholesale lots into Shorters Court where dealers in Anglo-American securities assembled after the close of the Street Market. Hatless, rain-drenched, bidding, shouting and selling on the street, the dealers created an uproar that attracted large crowds of water-logged onlookers and caused the borough constable to sound an emergency alarm. Shouts of "Sell—Sell!" could be heard several squares away. The market was to continue almost through the rain-soaked night. It was after midnight, twelve-thirty, before final New York prices were available, but even the obvious rally served to mollify the selling fever only temporarily.

In Montreal, despite a late rally, prices on the stock exchange, after a record turnover of 382,521 shares, established new lows for the year in thirty stocks. On the Curb, eleven new lows were set.

In Toronto, prices on the stock exchange dropped as much as ten points, but the late afternoon rally restored from three to five points selectively among the losers.

Strong selling was reported on the bourse in Paris, and in Geneva, Amsterdam, Berlin and Milan.

The foreign press reacted strongly to events in New York. Their stories were on the streets of foreign capitals by four o'clock, New York time.

They revealed what must have been long-smoldering animosity toward America's boom.

Said London's *Daily Express:*

> The crash of the New York Exchange has come, as it was bound to come. Stocks could not forever be forced up out of all proportion to the earning capacities of the undertakings they represented without a break coming sooner or later.
>
> Only the phenomenal prosperity of America as a whole and its expanding industrialism, have been able to support so long the antics of Wall Street speculators.
>
> The awakening of the diverse elements smitten by the gambling fever is rude and convulsive, and probably it will not in the least console them to know that until they did awaken—that is, until America's speculative fever was reduced to normal—there could be no financial stability anywhere.

The *Financial Times* (London) seemed mildly pleased with the turn of events in New York and referred to the "compensating factors," which, in the *Times'* view, meant that money would now return to London to be invested in gilt-edged securities or deposited in the banks.

The financial editor of the *Daily News* (London) was quite bitter about developments in Wall Street and said he was not sure but that this was merely "one of the capricious outbursts to which Wall Street is making us hardened." Nevertheless, he said, the bright side was that the crash would release a flood of foreign money "which the United States has attracted to finance its share of the purchases."

In Paris the French journalists also looked for a repatriation of French capital that had been used (for so long a time, it was lamented) for speculation in New York.

Declared *le Journal des Débats:* "We have long believed this debacle to be inevitable. An interesting conflict has now begun in America between the exigencies of the economic situation and the development of speculative operations."

Almost universally the foreign press blamed American speculators for attracting the capital of *their* nationals, and somehow did not regard their exporters of capital as speculators, too. Nor did they seem to regard as speculative the American capital that was being invested in increasing amounts in England, France, Belgium, Holland, Germany and Italy, much of it by corporations whose stock, on the New York Stock Exchange, was the object of speculative bidding.

Brokers and traders in Wall Street who read the late-afternoon tape dispatches on October 24, 1929, were introduced to this remarkable dichotomy that was to become familiar to large numbers of Americans when dealing with foreigners, especially Europeans, and that was to last until the onset of World War II.

Many brokers, even some of those connected with wire houses, who had decided that it was most prudent to remain silent when the market was in such obvious disarray, changed their minds and decided to speak out and clarify the situation after reading how easy it was even for foreign experts to misinterpret what had happened.

Bankers and other financial leaders throughout Wall Street issued statements expressing confidence in the soundness of the stock-market structure, despite the upheaval of the last few days. There was an effort to remove emphasis from the crash itself, and, instead, to speak of a broad general decline. Cheerful words were written and spoken. The worst had been seen, nearly everyone said.

The market itself was not weak, it was emphasized. Instead, the cause of the sell-off was the public's alarm over the steady liquidation of the past several weeks. No one explained why there had been so much consistent liquidation if, in fact, it was the liquidation that was solely responsible for undermining the confidence of investors.

Over the private wires to their customers, the wire houses again cautioned against scare selling at "sacrifice" prices.

Don't give it away, was the advice. The implication was that if you held onto it and didn't sell it, you'd get more for it in the future. In effect this was good advice, for if there is not much stock of any one issue offered for sale, it stands a good chance of increasing in value. Unsatisfied bids boost prices.

The fundamentals (of the market) remained unimpaired, declared Charles E. Mitchell, the vocal chairman of National City Bank. "I am still of the opinion that this reaction has overrun itself," he added.

In Cleveland, Leonard P. Ayres, vice president of the Cleveland Trust Company and nationally respected economist, said that the "tremendous development of industrial resources and solidification of banking interests makes the United States probably the only nation in the world which would withstand the shock of a $3,-000,000,000 paper loss on the stock exchange in a single day [Wednesday] without serious effect to the average citizen."

Mr. Ayres also pointed to increasing per capita wealth in the nation and termed it a "financial shock absorber."

Lewis E. Pierson, chairman of the board of Irving Trust Company, issued the following statement:

> Severe disturbances in the stock market are nothing new in the American experience. The pendulum always swings widely and it would seem as though the long-expected break should bring about an equilibrium.
>
> The position of the Federal Reserve Bank is unusually strong and the borrowings of member banks are moderate.
>
> Considering the record-breaking earnings in many industries, we may well remember that whenever fundamental values are lost sight of by the unthinking majority it is time for courage on the part of those investors who have a real sense of basic worth.

This, perhaps more than any other statement, struck the keynote, the theme, for statements that would be pouring forth for at least the next forty-eight hours.

The idea was that unthinking, panicky selling had taken place and that sober reflection would cause sensible investors, those who could, indeed, read a balance sheet, to get back into the market and cash in on the unprecedented prosperity of the nation's growing industrial economy.

In many ways the crash was a newspaperman's dream. It had possessed the decency to manifest itself early enough in the day so that editors had time to demand extra space for the big story and plan elaborate "spreads"; publishers could make arrangements for an extra run of the presses and provide for distribution of the additional copies they knew they would sell; and writers had a chance to dig into the files for the facts and figures to make interesting comparisons.

The "Wall Street editions," usually on the streets between four and five o'clock with closing prices, were forced to go to press with the deeply depressed noontime prices, and some carried stories comparing the crash of 1929 with those of 1901, 1903, 1907 and 1920—but none, it was concluded, had been so wide, so deep, so violent, so destructive, as that of Black Thursday. This was the crash of all crashes.

Freshest in memories was the general business decline of 1920, an upsetting period that had been reflected strongly in the stock market, first in the spring, then again in November and December. Four important segments of the economy had been seriously involved—retailers-wholesalers, manufacturers and banks.

There had been severe inflation of prices, along with shortages of many goods, during World War I, and the high prices continued long after the shortages had evaporated, through 1919 and into the spring of 1920. Then, suddenly, there were enormous inventories of goods that had been made and stored in warehouses and on shelves at high wartime prices. They could not be sold because competing goods at reduced prices were coming onto the market. The banks had extended immense sums of credit in the high-cost merchandise.

The cost of money soared. Prices of merchandise plummeted. A number of banks in the West failed. Business failures generally increased sharply. It all combined to cause dumping of stocks and wild selling in the stock market.

The cause of the trouble was known, however, and it was reasoned—accurately, it turned out—that the problems would end as soon as the distress merchandise was cleared out. Banks had not yet thought of consumer credit as a means of liquidating merchandise, and the high money rates demanded by the nervous lenders came under wide and deserved criticism. The episode may have given rise to the discount store. It also certainly caused wise heads to begin to think in terms of easily repayable installment loans for consumers.

The big break in the stock market of October 1907 was also caused by tying up capital on a large scale. There had also been unbridled speculation in all of the markets, including commodities, where Eastern interests had tried to get "corners" on some of the grains and fibers in the futures markets. There was panic selling, and several brokerage firms were bankrupted in the melee.

In 1903 the securities markets broke after suffering what was described quite seriously as "indigestion." So many new issues of new corporations were offered that the underwriters and brokers who bought them couldn't digest them all. They had extended so much fresh capital in taking over the underwriting of the new securities that when several of them turned out to be somewhat less than what they were represented and were unsalable, they had no alternative but to dump their other stocks into a declining market, causing a precipitous crash. It was a tech-

nical affair, however, and though the professionals may
have been poorer, they were unworried.

The crash of May 9, 1901, had greater similarity to the
one of Black Thursday in that it had been preceded by a
long period of sometimes frantic speculation, sending
prices of securities so high that it worried even the least
conservative Wall Streeters. There seemed to be a general
belief throughout the nation that there was no top to the
market, that prices would keep rising indefinitely.

The denouement came when two of the largest banking
houses engaged in a battle to seize control of Northern
Pacific Railway, sending the price of that railroad's stock
up to $1,000 per share. The two competing banks
managed to get a genuine corner on the stock, and other
brokers, caught on the short side of Northern Pacific, had
to dump other stock to cover their losses.

In a few hours on that earlier Black Thursday, prices
across the board were eroded as much as thirty percent,
and, it was said, on their books, half the brokerage houses
in the Street were insolvent.

The banking houses, having been on the long side of
Northern Pacific, had plenty of cash, so they began actively to buy the stocks that were then at bargain prices,
and thus retrieved balance for the market and saved the
brokers' hides.

Catching their second breaths over late afternoon
snacks, brokers and other Wall Streeters read of the ancient crashes and noted the comparisons, and knew that
no other crash in the history of the auction market in
securities had been so severe.

An hour after the market's close, however, most were
still convinced that a genuine recovery had been started
by Whitney and that it would continue on the morrow.
They were equally certain—profoundly so—that the na-

tion's prosperity was intact, that consumers would continue to consume, that manufacturers would continue to manufacture, and that profits would be made in the process. Most who thought about it could see it no other way. The men who were in their midforties had spent most of their lives in the industrially expanding twentieth century and could not believe that a stock-market crash could have more than temporary significance. Older men who had been mature when the depression of 1895–97 had occurred, could find no disturbing similarities or corollaries, for surely this market was better financed than any other in history, and the industrial complex was modern and sophisticated.

No, America was strong and growing stronger. Nothing could stop her, certainly not a "shaking out" of some of the less-provident speculators in the stock market—that is, admitting that some had been, indeed, improvident, and not all would acknowledge that to be the fact.

In the senior partner's office at Raymond & Company, Ed Newbord was finishing a phone call with his wife.

"I simply didn't think I should sell it, Kay," he explained. "After all, it's still 46½—exactly what it closed at yesterday—and that omits the fact that it did go to 47 today before losing a half a point before the close. In this market, it means that Coca-Cola is holding up as one of the best stocks."

He listened a few moments, then said, "Oh, all right. If you insist, I'll sell it first thing in the morning. You've got one of the few stocks that did well today without any support from the banking group, and you want to sell it just to be fashionable. Okay, we'll sell."

He replaced the receiver as Angus Felt came into his office with some typewritten sheets.

"Ah, Angus, you have it ready? Good. Good. Will you get Jules in here, too, and we'll go over this."

Newbord began to read the "overnighter" memorandum that would go out on his firm's private wires:

In spite of heavy losses sustained by many issues due to unprecedented selling in Thursday's market, we direct your attention to the remarkable recovery displayed by a large number of key stocks during the final hour of trading.

Beyond doubt, in our opinion, this indicates clearly that purchasing power remains in the stock market and will exert an upward pressure on prices in future trading.

In the opinion of our analysts and technicians there is no valid reason for liquidating further at this time, and, in fact, there are numerous reasons for making wise selections from the wide variety of favorably priced stocks now available.

These include the following facts:

1. Security values, except for isolated instances, are not likely to drop much lower.

2. Most existing stock prices are the best, from the purchaser's standpoint, that have been quoted in many months.

3. The nation's economy, according to every official authority, including the Secretary of the Treasury, is in excellent condition:

    a. Steel production is at peak capacity.

    b. Manufacturers' inventories are not too high and said to be moving well.

    c. Machine-tool production is near a record.

    d. Housing starts are expected to increase in 1930.

    e. Consumer prices are considered to be both fair and stable.

    f. Both rail and utility earnings have been increasing.

4. Measured by any standard, both the stock market and the nation's economy merit your confidence.

Following is a list of stocks that we recommend for your consideration.

Newbord passed the sheets of paper back to Angus Felt.

"I like it," he said. "I think it's fine. You might want to change one word. In the second paragraph, I think it is, you say that purchasing power remains in the stock market. How about making it *abides* rather than *remains?*"

"Sure. Fine."

Jules Barnish, reading from a set of carbons, said, "I'd eliminate the whole second paragraph."

"What!" Newbord was shocked.

"You lose nothing by striking it out," Jules said, "and then you don't have to stick your neck out. How do you know there's purchasing power there? The peanut vendor down on the corner may have a whole wagon full of first-class peanuts and offer them at bargain prices, but that doesn't mean he's going to sell them unless a lot of people want peanuts."

"There was plenty of purchasing power there this afternoon," Newbord said. "I really believe that if the market could have been kept open for another couple of hours, all of the serious losses could have been recovered."

"I don't."

"I know you don't and I can't understand why not. Anyway, we owe it to the Street and to our clients to send this out and do what we can to restore confidence in the system."

Jules shrugged. "There's nothing wrong with the system that an honest price adjustment won't correct," he said.

"Okay, Angus," Newbord said, "send it. Soon as possible."

At four o'clock Harry Weedon emerged from the Times Square station of the Main Street Flushing IRT subway line after spending the day in a factory in Long Island City. People had been talking about the market off and on all day and he was vaguely worried about it.

He bought an evening paper from the first news kiosk he encountered and turned quickly to the listings. He noted, as his eye ran down the column, that they were twelve o'clock, noon, quotations. He came to Westinghouse. Opened at 190, high was 190, noon price 160!

Great Heavens!

A misprint. It had to be a mistake. He bought a different evening paper and turned quickly to the listings. Noon price: 160.

What could have happened? His profits were wiped out. Wiped out! He knew, without doing the arithmetic, that they had called his loan. Correction, loans. Plural.

Harry headed into the Schulte Cigar Store at the corner of Forty-Second Street and placed a long-distance call to Helen.

"Oh, Harry," she said, "I've been looking for you all day long. Where have you been?"

"Never mind that, Honey. Have you heard what happened to the market?"

"Of course. Raymond & Company has been calling and so have the banks."

"I might have known."

"But Harry, I've been thinking. I've just heard the noontime prices on the radio—the tape is running very, very late—and it's 160. Suppose they do sell us out? Our four hundred shares will bring $64,000, and you only owe about $25,000 or $30,000. If you margined the shares for fifty percent, you'll still get about $32,000 for our stock and you can pay off your debt. I've been figuring it out, Harry, and we're going to be all right. Maybe even have a little money left. I don't know why they're so excited about it."

"Helen, Helen, it doesn't work that way. And I didn't tell you, but last spring I bought two hundred shares more at $290 a share on ten percent margin and I put up all of our other stock as collateral."

"Oh, Harry. Gawd!"

"We're wiped out, Helen. I don't know how badly, but we're wiped out. I'm certain of that."

"Oh, Harry."

"Now hang on, Honey. We'll make out all right. I've got to run now because I'm going to catch the Detroiter at six-thirty. Helen? You all right?"

"Yes, Dear. I'm all right. Come home."

"How are the kids?"

"They're fine. Just fine."

"Okay, I'm coming. Just as fast as I can."

"I love you, Harry. Don't worry about things. We'll be all right."

"I love you, too, Helen," Harry shouted, then blushed as he realized that people in the cigar store could hear him through the thin partition. "Good-bye dear—I've got to rush."

In Providence, Eddie Gallant bought a copy of the 4:15 edition of the *Evening Bulletin,* and found, instead of the usual closing prices, the noontime quotes. He skimmed down the listings to Radio Corporation and learned that it was 44½. He realized instantly that he had been sold out, for his first purchase had been at 60 and others had ranged up to 112.

But when he turned back to Commercial Solvents, he smiled. It had opened at 448 and the noon low was reported at 425. He had bought it at $100 a share. By golly, he thought, he should have bought ten or twenty more shares while it was on its way up. Good old Solvents was going to see him through. That candy butcher at the Old Howard knew what he was doing, all right.

It was shortly after two o'clock when Marcy Fitton hooked and landed the giant Large Mouth bass in Lake Texoma. He grinned foolishly all by himself out there on the water and took a bottle of home brew out of the net bag that was dangling in the cool depths off the dinghy's transom. He toasted the big fellow flopping about inside the boat, and drank a hearty draught, being extra careful not to disturb the foul-smelling yeast in the bottom of the bottle.

On the farm Carrie was busy in the summer kitchen bringing chili sauce and ketchup to boil simultaneously on different burners of her oil stove. Thus occupied, she missed the news broadcast.

She didn't hear the announcer say that Insull Utility Investments, which they had bought at 125 the first time and 155 the second time, had hit a low of 67½ at noon, or that Spalding, which they had purchased at 63, had dropped down to 45½.

Like her husband, she was smiling, for she enjoyed her aromatic chores. She liked the feeling of thrift and prudence she got when she was putting up preserves and sauces for the wintry months ahead.

CHAPTER 13

Thursday, October 24, 1929

6:00 P.M.

~~~~~~~~~~~~~~~~~~~~~~~~~~~~~~~~~~~~~~~

By six o'clock the front office and sales people were at their most conveniently located financial-district speakeasies. There was a festive air, not alone because the Street had apparently withstood the biggest sales assault of all time, but because fantastic commissions had been earned that day. The salesmen, customers' men and registered representatives may have lost money on their personal investments in the market's decline, but they had set a daily record for earned commissions.

It was a simple but absolute irony that while millions of Americans were facing bankruptcy, or thought that they were, and the general partners of the brokerage houses—the real owners of them—counted personal losses into the millions, the workers of Wall Street, both those who received wages and those who worked for commissions, reaped rich dividends from the market break.

Not only were sales commissions piling up, though on a declining scale as stock prices dropped, but the tens of thousands of clerical and administrative workers had been ordered to work overtime, as they had every night that week. The Saint George Hotel in Brooklyn, nearest accommodation to Wall Street, was booked solid by workers who knew it would be late when they finished. Some, indeed, got to Brooklyn when the first gray streaks of the dawn of October 25 were limning the horizon over Long Island.

By five-thirty, most front-office people had parceled out the assignments and delegated those who were to remain in the still-jammed board rooms, and in droves they sought the darkened, quasi-illegal oases that were peppered throughout the area, there to slake great thirsts acquired through a long and grueling day.

The slaking was done with martinis made from gin said to have come by boat from London but that possibly came from a Westchester bathtub, or with whiskey that was said to have come from Canada but that may have originated in Maryland, or with genuine applejack (a product in which Mr. Richard Whitney was to become financially interested as an investor) that came straight across the river from New Jersey. The beer, everyone knew, came from Brooklyn, and it was good. "Needled" beer, against which citizens were warned, was found only in the tourist traps farther uptown, or possibly in some of the shabbier of the neighborhood hideaways that were scattered by the thousands throughout the five boroughs.

In a fine club overlooking the river, Paul Mazur, highly respected partner at Lehman Brothers, turned to his companions and asked the question that was being voiced at that hour throughout the district: "Who's to blame?"

None of his party answered him. Several shook their heads, implying that the entire situation was too much to assess and was beyond analysis.

Earlier in the day, at luncheon, Mazur had addressed leaders of the textile trade and told them that the slump in the stock market would probably slow down or possibly halt the number of corporate mergers that had, in the last few years, supplied great gusto to the market.

Mazur had also said that the rapid development of investment trusts was beneficial and had aided the trend to merge because of the trusts' ability to handle large concentrations of a company's securities.

As the light of the historic day faded over the New Jersey flatlands and New York's famous skyline came aglow from the light through millions of windowpanes, Mr. Mazur and his friends talked about the role of the investment trusts in buying the securities of new corporations and in helping existing corporations to expand by creating a ready market for their stocks.

It was the opinion of those gathered there that while there was much to learn about the influence of investment trusts on the market, most of them had not contributed either to the orgy of speculation that had preceded the crash or to the frenzied selling that had precipitated and characterized it.

Subsequent studies verified this judgment.

Indeed, on October 24, the investment trusts had put in a busy day. It was estimated by some that trust bids to buy had exceeded $500,000,000 in purchases.

This promoted the inevitable conclusion in some quarters that if it had not been for the investment trusts and their almost automatic buying with "scale orders," prices would have tumbled more precipitously and ended up lower than they did, rendering the crash wider and deeper. More than forty years later executives of investment trusts would be citing those facts during another period of high speculation at a time of tightening money policy.

The trusts . . . the unchecked speculation . . . the easy margin loans . . . the seemingly indecisive role of the Federal Reserve Board . . . the zestful participation in the speculation by the banks—all of these factors were chewed on and discussed in the course of the unending "cocktail hour," which was ultimately to enrich the owners of the speakeasies in the financial district with the biggest day in their histories.

Edward Newbord was sipping his fourth Pine Valley, a tall cool drink named for the New Jersey golf club, and concocted of gin, powdered sugar and bruised fresh mint leaves poured over cracked ice and blended in a large steel tumbler in a machine like those used at soft-drink fountains to make sodas and frappes. He had a date to meet his firm's general counsel at the Metropolitan Club at eight-thirty for dinner, but like everyone else on Wall Street, he was caught up in the postmortems of the day's events.

"It's the urge to merge," he said. "Too many corporate mergers. There have been nearly twelve hundred of them so far this year. It's too many. All those bank mergers, for instance."

"They created a lot of working capital," Jules reminded him.

"Well, to tell the truth," continued Newbord, "I don't mind bank mergers so much. A bank is a bank. When one bank merges with another bank, what you get is a bigger bank, though it does remove one bank from the competition. What bothers me more is the trend toward creating hodgepodge corporations out of unrelated companies— conglomerates, I suppose you might call them.

"You buy stock in a company because it makes good wheelbarrows and you think that there's a good market for wheelbarrows and that this company's wheelbarrows will sell well. Then before you know what's happened, your wheelbarrow company has bought a company that makes bicycle seats, and another that operates a fish-canning factory, and another that spins silk thread. You own stock no longer in a wheelbarrow company but in a sprawling corporation that performs several different functions in several different markets.

"All of you analysts tell me," Newbord shook his finger at two drinkers sharing the table, "that it broadens the base, creates more working capital and reduces the risks. But I'm not so sure.

"It creates a corporation that is dedicated solely to profits rather than to the performance of a marketable service or to the creation of an identifiable product. In many ways it defeats the purpose of brand names, for it is implied that, for instance, the radio made by one manufacturer is no better than the radio made by another, even though the second producer may be basically involved in the manufacture of shovel handles.

"From our point of view in Wall Street, the emphasis of market analysis of the conglomerate is placed exclusively on the management and the financial structure, and not on the markets it serves or the product it makes. What I'm saying, I guess, is that a chemical company ought to make chemicals and stick to chemical markets. In that way we can judge its investment value, and the fellow who wants to invest in chemicals can do so.

"A fellow might want to buy stock in some chemical companies because he wants to diversify his portfolio and also because he is convinced that chemicals face a bright future. But if chemical companies get into railroading and owning timberlands and making automobiles and bottling soft drinks, he won't be able to buy the stock of a chemical company, per se. Let the diversification be done in the portfolio, not with the corporations."

"I agree with what you say," nodded Jules Barnish, "but I don't see how you can stop mergers, particularly in a rapidly industrializing economy."

"Well, they're beginning to get tough about holding companies," Newbord said. "Maybe someday they will toughen up the rules about mergers."

"Some mergers are mere devices for getting around the new restrictions on holding companies," Jules observed.

Throughout the decade that was drawing to its close, holding companies had provided the subject for innumerable discussions in Wall Street. Holding companies were flourishing, many of them propped up by combines of investment trusts that worked in uncommon harmony in supporting the securities of holding companies that, in turn, owned giant combines of other corporations.

Samuel Insull headed a holding company that embraced electric utilities ranging from Michigan and Illinois, through the Midwest and down into Texas, a combine of "independent" companies valued at two billion dollars.

The idea of the holding company had been hatched in New Jersey before the turn of the century as a device to attract additional tax revenues. It had spread to most other states and was, by the 1920s, an important and profitable institution.

The formation of corporate trusts (thinly disguised cartels for dividing up markets) had been frowned upon by the Justice Department as well as by stock-exchange officials. The advent of the holding company, therefore, presented a convenient and profitable way of circumventing the onus of the trust.

A group of competing companies could organize a holding company that would buy the stock of their companies and thereby control the operations and the markets of all of them. This was done, in fact, without much hard cash, because the "purchase" of the Treasury stock of the various companies was done by exchanging shares in the holding company for the securities of the companies it was buying.

When the investment trusts came along they were naturally attracted to the giant combines that could control whole markets without bothering to go through the formality of creating a cartel, and they bought huge blocks of holding-company stocks.

Those holding-company stocks sometimes carried a high market value, quite out of reach of the general public, because they represented the combined worth of several thriving corporations.

"Well," Jules declared, "you can't pin all the blame for the crash on holding companies or too many corporate mergers."

Newbord raised his hand to check the conversation. Angus Felt was making his way between the tables, having some difficulty with the dim light.

He stepped beside Newbord and handed him two pieces of yellow notepaper, which the managing partner promptly read.

"Hey, listen to this," he commanded. "They're meeting again—the big bankers—over at J. P. Morgan's. Whitney, Mitchell, Wiggin, Potter and Prosser. Same group that met this noon. They're in session again."

"In session, but not in season," Jules commented. "What do you think it means?"

"It can mean only one thing. More support from the bankers for tomorrow's market."

"Umph."

Newbord read the other note and then leaned back to laugh.

"Well, it's an ill wind that blows no man some good," he quoted. "Somebody made a neat pile out of today's market."

"Who was that—Ben Smith?"

"No. Governor Roosevelt. Old Franklin D. Roosevelt came out ahead of the game. New York State made $350,-000 today in stamp taxes on the transfer of stocks."

Jules repeated an earlier opinion. "Umph," he said.

CHAPTER 14

In Search of a Culprit

〜〜〜〜〜〜〜〜〜〜〜〜〜〜〜〜

Who *was* to blame? Someone had to be. The American public would not—could not—accept the notion that a weakness in human nature had led to unbridled speculation; that mankind's desire to get something for nothing, to realize profit without work, had caused seventeen million Americans to invest money that wasn't theirs in enterprises that they hoped would gain them wealth without having to expend toil, concern or responsibility.

Having done so without too many reprimands, the American people tended to blame those who had allowed them to do it.

They blamed the Federal Reserve Board.

They blamed brokers who had extended loans atop margins.

They blamed bankers who had loaned the money to brokers so they could lend it to speculators.

They blamed international bankers.

They blamed investment bankers.

They blamed Jewish bankers.

They blamed British bankers.

They blamed newly discovered Communists.

They blamed newly discovered fascists.

They blamed Herbert Hoover, and some laid it all on the doorstep of New England farmer Calvin Coolidge.

Ultimately they blamed industry, biting the hand that had fed them. In this manner they extended the blame to real people: Henry Ford, John D. Rockefeller, the Du Ponts, the Morgans, and known "economic royalists."

Not many of the horrified and disillusioned "investors" could realize on October 24, 1929, that they were participating in one of the most momentous events in all modern history and that before long they would create their own special purveyors of hate and distrust—Rev. Charles Coughlin, Gerald L. K. Smith, Huey Long, Theodore Bilbo, William Z. Foster, Earl Browder—whose motivations, whose *raisons d'être,* could be traced back to the brutal disenchantments of Black Thursday.

Neither could they even guess, most of them, that the market crash, which turned out to be preliminary to a general, broad, deep and prolonged decline in stock prices, would cause such economic upheaval in America and much of the world as to set off a reexamination of social values and national goals that would last for four decades and more—a reexamination that would alter not only the course of history but also mankind's philosophies and ideals, and that would bring fresh thinking to a more hopeful life for the individual's brief sojourn on Earth.

Why the market crash commenced on Wednesday, October 23, thundered into headlines and history on Thursday, October 24, and bottomed out on Tuesday, October 29, is probably, as *Time* magazine said the following week, unimportant. It was simply that the time had come. All of the factors that bring about a crash were in proper combination.

There was, and had been, a transcending feeling of

guilt. In addition to acumen, thorough knowledge and considerable skill, a successful investor needs courage and a profound belief in what he is doing. America's speculating public, lacking knowledge and market sophistication, was devoid of courage in the face of adversity, and it identified its unearned profit as something in league with sin.

It is probable that many investors had anticipated the great sell-off that came on Black Thursday, for surely there had been numerous signs of impending trouble. Possibly, many subconsciously awaited the market break as a day for cleansing away their sins, for washing away the guilt they felt about their unworked-for paper profits. The sharp slump in September had warned off many of the professionals, and it was discovered later that quite a few of the men who made careers out of investing, had liquidated on the crest of the fluctuating rise in early October.

The crash occurred—any crash will occur—because of the undermining of popular confidence in the market. The enthusiasm did not end suddenly on October 23 with an ice storm in the Midwest. It had been waning for some time, the nibbling process having started back in the spring.

Until then nearly everyone had seemed to believe that there was a limitless economic future for America, that the stock market had no top and that prices could continue to rise endlessly, or, as one wag put it, "Gains without end, Amen."

It was not to be until years later that ordinary businessmen and investors would accept what the economists had been saying all along, that 1929 was, indeed, a remarkable year, and had set a high record mark, not only in stock prices, but also in nearly every other economic category.

Regarded by itself, this was an important fact, but it was to be ignored by investors for nearly twenty years, during the Depression and two wars, while the market was shunned by all but a few stalwarts, who may or may not have been visionaries.

The prosperity that had started in 1925 smashed through to new records in 1927. Small-town merchants who had for years been able barely to make ends meet suddenly were putting money into savings accounts or expanding their businesses. New cars crowded the highways, many of which were axle-deep with mud. Shop and mill workers forgot about shortened workweeks or those former unconquerable piece rates, as they worked straight through Saturday noon. Overtime pay came into being. Even on the small farms there were abundance and pocket money. Life was good.

"The Coolidge prosperity," the newspapers called it, and the taciturn, tight-lipped Yankee in the White House felt called upon, in the fall of 1927, to express himself about it.

America, he told the world, was "entering upon a new era of prosperity."

"New Era!" cried the press, "a New Era is born!"

And so it was. "New Era" became a much-used and ultimately an overworked phrase. There were New Era restaurants, New Era laundries, New Era duckpin alleys, New Era ice cream parlors, New Era theaters, New Era groceries, New Era poolhalls, and so on, ad nauseam. In New Orleans there was even a New Era house of pleasure. The slogan was used as a name for a high percentage of all the new small businesses that were started during 1928.

America embarked on a New Era kick.

Everyone believed in it; it meant limitless prosperity.

The factories hummed late into the nights; inventors came up with new gadgets and devices; the stores were crowded with shoppers with cash in hand; the railroads expanded and added elaborate luxury service; trolley lines were run farther into the country to bring the folks into town to the shopping areas and to link up with lines serving other nearby towns.

Some papers printed a story saying that one could now travel by trolley from Boston's North Shore all the way to New York and thence southward to Washington. It wasn't true, but it was almost true. With some short railroad hops it could have been done; in fact with just a little supplemental railroad service, one could take a trolley car most of the way from Boston to Milwaukee. Or from Washington to Milwaukee.

To the more serious students of the nation's finances, the slogan "New Era" meant an end to the classical economic cycle of boom and bust. It meant that forevermore there would be continuing prosperity.

It mattered not that mankind had striven for this elusive status since barter was first devised. America, magical America, had found the golden key that opened wide the doors that heretofore had held only promise. Here, in this burgeoning land, prosperity would spread its benign yet stimulating influence over all until the end of time. The wealth, the savings, the industriousness and the inventiveness of the great American people would see to that.

There was no stopping the great American economic juggernaut.

Having accepted this credo, which went far beyond anything the dolorous Coolidge had said or intended, the rank-and-file Americans, their new savings burning holes in their pockets, set about the task of learning more about the nation's economy, so they might better understand this prosperity. In so doing, they discovered Wall Street. Here was the way, it seemed, to share more directly and actively in America's prosperity.

The reasoning was simple, fundamental and valid: America's growing consuming population needed new industries; new industries needed new capital; new capital was provided by selling shares of the corporations to the savers; thus the savers could share in the profits of the new corporations. Most didn't start out being speculators. Rather they were investors. The force of their numbers on the market, the impact of their wealth, gave stock prices such a precipitous rise that speculation was an inevitable result.

They trooped to the stock market in droves all during 1926, 1927 and 1928.

There they discovered something else, credit. They learned that they could borrow money from their brokers and buy more stock than they had intended. The brokers wanted only a cash margin, sometimes a mighty thin cash margin of only ten or twenty percent. The balance could be borrowed. The brokers in turn borrowed their money from the banks in the increasingly active call-money market, but not many of the new investors knew much about that, or gave it much, if any, thought.

Herein, perhaps, was the catastrophic flaw in the exciting economic evolvement. The brokers, accustomed heretofore to dealing with more sophisticated traders, most of whom were well secured by other collateral or assets, accorded the same margin privileges to millions who were so unworldly they should have left their money in savings accounts.

The brokers, sometimes made painfully aware of this by the questions that were asked them by the new breed of investors (that is, one thought that Cuba Cane, among the largest of the sugar companies, made walking sticks and crutches), consoled themselves with the knowledge that they were fairly well protected because in a falling market they had the right to sell their customers' stock to cover the loans.

Though this was a comforting bit of knowledge, it was seldom put to the test because the market kept rising, and when it did, the borrowers borrowed more on their borrowings and bought additional stock on margin.

Thus, by 1928, banks' loans to brokers had risen to record heights.

To some, the credit structure in Wall Street began to look a bit odd—top-heavy, was the term most often used —and these concerned observers looked to the Federal Reserve Board to exercise its great politics-free powers in reducing the amount of credit available.

The board had two devices at its disposal for accomplishing this, and they could be used in concert or singly.

• It could raise the discount rate—that is, the amount of interest charged to banks to borrow from the Federal Reserve Regional Bank.

• It could reduce the amount of reserves required by banks as decreed by the Federal Reserve Board, thereby cutting back on the amount of money available for lending. In order to make a loan, a bank must have a certain percentage of its liquid assets in cash reserve, and the size of these reserves, called the "Reserve Requirement," is determined by the Fed.

By raising the discount rate and reducing the amount of reserves, the Fed could "tighten up" the money supply and make credit harder to get. By lowering the discount rate and raising reserves, it could cause "easy money" conditions, and expand the availability of credit. Charged with maintaining monetary stability, the Fed had the obligation to use either or both devices to prevent either inflation or depression.

By the spring of 1928, news reports of the meetings of the Federal Reserve Board were as eagerly awaited as were accounts of the baseball games, and by as many people. In bars and barbershops and at Sunday dinners across the land, the doings of the Federal Reserve Board were cussed and discussed, probed and analyzed by an army of late-come "experts," some of whom had not known of the existence of the central banking system before their forays into the credit structure of the stock market.

By early summer, most Federal Reserve Board watchers were convinced that the Fed would be forced to raise the discount rate and lower reserve requirements in order to calm down the call-money market in Wall Street.

When the board did nothing about the swelling call-money market in June, and failed to mention it in the early part of July, rumors sprang up and spread rapidly that the Fed at its last meeting in July was going to deal a very severe blow to easy money.

Accordingly, on the afternoon of July 27, millions of Americans listened to their radios (some of which were all-electric, requiring no batteries), or waited for the "Market Final" editions of their afternoon newspapers, to learn what action the Federal Reserve Board had taken. They knew that the announcement of whatever had happened at the meeting would be withheld until after the close of the stock market at three o'clock.

They were rewarded with one of the most spectacular surprises in all economic history. The Federal Reserve Board did exactly the opposite of what had been expected. It *lowered* the discount rate and *raised* reserve requirements! It made easy money easier to borrow!

Banks could now borrow from the central system at a lower rate to create higher reserves, which, in turn, would permit them to lend out more funds than they had been able to do, at an even more favorable rate of interest to the borrower than heretofore!

At first, when radio stations "bulletined" the information by interrupting programs in progress, listeners assumed that somewhere along the line the message had become garbled and the facts transposed.

With repetition of the broadcast, however, and confirmation in type with the arrival of the late editions, the public accepted the truth.

The United States government had endorsed the speculators! The speculators had won!

Contrary to public belief, the Federal Reserve Board did not regard the market as too speculative, otherwise it would have taken the long-expected action to curb credit.

People reminded themselves that here was a federal superagency, austere, aloof, created by Congress in such a manner that it was not even answerable to the President, and staffed by experts who were free to act as their consciences bade them in determining what was best for the nation's economy.

These experts had said, in effect, go to it, speculators! There's lots more room to expand! Ah, the New Era, it made its own rules, because it was different from any other period in mankind's history.

As the market surged ahead in the next few days, with investors happily aware that more money was available for borrowing when needed, few bothered to take a second look at the almost unbelievable move by the Federal Reserve Board. Absorbed in making money, at least on paper, people forgot to ask what had motivated the board members.

Behind the decision was America's deep involvement in the effort to restore a sound economy to war-ravaged Europe so that, among other things, Germany could pay her reparations, and the Allies could repay their war debts to Uncle Sam.

Unaccustomed to foreign adventures, much less to foreign responsibilities, few Americans thought about it.

In 1924, a plan that had been developed by American financier Charles G. Dawes, later vice president of the United States, permitted Germany to pay her reparations by mortgaging her industries and railroads. Deeply involved in this and the subsequent negotiations was Wall Street's John Pierpont Morgan, close friend of Britain's chief negotiator and richest man, Lord Revelstoke. Almost as deeply involved was the governor (president) of the Federal Reserve Bank of New York, Benjamin Strong, a "Morgan man" in that he had been handpicked for the job by J. P. Morgan. As deeply involved in the German reparations problem as Strong was Strong's closest friend, Montagu Norman, governor of the Bank of England, Britain's Central Bank, broadly similar to our Federal Reserve System.

In 1925 Ben Strong had played a major role in assisting Montagu Norman in getting Britain back on the gold standard. To accomplish this, the American Federal Reserve loaned Britain $200 million, and the House of Morgan, through Strong's intercession, loaned another $100 million.

Because of this background, Strong, who was the dominant and most forceful banker on the Federal Reserve Board (perhaps the most competent banker in the nation at the time), resisted raising the discount rate because he knew this would boost interest rates and attract gold from Europe. This would weaken the economies of the European nations, he knew, and would jeopardize, if not scuttle, all chances for payment of reparations or war debts, and would undermine Britain's foundation on the gold standard.

What Strong wanted from the Federal Reserve Board, Strong usually got. He was the soundest and most experienced banker on a board that, at that time, harbored some undistinguished political appointees.

As the nation's leading banker, Benjamin Strong would have put America's economic interests first had he thought they were being weakened, just as his friend Montagu Norman would have placed England's welfare above all else. Strong reasoned, however, that the greatest threat to the American economy was not overspeculation in Wall Street but the possible bankruptcy of America's trading allies and debtors.

He thought that he *was* putting America's interests first.

Strong, not given to communicating with the "outside world" where central bankers were not involved, must have felt extremely isolated as he maintained his fight to keep Europe economically sound . . . for America's sake.

Secretary of Commerce Herbert Hoover wanted a higher discount rate and a restrictive credit policy, and, after some grumbling around his own department, had finally made a formal presentation to President Coolidge asking that the President intercede with the Federal Reserve Board. The President took no action. He was justified in refusing to do so; the law forbade intrusion by the executive branch into the policy matters of the Fed.

Treasury Secretary Andrew Mellon, a banker and businessman, was all in favor of what he called the "expansion" (meaning an easy-money-ample-credit policy), which he felt was adding solid muscle to America's growing industrial empire.

There were farm-bloc senators, however, led by Virginia's Carter Glass, who favored some kind of change in policy, though they were not specific about how it should be accomplished. Their complaint was that all available credit was being siphoned off by Wall Street, leaving little for farmers who needed it to live on and to do a little expanding of their own.

Apparently the sole public official who was concerned with the larger, the international, picture was Ben Strong.

Nothing had been done by the Fed during the winter and spring because Strong, suffering from tuberculosis and other complications, had been in a sanatorium in South Carolina. He mustered his strength and his forces in July, however, and the result was the unexpected decision to lower the discount rate and raise the reserve requirements.

In the world of finance, the Fed's decision seems to have been misinterpreted. It was not an endorsement of speculation, a green light for speculators, as was apparently universally believed. It was a device to help Europe keep her gold so that the Germans could make their reparation payments and the other nations could pay their war debts to the United States.

Less than a month after the July decision, the discount rate was lowered again, from 4 to 3.5 percent. The Chicago Federal Reserve Bank didn't go along, as was its option, so Strong got the Federal Reserve Board together to vote on ordering the bank to comply. The board voted the order; the Chicago bank complied.

The market zoomed skyward.

Brokers' loans leaped up from less than $3.3 billion to nearly $4.5 billion.

Total U.S. income was about $90 billion.

But Professor Irving Fisher of Yale, a bull-market enthusiast, noted that about eighty percent of all Americans, or ninety-three million, were earning just enough to make their living expenses. So Americans were far from rich—but with the market going the way it was, they were going to get richer.

There was a break in the market in July 1928. It was the most frightening thing that had happened to speculators in a long time, but they forgot about it a day or two later when everything got back to normal and the upward thrust was resumed.

Here and there, in 1928, there were vocal objections to speculation and, in fact, to the stock market itself. They came mostly from farm-state folks and their stalwart U.S. senators—LaFollette, Capper, Borah—and from localities in the Bible Belt where bedrock Protestantism prevailed and the people prided themselves on their Prohibition Amendment and mistrusted the cosmopolites of the East Coast who drank, consorted and gambled in the paper stock certificates of Hell-destined corporations.

Benjamin Strong died in October 1928, after reversing his easy-money monetary policy, but with his hand still at the helm of the Fed. He could begin to see, toward the end, that a complete switch in policy was needed.

The low discount rate and high reserves had resulted in such a spectacular stock market that it was attracting European money, anyway, if not its gold. The Strong ploy had been so successful it was defeating its purpose.

Strong succumbed to a painful death after a life of great personal disappointments and tragedies, but was destined to be talked about in banking circles for many years thereafter as one of the most astute leaders of central banking in the world.

From his deathbed in London, Strong prodded the Federal Reserve Board into slowly reversing its position. In three steps in 1928 it raised the discount rate back to five percent. It did not lower reserve requirements but effected the same result by selling an unprecedented amount of government bonds through its Open Market Committee activities, thus reducing the amount of reserves available.

Americans were diverted in the autumn of 1928 by the extremely bitter campaigns waged by both Herbert Hoover and Alfred E. Smith. They did notice, however, that interest rates were climbing higher. Bankers' loans were costing more. So were collateral loans at the bank. Call-money rates, it was noticed by those who bothered to look, were skyrocketing.

Speculators seemed quite happy that Hoover had won the election, for he was a New Era man—or so they thought—a formal successor to prosperity-creating Calvin Coolidge, and a man who would, he had promised, keep the chartlines climbing.

The market roared onward, upward.

Brokers' loans climbed to new heights. Traders paid their brokers twenty-five percent more interest than they had during Ben Strong's easy-money days, but they didn't mind. What was twelve percent or even fifteen percent on a loan when you could double the money you borrowed within a month or so—sometimes even in a week?

As the year 1929 began and the decade prepared to enter history, the year-end editions of the newspapers, those annual financial and economic reviews and predictions, hailed the nation's seemingly unshakable prosperity and printed more fulsomely than ever the litany of optimistic and glowing forecasts from the nation's business and financial leaders. The dubious—the Paul Warburgs, the Roger Babsons, the Russell Leffingwells, the Norman Stablers—were not consulted. Good news was wanted; good news was printed.

With the January snows came realization of what the Federal Reserve Board's "new" policy meant. Dearer money drove upward the interest rates right across the board, right across the country.

Small businesses began to hurt. New ones foundered and folded. Anything but a Triple A–rated corporation found it difficult to float bonds or to acquire formal indebtedness. Municipalities and even larger governments were forced to withdraw their bond offerings. Housing starts slowed down; building construction of all kinds fell off; automobile sales began to look a little shaky.

A few people worried.

These things were there to see, these less-optimistic figures, but seventeen million Americans had their eyes riveted to the quotation boards in the brokerage offices. The stock market was romping away into ever-higher ground. The target of the Fed's "new" policy was completely untouched by it.

In February there were repeated reports and rumors emanating both from Washington and from Wall Street that the Federal Reserve Board, committed to its tight-money policy, was going to raise the discount rate even higher.

Instead the Fed issued two warnings, neither very stern or meaningful. One reminded that it was wrong for member banks to maintain speculative security loans with Federal Reserve credit. You couldn't, in other words, borrow from the Fed to lend money to brokers.

It was a mild tap, yet such was the sensitivity of the market that a sharp decline ensued.

There was a pause, a short vacuum, then Charles E. Mitchell, National City Bank's chairman, announced that his bank would put up twenty-five million dollars for the call-money market and, what's more, would borrow it from the New York Federal Reserve Bank.

He has "slapped the Federal Reserve Board squarely in the face," cried Carter Glass.

But the market responded and surged upward, ignoring the break.

It advanced steadily until March, when another break came, toppling prices and wiping out some small investors.

It sent call-loan rates up to 20 percent.

Perhaps now was the time for Washington to say something, do something.

The Federal Reserve could have asked Congress for power to raise margin requirements as a move to curb speculation, but it didn't.

President Herbert Hoover, inaugurated on March 4, could have reaffirmed his opinion, expressed two years earlier, that speculation was out of hand and should be throttled down, but he didn't.

The silence was too much for Paul Warburg. He issued his warning and scolded the Federal Reserve Board. It was ignored.

By mid-May the market was climbing into new and higher ground and, as one observer noted, "wasn't even breathing heavily from the exertion."

Bernard M. Baruch said the economy of the world seemed to be on the "verge of a great forward movement." This was interpreted as meaning a New Era for the whole globe.

At Yale, Professor Fisher declared that stock prices seemed to reach a "permanently high plateau." This was reassuring, for it was understood that if prices fell, they wouldn't have far to fall. The new floor was higher.

Mitchell issued additional statements of confidence.

Throughout the summer months the market climbed, shattering records. Here and there soft spots appeared, an imperceptible misfiring in one of the spark plugs. People listened instead to the powerful purr of the main engine.

On Thursday in the second week of August the tape watchers were worried because it had been rumored that the Bank of England was going to raise its discount rate. They watched fretfully during the forenoon while the board members met in London, then were cheered to learn that the members had decided against the raise. The attention shifted to the quotation boards and they watched stocks post gains right up until the closing gong.

Then, a few moments after the market's close, came the word: the New York Federal Reserve Bank had boosted the rate from five to six percent.

Next morning, stocks lost on a broad front, a decline that was deeper and wider than in March. Late in the day, though, some recovery was noted, and on Saturday, good gains were posted. On Monday, U.S. Steel, which within the fortnight had announced it was operating at 95 percent of capacity, reached a new high.

Labor Day had been a stolen respite, for stocks were pushing against their records, so powerful was their upward thrust, and speculators seemed unwilling to give up, even for a day, the heady excitement of making paper profits. All during the month of September, as the stock market embarked on its "New Year," the wildest kind of speculation boosted prices.

Other September indicators were less cheerful. Factory

output was down. Steel production was off. Foreign trade was lower than it had been in a long time. Home building and building construction of all kinds were genuinely depressed.

Some people began to notice, and in the waning days of September, the market began to lose ground.

It lost a little in October's early trading days, too. It lost, then regained, then lost again; each time the loss was a bit more severe than its predecessor, and each time the recovery was a little less than the loss had been. Those who kept charts plotted a slow, ragged descent.

On Monday, October 21, sell orders were so numerous that the tickertape fell behind.

Many people were undisturbed by this, for a substantial recovery had taken over before closing time, and from his aerielike perspective at Yale, Professor Irving Fisher hailed the drop as a beneficial "shaking out of the lunatic fringe of speculators." Many in that lunatic fringe had been sold out by the sharp drop.

It was the next day, Tuesday, October 22, when Charles Mitchell, returning from Europe, announced to reporters that the market was fundamentally sound and would correct itself.

So who really *was* at fault?

Was it the speculator, after all, rather than some individual or small willful group?

Was it the fellow who bought numbers rather than securities, and didn't know, in many cases, what function was performed by the company whose stock he owned? If so, it was not exclusively an American malady, as foreign newspapers implied, for investors from all over the world were playing the American stock markets.

Was it Ben Strong, who waited too long to force tight

money onto the economy so that it could cool the fevers of speculation, waited so long, in fact, that the patient could not respond to the treatment?

Was it the brokers, who allowed amateurs to "play" with margin accounts, when prudence should have restrained them?

Or was it the bankers, who took advantage of the Federal Reserve's policy and made loans uncommonly accessible to the brokers?

Perhaps, after all, it was a natural and necessary phenomenon, destined to occur when, for the first time in mankind's history, a nation progressed from a second-rate power to the foremost economic force in the world within the space of two decades, and at the same time created the greatest, richest, most productive industrial complex ever assembled.

Whether he was a true-blue and cautious investor or a come-lately unsophisticated speculator, the situation was just too compelling to resist for anyone who had a few dollars to spare.

So perhaps, after all, no one can be blamed, and the experience will be chalked up as an economic spasm, caused by America's violent growing pains.

CHAPTER 15

The Automotive Bull

At six-thirty o'clock the old man pushed through the revolving door and walked jauntily, almost youthfully, to the curb where his chauffeur was holding open the rear door of his twelve-cylinder Cadillac. A few minutes earlier he had told an associate, "Well, we're cleaned out— again. Broke. Flat broke. But we'll rebuild. There are many opportunities ahead of us."

He settled back in the seat and told the driver to take him straight home to New Jersey. He opened the *Post* to the financial section and squinted in the fading light, then put the newspaper aside. He didn't need more news of the market crash.

At age sixty-eight, William C. Durant looked, acted and felt (most times) twenty years younger. He was deeply disturbed by the events of the day, events he had predicted, but was not depressed. He had been broke several times before and had always recovered quickly. As the founder of the company that was the world's largest manufacturing corporation—General Motors—William Crapo Durant was the stock market's most irrepressible Bull and one of America's most optimistic financiers. Today he was nearly broke.

The "Automobile Century" had encountered a patch of very rough highway that day. He supposed that young Alfred P. Sloan, Jr. (then fifty-four) was having a tough day in the president's office in the General Motors Building on Broadway, and he thought, briefly, about hard-hitting Walter P. Chrysler, whom he had brought into General Motors management, and also of his old-time corporate feuding partner and former teammate, Charles W. Nash.

They should be made to realize, he thought, that the automobile business was just getting started. He had thought so in 1908 when he formed General Motors, and he still felt the same way in 1929. He knew that Henry Ford, who shared his vision, would survive the market crash and any depression that might follow, for he had only the year before introduced the new Model A Ford with a popular price ticket, and had already regained a good share of the market.

He knew them all, all the big men in the auto industry and many who were on their way up. There was a young man at General Motors now, working as general assistant treasurer, and Durant figured they had better keep an eye on him. His name was Ernest R. Breech.*

The automobile industry more than anything else had contributed to the nation's unprecedented prosperity and had served a major role in sustaining it, Durant firmly believed. He also devoutly believed it would power the prosperity of the future.

As the greatest promoter of American business and probably the biggest individual operator in Wall Street, Durant controlled a "pool" of investments from faithful followers, a pool calculated to be valued at over one bil-

*Breech later became president of Bendix and then president of Ford Motor Company.

lion dollars. That is, he had controlled it, until today's market crash.

Today the pool had been drained.

He may have realized, as he was being driven out of the financial district, that a great period in America's economic history was drawing to a close and that he had been a leading source of the energy that powered its thrust. More likely he was even then planning other bolder business ventures, a pastime that occupied him until he was eighty years old.

Billy Durant was a money man. He knew how to raise it. He knew how to make it multiply. He was as much a part of his time as was the automobile he had pioneered, the Buick. What the Buick motorcar was to the sandy, rutted roadways of America, William C. Durant was to the entrepreneurs of Wall Street, the more imaginative of the big bankers and the planners among the business leaders.

As is proper for successful promoters, Durant started his career as a salesman—a traveling salesman who sold equipment to blacksmiths, saddleries, harness shops and feed and grain stores, mainly in the Midwest. Hitchhiking from one town to the next, he was one day given a ride in a fine, solid-feeling wagon. He noted the name of the manufacturer, Dort, and resolved to get in touch with him. He did, and a short time later he was president of the Durant-Dort Carriage Company. Ten years later, Durant-Dort Carriage Company was the largest carriage and wagon manufacturing enterprise in the world.

Before he was forty, Durant had acquired a personal fortune of more than a million dollars, so at the turn of the century he went to Wall Street, "just to study the place," he said. He informed friends that he was taking an "extended vacation."

After a suitable period of observation, Durant began to play the market a little, venturing into one industry after another and watching closely the formation of the big business trusts that resulted from combines and mergers. The latter fascinated him and he began then a love affair with the stock market that was to last him the remainder of his life, an affair that rewarded him frequently and lavishly, but one that sometimes hurt him cruelly.

Only six months earlier, in March 1929, David Dunbar Buick had died of cancer in Detroit, leaving his name on a popular and durable automobile, but ending a life that had been plagued by bad luck, frustrations and failures. "It was the breaks of the game," he had said, philosophically, as he departed for the hospital for what he knew was terminal care. "Money isn't that important." The survival of Buick's motorcar and its rise to become the most popular model in America were due, in major measure, to the efforts of William C. Durant.

David Buick was a partner in a profitable plumbing company in Detroit when he became interested in the experiments with the horseless carriage being conducted by Henry Ford and R. E. Olds. Not long after that, he assembled his first workable gasoline engine. He believed he could manufacture them profitably. It was 1900, a new century was getting under way, and David Buick believed that "automobile machines" offered the most promising future in the industrial world.

He backed this belief with all that he owned.

He sold his partnership in the plumbing firm, sold also his rights to a bathtub-enameling process, raised one hundred thousand dollars, and started setting up his factory in an abandoned barn. His one employee was his son. The Buick Manufacturing Company was incorporated two years later, and from the outset it suffered from a shortage of capital.

In 1903 the Briscoe brothers put more money into the company, changing the name to Buick Motor Car Company, but they, too, found that the capital was insufficient. It did no good to appeal to the banks; bankers wouldn't talk to them about the Buick dream. Ford was in the process of organizing Ford Motor Company, and financial prospects didn't look good for him, either.

Then the Briscoes and David Buick learned that a wagon maker in Flint, one James H. Whiting, was interested in entering the automobile business. He, too, thought it held promise.

A deal was consummated and Whiting joined forces with the Briscoes and Buick. Again the name was changed, this time to Buick Motor Company, and the plant was moved to Flint. That year the company turned out sixteen cars priced at $1,200 each. The Buick was competitive in price and quality with the Olds, and it became established in the marketplace, but Whiting learned during the next two years that more capital was needed.

What was really needed, Whiting decided, was to go public, and he required a man who could promote the company—raise money and sell cars at the same time. As a competitor in the wagon business, Whiting knew Durant and held a healthy respect for him as a money raiser, a manufacturer and a promoter. He contacted him.

Durant made one visit to Flint and took to automobiles the way he had to wagons ten years earlier. He bought control of Buick Motor Company.

The year was 1905. Durant may have liked them, but most people had a well-founded and thoroughly deserved mistrust of automobiles. Even when they worked well, which was not consistently the case, there were few roads to drive them on. There were not many mechanics around to service the confounded machines when they didn't work right. They smelled. They made noise. They frightened horses, chickens and people alike.

Yet, despite this general attitude about cars, Billy Durant raised a half-million dollars for Buick Motor Company in the relatively small city of Flint, Michigan, in one day. The money, he told investors, was for expansion.

The expansion resulted in the production of 627 Buicks that year. It was only the beginning, Durant told his backers. Production swung into higher gear. The Wall Street panic of 1907 didn't cause a ripple at Buick. In 1908 Buick emerged as the leading motorcar producer in the country and its factory was the largest industrial plant in the world. There were 8,487 Buicks built in 1908, compared to a production of 6,181 Fords and 2,380 Cadillacs.

And Buick became profitable. It earned $400,000 on $2 million in sales in 1906; about $1.1. million on $4.2 million in sales in 1907; and $1.7 million on $7.5 million in sales in 1908.

Buick led the industry.

It had the two most important basic ingredients for success in the dawning world of Big Business—growth in sales and increased profits.

Durant had been the biggest wagon maker in the world. He was now the biggest automobile manufacturer. It wasn't enough. Big Business could become bigger in burgeoning America. Great profits could become greater.

Thus, on September 16, 1908, William Crapo Durant

incorporated General Motors Company. Into General Motors he brought Buick on October 1, 1908; then Olds (now Oldsmobile) on November 12; and then, in 1909, Oakland (now Pontiac) and Cadillac.

The creation of the trusts that Durant had watched so carefully on Wall Street, and in which he had made modest but profitable investments, now served him as blueprints while he organized his own empire.

By various methods, mostly involving the exchange of stock, Durant, between 1908 and 1910, brought into General Motors some twenty-five new companies. Eleven were automobile companies; two were electric-lamp manufacturing outfits; and the remainder were companies that manufactured auto parts and auto accessories. Most of the automobile manufacturing companies acquired by Durant were bought for their engineering designs; they had little to offer in the way of plant or production facilities.

Durant also made a bid to buy out Henry Ford. If his bankers had been endowed with a bit more vision, Durant would have succeeded, thus exciting speculation on what would have happened to the great American automotive industry.

Ford's price to sell was $8 million, of which $2 million must be in cash. Durant's board of directors approved the purchase, but when he went to the bankers to borrow the cash, he was turned down. "The Ford business," they said, "is not worth the money." Ford had earned in 1908 a profit of nearly $2.7 million on sales of $9 million, which must have been one of the finest profit pictures in the nation.

Perhaps 1908 was the pivotal year for America's future prosperity—the prosperity that was to be postponed by war but that was to mushroom into the economy in the 1920s, and to come to a sudden halt on October 24, 1929.

It was the year that the automotive industry became the biggest single economic force in the nation. It was the year that Durant formed General Motors and that Henry Ford introduced the Motel T. The two separate acts, made by two not-too-friendly men in the same city, unleashed a dynamic force on the American economy that was to be even brighter and stronger more than half a century later.

Because of those Detroit-built machines:

• Consumer credit was devised, changing the entire financial structure of the nation.

• Mechanical engineering and draftsmanship became recognized sciences in the schools and colleges, opening many other doors.

• Hundreds of millions of dollars were invested in oil wells in search of the fuel for the vehicles.

• Whole cities were to change; suburbs were to spring up, linked to urban areas only by automobiles.

• Roads and bridges were to be built to accommodate the outpouring of autos and trucks; then they were to be torn down and replaced with turnpikes and better bridges, only to be torn down once more to be replaced with superhighways and superspans.

• Enormous truck fleets would move commodities, goods and products to even the most remote parts of the land.

• Tire manufacturers were to range the world creating plantations in the hotter, more humid countries so that millions of cars could ride on rubber.

• The steel industry was to double, then quintuple capacity.

• Chemical industries, machine tool industries, metal-fabricating industries were to grow and to flourish as they supplied components to the automobile.

• Tens of millions of jobs were to be created directly or indirectly because of the automobile.

• Tanker fleets and freighter fleets were to be built to service the automobile industry. Railroads were to fan out from Detroit to the rest of the nation.

Being a buccaneer and an "individual-type" industrialist, it is possible that William C. Durant never thought of the broad perspective of the car that he had helped to create and that seemed to be ending a phase on the evening of October 24. That other strong-minded individualist, Henry Ford, out at his enormous Highland Park plant, probably accorded the market's crash only passing attention, for he was en route to a record-setting year, and very busy.

Alfred P. Sloan, Jr., General Motors' president, did think about it, as he wrote later. He was, perhaps, a more perceptive man than Durant, in that he possessed the administrative and management talents that Durant had lacked, and he saw the empire that he headed as more than bricks, mortar, machines, markets and profits. He perceived, as possibly Durant did not, just how much Durant and other pioneers of the automotive industry had contributed to the national well-being and to the accelerated stock market.

Durant had been one of the first to try to capture an entire consumer's market, and in doing so he pioneered in both corporate and manufacturing diversification, a philosophy that was to bring about many acquisitions and mergers in the corporate world in the quest by Big Business to grow bigger during the speculative 1920s.

His marketing efforts were illustrated by the wide price diversity of his cars—Buick, Olds, Oakland, Cadillac and, later, Chevrolet.

Durant's diversification also stemmed from his desire

to cover every engineering development—developments that were legion at the time—so that General Motors would have a head start, at least in the laboratory. Because of patterns or designs or unusual engines, Durant acquired the friction-drive Cartercar, the two-cycle engine of Elmore Manufacturing Company, the Marquette Motor Company, the Ewing Automobile Company, the Randolph Motor Car Company, the Welch Motor Car Company, the Rapid Motor Vehicle Company and the Reliance Motor Truck Company.

Thus he gained a lead in the technical advancements for engines.

The practice in those days was to concentrate on engines and, perhaps, bodies, and to buy all parts and accessories from private suppliers. Durant, father of the integrated industrial plant, thought this was impractical, so he brought under the General Motors wing a number of component manufacturers. These included the Northway Motor and Manufacturing Company; the Champion Ignition Company, later to be known as AC Spark Plug Company; the Jackson-Church-Wilcox Company, a manufacturer of parts; the Weston-Mott Company of Utica, manufacturer of wheels and axles; and several other smaller suppliers. He also bought the McLaughlin Motor Car Company, Ltd., of Canada, giving birth to the McLaughlin-Buick car in Canada and acquiring for GM one of its most able executives in the person of R. Samuel McLaughlin.

Within a two-year span, Durant had made of General Motors a fully integrated company, one that manufactured and supplied itself with all of its component parts.

All of this acquisition imposed great drains on the company's capital supply. Durant wasn't bothered; he was building for the long haul. In neglecting to give consideration to the immediate future, he failed to consider the fact that his company was becoming so thin on capital it would be able to withstand no reverses whatsoever.

One of his purchases was the Heany Lamp Companies, bought with General Motors securities for $7 million—more than the cost of Olds and Buick combined. Heany's principal asset was one item—an application for a patent for tungsten lamps. When the patent office declined to issue a patent and denied the application, the company was valueless.

This, combined with the thin capitalization, forced Durant to the wall, and he was soon overextended and in serious financial difficulties. He appealed to the banks and was turned down repeatedly. Finally an investment banking group headed by James J. Storrow, of Lee Higginson Company of Boston, and Albert Strauss, of J. and W. Seligman and Company of New York, agreed to take over the refinancing of General Motors through a voting trust. There was no alternative but to have the group set up the trust and take over command.

Thus, in September 1910, exactly two years after he had created General Motors, W. C. Durant lost control of it. He remained as a vice president and member of the board of directors, but he was allowed no voice in management.

He was, however, allowed to make suggestions. One of them was a recommendation to Mr. Storrow that he hire as head of the Buick division, Charles W. Nash, who for twenty years had managed the Durant-Dort Carriage Company.

The following year Nash hired, on the recommendation of banker Storrow, a two-fisted management man from American Locomotive Works, Walter P. Chrysler. In 1912 Nash was made president of General Motors, replacing an interim man named Thomas Neal, and Chrysler was made head of Buick division.

Nash would ultimately quit General Motors, the result of an invasion by Durant, and go to Kenosha, Wisconsin, to create his own auto manufacturing company out of a company that made a bicycle called the Rambler.

Chrysler in time would form his own company and acquire the thriving automobile production of the Brothers Dodge, and preserve for the American motoring public such durable and respected names as DeSoto, Chrysler, Imperial, Plymouth and, of course, Dodge.

Back in 1905, William Durant had pursued a dream wherein Americans bought a million motorcars a year, and in 1910, when he was dethroned at General Motors, he still thought the dream was attainable. He had no sooner stepped down from the presidency at GM than he contacted Louis Chevrolet, the daring French racing driver, designer and engineer. It was probably something he had been planning to do for General Motors had he not run out of company cash.

In 1911 Messrs. Durant and Chevrolet together started the Chevrolet Motor Company, the first step in Durant's return to General Motors' presidency. Within four years they built a coast-to-coast operation with several assembly plants and wholesale distribution offices across the country and in Canada. As Chevrolet Motor Company prospered, Durant increased the amount of stock and, wherever practical or possible, offered it in exchange for General Motors stock.

It was about this time that the Du Ponts, made cognizant of General Motors' need for cash, became interested in the organization. This resulted in one of the most remarkable corporate courtships in U.S. business history.

The intermediary was John J. Raskob, then treasurer of E. I. du Pont de Nemours & Company and personal financial advisor to Pierre S. du Pont, president of the company. Raskob was later to become chairman of the Demo-

cratic National Committee and one of the most vocal
Bulls in Wall Street, a partner with Republican Durant in
urging people to buy securities. "Any American can become rich," Raskob said, advising everyone to get into the
stock market.

On Mr. Raskob's advice, Mr. du Pont began to buy General Motors shares for his own account. On Mr. Raskob's
further advice, Mr. du Pont became personally interested
in the spectacular rise in sales of the Chevrolet motorcar
and its "Baby Grand" touring car and "Royal Mail" road-
ster, and he came to know Durant.

The bankers' voting trust was to expire in September of
1915, and a new director was to be elected to the board to
replace Mr. Storrow. Pierre S. du Pont was slated to be
elected chairman of the board and Charles W. Nash was
scheduled to be reelected president—or so most people
thought.

As the meeting convened, Durant, still a board member, strode into the room followed by helpers carrying
several cases of stock certificates and proxies. These he
placed on his desk.

"Gentlemen," he announced, "I have control."

There was nothing more to be said or done.

Durant offered Nash a second-in-command job at General Motors, but he declined. The records do not show it,
but it is regarded that he left in somewhat of a huff. History shows that Nash had turned in a good stewardship
during his tenure as GM's president.

Durant immediately set about consolidating his relationship with the du Ponts and, aided by Pierre S. du Pont,
he changed General Motors from a holding company to
an operating company, owning and operating all of its
divisions.

With John J. Raskob as chairman of GM's finance committee and Pierre S. du Pont as chairman of the board of directors and financial fountainhead, Durant was the only non–du Pont man on the powerful finance committee. He was back in the drivers' seat as president, however, running management.

Expansion was the theme. As Durant set about acquiring companies and expanding operations, the du Ponts arranged for more and more money to be poured into the swelling General Motors structure. Over a period of three years the du Pont Company itself bought $49 million worth of General Motors stock, acquiring for itself 28.7 percent of the ownership of the outstanding common stock, which was more than effective control.

Chevrolet was consolidated into the GM structure. Then Fisher Body (with forty percent ownership remaining with the financially astute Fishers). Durant also got interested in tractors and acquired Samson Sieve Grip Tractor Company of Stockton, California, the Janesville Machine Company of Janesville, Wisconsin, and the Doylestown Agricultural Company of Doylestown, Pennsylvania, all of which went into General Motors' Samson Tractor Division.

With his own personal check for $56,366.50, Durant bought the Guardian Frigerator Company of Detroit, paving the way for formation of GM's Frigidaire Division.

Durant started General Motors of Canada, Ltd. He launched General Motors Acceptance Corporation to help people finance the purchase of their cars and to prod the foot-dragging banks into offering automobile loans. He acquired a group of Dayton companies headed by engineering genius Charles F. Kettering and brought Kettering into the organization.

Virtually dozens of manufacturing divisions were established to supply basic parts for General Motors cars,

such as wheels, axles, gears, crankshafts, radiators, brake
drums and the like. Another large group of companies
was assembled for the manufacture of parts and accessories for the widening line of GM cars. To head this
spreading operation, called United Motors, Durant hired
a brilliant young science graduate from Massachusetts
Institute of Technology who had distinguished himself in
the roller-bearing field—an important component part of
the automobile. His name was Alfred P. Sloan, Jr.

Then, in the spring of 1920, the postwar inflationary
balloon burst and a depression quickly descended over
the land. Again, Durant had not planned for short-range
contingencies. He was caught out with what suddenly
was viewed as overexpansion.

He had amassed a personal fortune of $100 million with
his ventures and he poured it all into the market in an
effort to support General Motors stock, but it kept falling
—from 42 earlier in the year to a low of 12¾.

His lone support was not enough.

Durant's deep personal involvement with the giant corporation he had created was such that it jeopardized the
corporate credit—so the bankers said.

The du Ponts and J. P. Morgan got together to finance
a settlement with Durant's brokers and to take his stock
out of the market. They bailed him out, and he emerged
almost as wealthy as he was before his heroic effort to
save the company's stock.

But he was out of a job. He was asked to make his
second—and final—exit from the company he had sired.

He left behind for General Motors a legacy of seventy-
five huge plants in forty states, an industrial empire that
was to grow faster and larger than any other in the world.

Durant was sixty years old when he left General Motors
for the second time. He could have retired and lived well.

A year later he was back in Wall Street announcing that he was going to launch Durant Motors, Inc., and had already lined up several powerful friends to join with him.

The "Durant" and the "Star" were good cars, and in 1923, 1924 and 1925 the sales were satisfactory if not spectacular. The stock of Durant Motors stood at 84 and it was actively traded. But the tough competition from General Motors that had brought the Model T Ford to a stalemate also wreaked problems on the Durant sales. Durant's child had grown up to smite the parent. Durant sales fell, and its stock dropped down to around $6.

The cars continued to be made into the 1930-model year, but Billy Durant knew as he rode home that October night in 1929 that it was to be the last car model to be put out by Durant Motors, Inc.

It was consigned to the automotive Valhalla where reposed the Jordan, the Hupp, the Willis-Knight, the Willys-Overland, the Graham-Paige, the Elcar, the Maxwell, the Auburn and many others, and where soon would be dispatched the mobile symbol of the 1920s, the Stutz Bearcat.

From about 1925 on, Durant had run a large, important and much-publicized stock-market pool, worth, it was said, well over a billion dollars. Active with him in the pool were the exceedingly well-to-do six Fisher brothers of the Fisher Body Division of General Motors—Fred J., Charles T., Lawrence P., William A., Edward F., and Alfred J.

His trading pools involved Fisher Body's separate operation, and Cast-Iron Pipe and Radio Corporation of America. His own millions were involved in the trades, supported by the millions of dozens of other multimillionaires who followed Durant, believing him an invincible winner.

Mostly they were Westerners and Midwesterners, though Durant did attract some notable Eastern Establishment investors. Durant's fellow pool members were dubbed "the Prosperity Boys" by envious outsiders.

One Durant pool in the spring of 1929 was in Radio stock, and it was reported to have made a profit of $5 million in one week. His associates in that Radio pool were reported to have been Percy A. Rockefeller, John J. Raskob, Mrs. David Sarnoff and Walter P. Chrysler, and others.

Durant was not one of those who thought the Federal Reserve should apply restrictive policies, and he fumed when the discount rate was raised finally. Fuming for Durant was not commensurate with the rest of his personality, for he did not like profanity, and he was, incidentally, a strong prohibitionist, abiding in one of the "wettest" areas of the country.

When rumors built up in July that the Fed was going to tighten the money market further, Durant put on a "disguise" consisting of a floppy hat and a false mustache and took a train to Washington to make a personal appeal to President Hoover to intervene. The Federal Reserve Board policies, Durant told the President, were going to hurt the market and cause professionals to liquidate their stocks.

If he was forced to dump the more than $1 billion in stocks that he controlled, he told the President, it would cause a nationwide economic catastrophe, a serious depression.

On the night of October 24, 1929, Durant heaved a tired sigh and settled deeper into the soft cushions of his limousine. Since ten-thirty in the morning he had been dumping millions of dollars' worth of stocks into a weakened market.

He wondered if this time Mr. Hoover would believe him if he should tell him the truth about market operations.

He hadn't in July.

No matter. Durant figured it wouldn't be hard to re-build his Wall Street empire.

He tried to recapture it until he was eighty years old, but he never succeeded.

CHAPTER 16

Thursday, October 24, 1929

8:00 P.M.

~~~~~~

Edward dePlassance Newbord, his anonymous and un-
pretentious gray fedora waiting atop his desk, was about
ready to leave for dinner at Jack & Charlie's. He fingered
the edges of the sheet of paper on which had been compiled a neat row of figures. It had been handed to him by
special messenger a few minutes earlier, a runner em-
ployed by a neighboring commission house. It had been
in an envelope marked "Personal and Confidential."

Revealed in neat, typewritten numerals was the history
of yet another substantial financial loss that Ed Newbord
had incurred in the day's market. A pool operation in
Montgomery Ward stock, in which he had been one of the
largest operators, had been wiped out, its margin called
by his own firm, and there was nothing he could do about
it except pay the debt, if he had enough cash left to do it
with.

The operation of a pool was not an officially recognized
or sanctioned function, yet it happened all the time, was
generally recognized by the more sophisticated segment
of the trading public, and progress of the larger ones was
reported, albeit obscurely, in the press.

Its purpose was quite simple—to gouge the public by

inducing speculators to bid up the price of a stock, and then to sell out before the floor caved in. If the structure toppled with the pool operators still aboard, they were more severely hurt than their intended victims because they had more invested in the phony price. That is what had happened to Newbord and his pool partners.

The trick, always, in running a successful pool was to find the right stock, and Newbord had been sure that Montgomery Ward was the one.

It possessed the proper ingredients. It had been increasingly active and had tacked on some good (and legitimate) gains. A number of favorably bullish stories about its financial condition and its merchandising successes had appeared in the press.

Moreover, Montgomery Ward owed the pool a special favor. It had tricked them earlier in the year.

The first step in organizing a stock pool is to select the parties to the conspiracy and bind them together with legal agreements, accept their pledges for certain amounts of money and credits, and swear them to secrecy. The second step is to get a manager, either a specialist in the stock, or a good, active trader in it, if such a person is not already a member of the pool organization. He receives either a special fee or an extra edge of the profits for his management.

Then the manager, as carefully and secretly as possible, must buy quantities of the stock for the pool. The trading must be controlled, if possible, so as not to cause either an undue rise in the price or a noticeable increase in activity. Thus it may take many trading sessions, with the trader stealthily stalking the particular market in that stock, to get the pool's securities in hand and ready for the next step.

Then the tactics must be changed abruptly.

With a substantial quantity of stock on hand that was bought in at a favorable price, the trader then starts buying sizable blocks of the stock, attracting as much attention as possible, hoping that it will push the price higher. A good manager waits until the price is rising anyway, then buys it in substantial quantities, with the expectation that this will push the price higher.

Betimes, it is expected that board-room denizens and tape watchers throughout the country, hungering for tips, signs and omens, will note these rises in the stock's price and decide that it is a "hot" issue and the time is ripe to buy it.

As often as not they do exactly that, even if they are suspicious that it is a pool operation that is pushing the stock's prices higher, for there is ever the inexorable temptation to try to guess what the pool managers plan to do and to jump aboard and get a free ride on their manipulations.

The final phase is a straightforward operation. Its requirements are to unload the pool's stock quickly and quietly while the price is still high, selling it to the people who have become lured to it and enamored of it by watching the price climb on the inscrutable tickertape.

If it succeeds, pool members can sit around reminding themselves of the famous quotations that have been made about the gullible who offer themselves as prey to the confidence man's game. These can include such worthies as Phineas T. Barnum's "There's a sucker born every minute"; W. C. Fields' "Never give a sucker an even break"; Texas Guinan's "Hello, Suckers!" and Eino Forstner's "Select your fat suckers wisely; eschew all others, for they may become nuisances."

A more sophisticated touch might be added profitably with the addition of some short selling as the final fillip but this has always been regarded as exceedingly tricky and possibly too revealing, because short sellers must be listed with the stock exchange.

A manager's skill determines the success or failure of a pool. He must time his buying carefully, and do his selling with surgical precision. A stock that is selling for 50 may be pushed up to 60 by pool operations, but despite a ten-point spread, the operators can fail to make a profit, or can even lose money, if the buying and selling aren't handled keenly.

The successful pool manager must buy the stock so that he nudges up the price only a point or two at a time, and then gives it a shot in the arm at the end. In the case of the stock moving from 50 to 60 points, he might be able to buy twenty-five percent of the stock at 50, the next twenty-five percent with a point spread ranging from 51 to 55, making the average cost 52½, the next twenty-five percent with a point spread of 56 to 58, making the average cost 57, and then the final twenty-five percent at 58, in hopes that it would boost the price to 60, at which point he would begin to sell, gently at first, and try to unload it all before it got back to, say, the break-even 58 of the last purchase.

In the spring, when Montgomery Ward had been recovering from a low of 50 and rapidly rose to the 70s, Ed Newbord had joined a pool managed by a friend who was an active trader in the stock, and had watched, pleased, while the friend carefully maneuvered it up from 74 to around 86 and had then given it its shot in the arm, sending it to 90.

The pool had started to dump at that figure, causing the stock to stop its rise for a day; but then, despite the dumping, it had continued to rise, and had gone on up through the hundred mark and in September had reached 156⅞.

Though no one lost on the deal, the pool members were disgusted to think that they had jumped out of a stock at 89 and 90, when they might have stayed with it up into the 150s.

After several meetings the pool's members had decided that two things had been wrong. First, they had mis-judged Montgomery Ward's market potential, and sec-ond, quite obviously another pool had started operations just at the time they sought to sell out their pool. Those things happened in a hot market. It turned out, of course, that they were wrong, too, about the second pool. The public simply responded to the rise in Montgomery Ward, and kept right on responding.

The trouble was, Montgomery Ward had done it to them again.

The same pool had reorganized and only the week before had started buying Montgomery Ward when it was selling in the nineties. Newbord had pledged a large sum of money, using thirty percent cash, and borrowing the remainder. The cash and credit had been absorbed on Wednesday and his loan had been called on Thursday when the stock plunged from 84 to 50.

He looked at the figures, a tabular recitation of the trades that had been made by the now totally dispirited manager, shook his head and sighed.

"If I ever pull myself out of this alive," he said aloud, "I'll live like a miser." But he knew he wouldn't. Like most of the leading figures of Wall Street who had sus-tained devastating losses that day, he was already think-ing of reconstruction of his empire. To drink but once of the strong waters of prestige, riches and lofty leadership afforded the titans of Wall Street was to make one forever afterward dissatisfied with the common troughs at which the thirsts of the less-anointed were quenched. Newbord could no more contemplate a nonextravagant life than he could envision himself hiring out to replace his own janitor. Indeed, he could not conceive of a nonroyal existence for himself. "As a man thinketh, so is he," he often quoted to himself when he would learn of some unfortunate who had stubbed his toe on the long ladder to the top and had plummeted to the dregs pile.

Miserliness for Edward Newbord, however, might mean terminating his liaison with Shanty Marlowe, whose garishness was beginning to bore him, anyway. Her return from the Caribbean cruise would be a good time to do it, he thought, a plot for severance half taking shape in his mind.

He might have to plan on fewer dinners at the Twenty-One Club, too, but he was certain that he had made more money from information he had learned while dining there than would be required to pay for the tab if he ate the Châteaubriand and drank six bottles of the finest champagne there nightly for the remainder of his business career.

He put into his top drawer the discouraging news of the aborted Montgomery Ward pool and picked up the latest wire advisory that was soon to be filed to branch offices and correspondent firms. It was a more carefully worded version of the advisory that had gone out earlier in the day and it was, like its predecessor, calculated to allay fears and restore confidence in the market. It was about all, Newbord thought wryly, that anyone could do. The rest was up to the public itself.

Earlier, Newbord had stood with Jules, Angus and a number of his firm's executives as the tickertape had printed out the quotation for the last trade of the day and had signed off at 7:08½ P.M., just four hours, eight and one-half minutes late. Boys continued to post the late-

arriving quotations on the wallboard for a room full of
speculators-turned-spectators.

"By the time those boys are through," Newbord had
said, more for the record than anything else, "you will be
able to note what is tantamount to a remarkable recovery."

"Yeah, remarkable," Jules had said, and had stared
back blandly when Newbord had frowned at him.

"It takes all kinds to make a market," Newbord said.

"It takes more buyers than there are sellers to make a
bull market," Jules reminded.

"We'll see. We'll see what the public thinks."

"Yep."

"The public is the final judge."

"Oh, sure."

After Newbord had turned from the board-room door
and had hurried down the hall to his office, Jules Barnish
went to his own leather-and-mahogany office, one wall of
which was booklined from floor to ceiling, and sat down
at his desk. From his inside jacket pocket he withdrew a
flat, wallet-sized notebook and opened it on the desk in
front of himself, his index finger flipping the spiral-
bound pages until he came to a blank one.

As with extreme caution he unscrewed the stubby cap
of his fountain pen, his eyes were remote with thought.
Jules intended one day to write a book, a basic philosophy
of Wall Street related against notable occurrences, and he
kept copious notes of his thinking about it. His instincts
told him that the time to write seriously on such a subject
might be nigh, for surely he had just lived through the
most calamitous day in the history of the Street, and just
as surely the public was as confused as it had been igno-
rant and naive.

A demagogue with political aspirations could find it

easy to wreak great harm on America's relatively "new" banking system, he realized.

Needed would be good common-sense analysis of what had happened. His instincts also told him that there would be investigations, that there would be scapegoats, and that ultimately there would be restrictive legislation of, possibly, several kinds, to preclude such a fiasco from happening again.

He wrote a few words in his pocket pad, scratched them out, then started again.

"The ideal market," he wrote, "is slightly bullish, with somewhat more buyers than there are sellers at any given time. Just as the economy fares better with a slight flush of inflation, so a market can enjoy better health with a slight push from the same kind of power. Just as too much inflation is harmful to the whole economy, too much bullishness can destroy the market structure.

"Money must come from somewhere, and a marketplace, to be viable, must give it somewhere to go. We have, on this day, October 24, 1929, cut off our source of money by bankrupting our suppliers of money—the small investors. We are at this point left with little to tempt new money back into the marketplace. We present money with no desirable destination; we offer no goals, no havens that promise rewards. Our wares, as displayed, offer little that appears attractive.

"Ahead of us stretches a barren period when only those whose wealth or special conditions force them to trade in securities will be our customers. The resumption of wide public participation in the stock market must await a new time when American industry has rebuilt the toppled structures of finance and confidence has been restored both to those who buy and to those who sell stocks."

As he capped his pen and restored it to his inside jacket

pocket, he reread what he had written.

He laughed aloud.

To the empty room he said, "Well, that's quite a bit different from the advisory we sent out. Ed Newbord would buy up my partnership and fire me if he should read this. Let's see what he thinks about it six months from now."

Eddie Gallant was in his dressing room getting ready for his 8:38 P.M. appearance on stage. Beside him, applying pomade to his carefully parted and smoothly slicked black hair, was George Clark, the male half of "Clark & Clark Moonlight Waltzers." Eddie was carefully daubing eye makeup to eliminate the shadows that the overheads and kliegs would make.

There was a pounding on the door, the authoritative knock of aging Pat McKennagh, boss stage manager. "Telephone, Mr. Gallant."

"Thanks, Pat. Be right there."

The phone was attached to the wall near the chief electrician's big control panel.

"Mr. Gallant?" the voice asked. "This is Frank Abruzzi of Raymond & Company in New York."

"Yes, Frank. Been trying to call you. Your lines have all been busy."

"I know. It *has* been a busy day."

"You're calling to tell me that you've called in my margin loan."

"Partly that, yes."

"You sold out my Radio?"

"Some of it; not all of it."

"You mean I still own some?"

"You do if you can raise $6,500 fairly soon."

"Well, I just don't understand this. If you sold me out,

you had enough to cover my loan, didn't you?"

"I'm afraid not, Mr. Gallant."

"Then why didn't you sell out the rest of it?"

"Let me explain, Mr. Gallant. I'll give you the figures over the phone, but we'll get a special-delivery letter off to you tonight. The real reason for my call was to find out where to send it."

"Send it to the Narragansett Hotel in Providence, but I still don't understand why. . . ."

"Let me go over the figures with you, Mr. Gallant, and then it will make sense to you."

"I hope so. It certainly doesn't now."

"You bought 100 shares of Radio at $60 at a net cost of $6,000 and you gave us a check for $1,000, leaving a balance owed by you of $5,000. Right?

"Next you bought 100 shares at $73, for a cost of $7,300, and you gave us cash of $2,500, leaving a balance owing on that transaction of $4,800.

"Your next purchase of Radio was at $97, and you bought 100 shares for a cost of $9,700, for which you gave us $3,000, leaving a balance owed of $6,700.

"Your most recent purchase was 100 shares at $112, for a cost of $11,200, and you gave us $4,200 cash, leaving a balance due of $7,000.

"Your balances, then, are $5,000, $4,800, $6,700 and $7,-000. They come to a total of $23,500. That's how much you owe Raymond & Company on loans."

"Right. I follow."

"You bought your stock at market prices that totaled $34,200. You paid cash for each transaction in turn. It totaled $10,700. The balance that you owed was $23,500."

"Yes. I agree." Eddie was making small notes on the wall with a pencil that hung by the phone.

"When prices broke this morning we offered two hundred shares of your Radio and we were able to get 62 for it. When prices continued to drop, we offered another hundred shares, but it wasn't bought until the price had reached 46.

"Now, the sale of two hundred at 62 brought you $12,400 and the sale of one hundred at 46 brought you $4,600, a total of $17,000. Deduct this from the $23,500 that you still owed us, and your balance due is $6,500. Follow?"

"I follow."

"Now you still own 100 shares of Radio and the closing price tonight was back to 58, so I'm glad for you that we held onto it. Ostensibly you have $5,800 in your account, if you can get a bid of 58 for your stock tomorrow morning. If we can sell it at 58, we'll apply the $5,800 to the $6,500 that you owe us, and you'll owe then a balance of only $700.

"What I'd suggest, however, is that you *keep* your shares of Radio and pay off the balance of your margin of $6,500 just as soon as possible. That way you'll have your stock and you'll be clear with us. There will be, of course, the commission charges, too."

Eddie's quick mind traveled right to the bottom line of what Abruzzi was trying to say. "In other words, there's no more margin available to me. I can either sell or pay off the balance."

"Er, essentially that's it."

"Why are you clamping down on my *credit?*" Eddie asked. "I still own ten shares of Commercial Solvents. It's been selling lower, like everything else, but it's around 425, isn't it? That's $4,250 available if you want it."

"We're not closing out *your* credit, Mr. Gallant, but nearly everyone's. When the market sustains such severe losses, our loans are called, too."

"I understand. But my Solvents. . . ."

"You might wish to hypothecate your stocks, Mr. Gallant."

"How does that work? What do I do to hypothecate?"

"Well, we'd allow you half the current market value of your stock and you would, in effect, assign your stock to us to own until such time as you pay off your indebtedness on it."

"You'd hold the stock?"

"Legally, we'd hold title to it, until you discharge your indebtedness."

"I see. . . ."

"Now, your Radio, let's say, is worth $5,800, on which we'd allow you $2,900, and your Solvents is worth $4,250, on which we'd allow you $2,125.

"That's a total of, let's see, now, $5,025. You owe us $6,500. So if you want to hypothecate your stock, you need to send us only $1,475.

"Then," Abruzzi continued, "you can buy your stock back for $5,025, plus interest, any time you wish to. You understand, Mr. Gallant, that if your stock should ever double in value, you can regain full title to it for only $5,025, plus interest."

"Yeah, I understand."

There was a pause.

"Or," reminded Abruzzi, "you can send us your check for $6,500."

Eddie thought ruefully of the $900 he had in his savings account.

"I'd like to go along and hypothecate the stock," he said.

"Very good, sir. I'll send you the papers to be signed. And then you'll get a check off to us in the amount of $1,475?"

"Yes. I'll do that. It'll take a couple of days for me to transfer from a savings account to my checking account."

He'd also have to borrow about $600 from his old man.

"That'll be just fine, Mr. Gallant."

"Okay. Thanks. Good-bye."

Eddie remained thoughtful at the phone, penciling in the figures he had written on the wall, being careful not to spoil the graffiti of Andy Gump and Mutt & Jeff that had been caricatured onto the plaster by a previous doodler.

So they had cleaned him out. And he had thought he was safe with his Commercial Solvents. Well—his natural buoyancy began to return—he was a big money maker these days. He'd get it all back.

Just let him get a chance at it.

And there was still, out there ahead, Radio. Not just Radio stock, but Radio. It was beckoning him. Eddie let the pencil drop to the end of its string and began to whistle as he turned back to his dressing room.

"Hey, there, George," he greeted as he plunged through the doorway.

"Hi, Eddie. Boy, that must have been good news to cheer you up like that. Must be you haven't heard about the stock market crash."

"Right on both counts," Eddie said, interrupting his whistling only momentarily.

"Well, it crashed, you know. Hit bottom."

"I heard something about it."

"But I thought you were in the market pretty deep."

"I *was*, George. I *was*. Some people know when to sell and get out."

"You lucky stiff," George said.

"Lucky, my foot. Skill, my boy. Pure skill."

In Wall Street, Frank Abruzzi replaced the receiver on his telephone, leaped from his chair and thrust his arms outward like an umpire calling a safe play at home plate, and shouted: "Got him!"

"What's that?" Marvin Gold, who also had been making customer calls, was always amused by Abruzzi's abrupt change in manner as soon as he finished on the telephone.

"He went for hypothecation. Ahh, that's a good piece of work."

Abruzzi felt that he had scored a big victory with a little customer. First, Gallant had decided not to sell his stock, a fact that would please old man Newbord if it ever got to him. Second, by hypothecating his stock he had committed himself to pay his remaining margin loan no matter how low the price of either Radio or Solvents might go. Even if it dropped to a dollar a share, he still owed Raymond & Company $5,025 after making a cash settlement of $1,475. Every little bit, Abruzzi thought, helped.

"Frank, you're a genius," said Gold. He neglected to add that he had just finished talking to Mr. J. J. Armstrong in the Detroit office about doing exactly the same thing with an account owned by a customer named Weedon, who held some Westinghouse.

On the clean and shining oilcloth that covered the big kitchen table, Carrie Fitton had lined up one dozen long-necked screw-top bottles of homemade ketchup, eighteen snap-on-lid eight-ounce jars of chili sauce, and two dozen quart Mason jars of stewed ripe tomatoes. They must all sit there overnight to cool slowly, and then receive a final lid, cap or cover tightening in the morning.

She was extremely pleased with herself. She softly hummed a tune.

The canning operation, requiring a full day of work, had been an outstanding success. Now, at six o'clock, the big kettles and steaming pans had been washed and put away, the redolent trimmings of the assorted vegetables and herbs had been carted out to the compost heap and

sprinkled with lime, grasscuttings and dirt, the summer
kitchen's oil stove had been scoured and burnished with
Gold Dust Twins cleanser, and she was tired. Not until
the very end of the season when she would pick a lot of
green tomatoes and make them into relish would she face
such a gigantic task in a single day.

The sun was low as Carrie arrayed the output of her
labors and snapped on the small light over the kitchen
sink. Her nails were stained and reddened from their
immersions in the bright liquors of her sauces, and she
scrubbed at length. Carrie did not believe that a farm
wife needed to look like a hired hand in from the fields.

As Carrie straightened from the sink she realized that
her back ached and her feet hurt. She really wanted to
take a bath but, she decided, it would be better to lie down
right now and rest those tired muscles.

With a last loving glance at her display of preserves,
she went to the bedroom and removed shoes, stockings,
dress, slip and garterbelt, and stretched out in her teddies
on the soft bed, emitting a great sigh. Her chores were
over. Her race had been run.

Carrie slept.

When Marcy Fitton returned to the farm a half-hour
later, he vaulted from the Model T truck and raced into
the house carrying a creel of four good-sized bass and
three white perch, eager to display the fruits of his prow-
ess to Carrie. He stopped briefly to admire her handiwork
on the kitchen table, then charged through to the living
room and, finding it empty, on into the bedroom.

Marcy stopped short and a grin spread over his face.
Before him was a scene of beauty he bet couldn't be du-
plicated anywhere. Carrie was asleep flat on her back,
her ankles crossed lightly, one arm thrown upward so
that a gently curled hand rested beside her cheek on the

pillow. Her dark, luxuriant hair fluffed casually about her face. Breathing deeply, she thrust her firm breasts hard against the filmy silk of the chemise with each indrawn breath. The garment itself revealed excitingly those zones that in daytime remain normally hidden from a husband's questing view.

For a moment or more Marcy was tempted to awaken her and request fulfillment of what her reposing body seemed to promise, but, with effort, he held himself in check. The cows could be heard in the barn, demanding that they be relieved of the accumulated production of their day's labors.

Instead, Marcy returned to the kitchen and searched in the drawer beside the sink until he found a sharp knife, which he put into his fish creel. Then, shouldering creel, he responded to the urgings of the herd of his friends in the barn. "Coming girls," he shouted from midyard. "Be with you in a minute, Rosie."

Because he was behind schedule, the cows had come into the barn by themselves and had gone to their own stalls, seeking food, water and relief in their heavy, sagging udders. At the other end of the barn, the horses had done the same, and now they were snorting and stamping their hooves, communicating to their master their displeasure with his dalliance.

Marcy put his creel of fish in the cooling room and then went from stall to stall, closing and fastening into place the stanchions, thus to prevent nocturnal wanderings by the several night people in the herd and to keep the cows from turning their heads to observe the milking process.

Before he fed them, he hooked up the milkers and got six of the cows started. Then he pitched fresh hay into the feed boxes. By the time he was finished, he was able to transfer the milkers to the remaining six animals.

After feeding the horses and putting fresh bedding hay in their stalls, he directed his attention to the fish. Using his sharp knife, he severed their heads with deft and expert strokes, slit their bellies, and with one clean cut removed float bladder and intestines. Then he scaled them until their skins were smooth, after which he washed them under the faucet and laid them, pink and fresh, on a folded newspaper to be placed atop the ice cake in the icebox.

Marcy knew that even the small amount of potash from the little pile of fish innards would be especially beneficial to the compost pile, but the two barn cats had made an appearance, so the parts were offered as a special treat to the barn's antimouse brigade.

Marcy left the cats picking choicely at their morsels and headed for the house, his own plump fish held before him with his two hands, like regal offerings. As he reached the door the phone was ringing and he hurried to get it so its sharp peal would not awaken Carrie.

It was the Eastern-sounding fellow from the stockbrokers, Pritchard.

"Mr. Fitton," he began, "I'd like to discuss your portfolio with you."

"Sure," Marcy said, "go ahead. Did you sell my Spalding?"

"Yes, sir, we sold your Spalding, and I think we got a good price for it under the circumstances."

"Fine, fine."

"We were able to sell it at 46."

"Oh, fine, fine."

"And then, of course, we had to sell your Insull Utility Investments."

"Those, too?"

"Yes. And we were able to get 82 for your two hundred and fifty shares."

"Well, gee, I don't know much about those things, but maybe you shouldn't have sold all of my shares of Insull, but just enough to cover my loan and pay it off."

"Oh, I'm afraid that you don't understand, Mr. Fitton. Let me explain."

"Wish you would."

"Our records show that you bought 200 shares of Insull at $125 a share, costing you a total of $25,000, for which you paid $5,000 in margin and took a loan for $20,000. Then you bought fifty shares at 160, for which you owe us $8,000. In other words, your loan account on Insull totals $28,000. Then you bought 100 Spalding at $63, costing you $6,300, but you paid $1,500 on margin, leaving a loan of $4,800. In other words, your total debt with the firm is $32,800."

"Yes, but I still don't understand. . . ."

"The proceeds of the sale of your Insull stock today total $20,500, and the proceeds of the Spalding sale are $4,600. That comes to a total of $25,100.

"In other words, Mr. Fitton, what I'm trying to say is that you now owe the firm $7,700, plus the regular commissions, of course."

"And I have no stock."

"Naturally not."

"Well-ll—"

"When can we expect to collect this loan, Mr. Fitton?"

"It'll take a few days."

"Very well, sir. I'm sure you'll work out the arrangements. I'll just make a note for the loan department to get in touch with you."

"Yea-yh."

"I thought you'd like to know the good news about our liquidation of your securities. I'll put it all in writing, of course. But that may take a few days. We're awfully busy here."

"Yeah."

"All right, then, Mr. Fitton. Thank you and good night."

"Good night."

Marcy turned from the wall phone and was startled to see Carrie standing behind him, her teddies and nakedness now shadowy beneath a blue transparent peignoir and her hair tousled so that its white streak was in startled contrast. Her eyes were large and luminous in the semilight.

"What's wrong, Marcy?" she asked.

"Well, nothing's really wrong, Carrie. Not really."

"What is it? Who *was* that?"

"That was Mr. what's-his-name, the stockbroker."

"Well?"

"There must have been one helluva market today, Carrie. They had to sell us out. Everything. And we still owe about eight thousand dollars that we'll have to get up in cash."

"Oh, Marcy. What'll we do?"

He sat down at the table, not answering.

"What can we do, Marcy?" She stood before him.

"We're knocked back a couple of years, Carrie. That's all there is to it. It's a bad setback. But if there's one thing a farmer is used to, it's setbacks. And if there's one thing a farmer is equipped to be, it's a gambler, and a losing gambler, at that. I gambled and I lost. Now no crying. Those are the rules of the game."

"Yes, but what will we *do?*"

"Well, we'll get a farmer's bank loan on the range steers for as much as they'll give us, which is probably about forty percent of their potential market value next spring. Then we'll get the balance in a second mortgage on the house and land. Our first mortgage isn't very big.

"That will give us enough money to satisfy the debt

with the brokerage people. Then next year we'll have to use what we can from our cash receipts, whatever they may be, to get that second mortgage off the house. So it really sets us back two years."

"Oh, dear, and you work so hard."

"Yeah." Marcy paused to test the new burden on his shoulders and found it heavy. "At that, Carrie, we're a lot better off than millions of people must be tonight. We've got some resources to hock so that we can get out of this eventually. How about those guys who have only a job? They must be cleaned out."

He sat in silence for a few moments, with Carrie leaning against the table.

"Those fish look nice," Carrie said.

"So do you. Even more edible."

"Marcy."

"And those canned goods, Carrie. They look mighty like a picture sitting there. Just look at 'em. We'll get by all right."

"Yes we will, Marcy. We'll get by."

"And there are many more important things than money." He reached under her peignoir and slapped her gently.

"Come to think of it, I guess there are."

"Come on in the bedroom and let's get freshened up before supper," Marcy said, and without waiting for an answer, headed for the door.

CHAPTER 17

Thursday, October 24, 1929

8:30 P.M.

Only a short time after he had boarded the train, before, in fact, it had crossed the Harlem River Bridge, Harry Weedon made his way to the club car and ordered a glass of ginger ale. With it balanced on the arm of his chair, he laced it with a serious shot of good Kentucky bourbon from the flat flask he took from his inside coat pocket.

He had drunk it slowly, sipping, staring moodily at the lights flashing past along the river, and only occasionally making a fleeting mental note of a town as, reversed in profile, it flicked by, beyond the reflecting windows. He spoke to no one, replenishing his drink by himself, and watched idly the mirrored silhouettes of people moving waveringly along the aisle.

With his third drink, Harry became aware that the man across the way was talking about it. Harry could hear the words, but his perception was numbed and they glanced off his awareness in fragments—"Dow–Jones" . . . "inside tip" . . . "should have sold then" . . . "naturally expected a rise" . . . "cleaned me out."

Raising his glass to his lips, Harry glanced at the speaker and saw that he had virtually captured a neighbor who, looking uncomfortable, seemed about to flee.

The talker was a fraud, Harry decided with the instant clarity of perception derived from good bourbon. He was too smooth, his clothes too perfect, his collar too white and starched, his shoes too shined, his pants creases too knifelike. His nails, seen when he raised his pudgy fingers to puff on an opulent-looking cigar, were manicured and buffed, pinkish glossed tips on fat sausages.

The man was lamenting his great losses of the day in the stock market, implying that they were titanic. He seemed almost smug as he indicated that he was not merely cleaned out, but also now just about destitute, totally insolvent, and without recourse.

Instantly Harry came to identify a new breed of American, one that evolved that day. He was the man who readily seized upon the great crash as the cause of his failure in life. Here was a pretender with a seemingly unchallengeable pretense. He liked to make believe that he possessed the capabilities for amassing great wealth, and had proved himself once, only to lose the proof in the market's betrayal. If it could catch the mightiest unaware, he lost nothing by admitting that he, too, like Durant, like Mitchell, had been caught napping. As Harry listened, he was willing to bet the man had never owned a share of stock in his life.

He was the first of a kind. There would be many like him in the years to come, some of whose progeny, having no way to disprove the parental claims to greatness, would innocently carry on the lie into the generations. Sometimes, in the future, the charade would be perpetuated only by implication, perhaps with the expression of the futile hope, "Oh, if only grandpa hadn't lost everything in the market crash. . . ."

Harry was at first disgusted, then angered at what he saw and heard. The crash was too real to him. For all he knew he was en route to the poorhouse, and faced the immediate prospect of bankruptcy; and here was this four-flusher, boasting, nay, literally *bragging,* about his losses.

He set down his glass, stubbed out his cigarette, stood and looked for the sign that said, "Dining Car in This Direction."

The dining-car captain, haughty, escorted Harry to a table for two, already occupied by a male diner who was being served his main course. The captain filled his waterglass and handed him the menu, first scratching off the special, as he muttered something. Harry observed later that it was the veal cutlet that had been penciled out.

Dining car prices were outrageous, he thought. Sirloin steak was $2.25. It included the soup-du-jour and two vegetables, but it restricted the dessert selection to pie, ice cream or rice pudding, unless you wished to pay extra. Even the lemon sole was $1.50 on the dinner.

Harry had an expense account, but his boss didn't want an item-by-item statement of costs, and being certain that the prices wouldn't be believed by the home-office accountant, Harry settled for the roast chicken dinner at $1.75.

He was sure that he always lost money when traveling for his company because of his failure to itemize expenses, but he had never kept a running tally to find out. The chicken came with creamed corn, Harvard beets, mashed potato, giblet gravy, cranberry sauce, and a tossed salad. Included also were the soup, which was minestrone, coffee, and the selection of desserts. Harry had vanilla ice cream, which was served accompanied by two wafer cookies filled with a confection.

He ate methodically and did not speak to his dining companion.

During his meal Harry strove not to think of the financial catastrophe that had overtaken him that day. Instead he dwelt on details of the new designs for the automobile heater that he had seen in Queens. He thought it would be a successful development not only in providing a constant source of heat, but also in providing it by means of a forced air that would cause the heat to flow gently throughout the car's interior without violating the theory of "no draft" ventilation. He was prepared to recommend it to his superiors.

His table companion, uncommunicative, finished his meal, paid his bill to the headwaiter, left a quarter tip and departed. It was getting late. No one replaced him.

When he was cleaning off the dishes, the waiter, a tall, lean, young black man, observed, "That was some market today, wasn't it?"

"It sure was."

"I lost me a little money, but not too much."

"Me, too. More than I can afford."

"I lose a dime, it's more'n I can afford."

Harry laughed. "You're right about that. I'm going to be counting every dime from now on." The steward chuckled and departed with his burden of dishes, the tray balanced on the flat of his hand over his right shoulder.

Harry had never been sure whether he should tip the austere headwaiter on a dining car, and if so, whether it should be on the way in or on the way out. Now, however, because he had, after all, been given a seat immediately, he decided he should give a half-dollar to the plump white man who was still straddling in mi-daisle, clutching a sheaf of menus.

He seemed slightly surprised, and Harry wondered if he had done the wrong thing. Then the man smiled.

"Thanks," he said. "I need this after the beating I got in Wall Street today."

"You, too?" Harry asked.

"Me—everyone." The man swept the air with his menus, indicating the whole train.

"You've got a sad bunch of passengers aboard tonight, then," Harry observed.

"You bet your Aunt Lizzie's shirtwaist we have," the man replied. "No wonder so many of them are ordering setups. They need a drink after today."

The train had departed its northward river course at Albany and now was headed west through the canal country and the Mohawk Valley. Before morning, Harry knew, as the train went nonstop through Canada, en route to Hamilton and Detroit, a nonpassenger would materialize mysteriously with some bottles of legitimate Canadian whiskey and some British Scotch and gin, that could be purchased for about two dollars above normal retail price. Harry suspected that the intermediary either was or was known to the minion who had accepted the half-dollar.

Now might be a good time to negotiate a bottle of Scotch, Harry thought. He quickly added another half-dollar to the man's always-available and ever-empty palm.

"Sir?"

"Would you happen to know if between now and any-time before we arrive in Detroit tomorrow morning, I could pick up a bottle of Scotch for my sick mother?"

"I'll be glad to try, sir, but, of course, even though we go through Canada, we don't stop in Canada. . . ."

"I understand, but I'd appreciate it if you'd try."

"I'll be delighted to, sir. Your berth number?" He had taken out a little notebook.

"I'm two cars to the rear, Car D-126, Compartment B."

"Ah, very good, sir."

"The name is Weedon."

"Fine, Mr. Weedon. I'll make some inquiries."

"Suppose, to save you trouble, I should pay for it now?
Then you can give cash to your, er, contact."

"That would be very sensible."

"D'you know, offhand, how much it would be?"

"The bottle of Pinch, sir, is twelve dollars."

"Fine. Here's fifteen, just in case, and I don't want to be
bothered with any change."

"Yessir. Thank you, Mr. Weedon."

Harry turned away knowing that when he was awakened in the morning he would be handed a package that
would fit into his suitcase. The transaction was official,
else the money would not have been accepted. The ethics
of the game decreed that it be discreetly handed back,
otherwise. Such was the honorable state of bootlegging in
a higher-class deal.

As Harry turned, he caught the knowing wink of the
steward who had served him. He smiled and winked
back.

"Good luck, sir," the steward said.

"Thanks."

Harry noticed his name badge. Rudy Rose, it said. He
made a mental note to remember it, for he was certain
that Rudy Rose would be an important man on the Detroiter in years to come.*

*His hunch was right. Rudy Rose, who became the Detroiter's chief steward,
retired at age 66 from the Penn Central Railroad's Dining Car Service on
September 30, 1970, having worked in the service, man and boy, for 49 years,
the last years, since the demise of the New York Central's Detroiter, as bar-car
steward on the Brewster-Pawling branch of the line's Harlem Division. His
memories are summed up in a terse statement: "The Detroiter was the best
train on the railroad. It had high-class passengers. Most of them were good
businessmen and well-to-do-salesmen, not phonies and hucksters, like on some
of the other crack trains."

To Helen Weedon the day had seemed a hundred hours long. She had flopped down on the living room sofa to stretch aching legs shortly before Harry had called from New York. She knew he would have to move fast to get back to the hotel, pack, and get aboard the Detroiter for its six-o'clock departure, so she hadn't bothered him with the many details that seemed to her to be accumulating into an overwhelming burden.

With throbbing head she had diverted Rick's demands, when he had returned from school, by inducing him to play with a neighborhood boy, down the block.

The child had received a new electric train for his birthday a month earlier, so the diversion was easily accomplished. Not so easy was the handling of four-year-old Debbie, until she became preoccupied with cutting out the dolls and then the fashion ads in the *Pictorial Review*. She had subsided in her second-floor bedroom with her blunt-nosed scissors amid a confettilike shower of paper scraps and a leaking pot of mint-smelling paste.

A reconciliation had taken place at her sister Kate's home. John, sobering, had sworn off the stuff, promising never to touch another drop until national law permitted liquor to be consumed legitimately, and then only in the company and with the permission of his wife.

Informed of this sweeping pledge, Helen had refrained from saying what she thought—that it was impossible for John to keep, and he couldn't be expected to survive without some form of celebratory libation through such upcoming holidays as Thanksgiving, Christmas and New Year's. Instead she said that she was pleased with both of them.

After Harry's call, Mr. Armstrong had phoned from the Raymond & Company office. Helen had copied down the facts and figures that he had given to her, hoping to have everything in order for Harry when he arrived in the morning. She knew that if he went to work, it would not be until after lunch.

Ordinarily she might have expected a different kind of reunion from the one that seemed in prospect.

Raymond & Company had sold the 380 shares of Westinghouse, plus the other 200 shares that Harry had bought, all in one sale. They had received 175 per share, Mr. Armstrong said, which, considering the fact that the price of the stock had dropped to 160 during the day, was a stroke of luck.

The amount due Raymond & Company was $68,200 on loans, Mr. Armstrong said, but she needn't worry, for the amount was covered, and a statement of account would be mailed out in the morning, soon as the office "untangled itself."

Helen had taken Gregg in high school, and she filled several pages of an old shorthand book as Mr. Armstrong talked.

From other calls she had learned that she and Harry owed a total of $12,000 to two banks, and that they now had a mortgage of $7,000 on their house.

All of the basic information was neatly transcribed now onto sheets of yellow notepaper.

When the kids had shown up at suppertime, she had been struck with a brilliant idea. She called her sister Kate, and suggested that since John would be sleeping it off all night, it would be nice if Kate took the kids until morning. She would pick them up right after breakfast, she promised, on her way to town to get Harry at the station.

Kate had agreed, and after packing two small bags, Helen had bundled them into the car and delivered them in front of Uncle John's big console radio set, where Aunt

Kate had popcorn and sliced apples waiting.

Back home, Helen had decided she should dig out the original bank notes and loan agreements from Harry's "file," a big oak-tag reddish-colored folder that he kept in the big drawer of his desk.

At the desk she had been temporarily distracted by discovering a snapshot of bathing-suited Veronica Modlewski, whom Harry had dated in his senior year at high school. After a few moments of hurt and anger, however, she had decided that if Harry wanted to look at a fifteen-year-old snapshot of Veronica now and then, he should be allowed to do it undetected, or at least believing he was. Veronica now lived in Sandusky, the last Helen had heard, was porcine, loud, and the mother of a half-dozen children of a construction foreman.

Because she had exercised so much nobility at the end of such a long, emotionally upsetting and fright-filled day, Helen decided she needed a drink. There was gin in the cupboard—two bottles of it. She looked at the accompanying soft-drink bottles of soda pop. There were Moxie, Orange Crush, Cherry Smash, Nu-Grape, Coca-Cola and Drury's ginger ale.

She elected to try gin and ginger ale, and pouring a liberal three-fingers of Gordon's into a tumbler, she added ice and filled it with the piquant and gingery Drury's. She put two sharpened pencils on the kitchen table, a fresh yellow pad and all of her accumulated notes beside them.

Sipping at the glass, Helen began to do her arithmetic.

In only a few moments she pushed back her chair and shouted, "Holy cats!"

She stared at the pad, drained her drink, and rushed to the cupboard to replenish it. Then she returned to the kitchen table to check her figures again.

The amount they owed Raymond & Company came to $68,200.

The sale of the stock, 580 shares of it at 175, had yielded them $101,500.

Raymond & Company would now be sending them a check of $33,300—minus, of course, its commissions.

Helen had no way of knowing it, but Mr. J. J. Armstrong had made a mistake that day that had been compounded by hundreds of other brokers, involving hundreds of thousands of other stockowners. He had panicked, and in doing so had liquidated customers' accounts that needn't have been closed out. As Jules Barnish had feared, many customers had been forced out of the market who shouldn't have been, and would not return for years.

Helen went over the figures again and in her excitement, again emptied her glass. Oh, if only she could call Harry with the good news. But there was no way she could do that.

As she mixed her third ultraliberal drink, slopping a little Drury's on the countertop beside the sink, she wondered whether she could send a telegram to Buffalo and have it put aboard the train there. Now that she thought about it, she was sure she could, if she just figured out the way to do it right.

Why, she calculated as she sat back at the table, they could even pay off the $12,000 in bank loans and the $7,- 000 for the mortgage and still have $14,300 *in the bank* —and with their home owned free and clear!

"Yip-pee!" she shouted aloud, and drank a toast to the freedom she felt after her day filled with fears and haunts.

Sipping her drink, she began work on the telegram she intended to telephone to Western Union: "STATIONMASTER, BUFFALO, N.Y., FOR CONDUCTOR TO DELIVER TO PASSENGER

HARRY WEEDON ABOARD TRAIN #61, DETROITER, DUE BUFFALO [she consulted the bound timetable] 11:00 P.M. . . ."

The doorbell rang.

Helen set down her empty glass and let the pencil roll to the floor as she made her way to the front of the house, steadying herself against the wall a couple of times.

Joe Francoeur stood there, grinning.

"Why, hello, Joe," she said. "Come in. Come in."

"Helen, I've just been out walking the dog and I thought I heard a holler or a shout over here. Is everything all right?"

"Oh, Joe, everything is not only all right, but lovely. Ab-so-lute-ly love-ly. C'mon in and have a drink."

"Why, sure," said Joe, smiling broadly. "Sure, Helen, I'd love to."

"Were you peeking out the window when I was out front this morning getting the newspaper?" Helen asked.

CHAPTER 18

Friday, October 25, 1929

THE MORNING AFTER

~~~~~~

The night of October 24 had passed slowly for many Americans. Strangely, more people stayed away from bed, it was estimated, than on the preceding New Year's Eve; more even than on the 1928 national Election Night, when returns had been broadcast for the first time from coast to coast to radio receivers in living rooms across the nation, around which were huddled "election parties."

Oddly, too, there was much revelry. Impromptu market-crash parties sprang to life in the better-known speakeasies in every metropolitan center of the land. An unprecedented amount of liquor was poured "on the house" by proprietors and operators of gin mills and booze joints, many of whom had shared in the day's great financial losses.

As the night hours accumulated, loud dissertations on economics and high finance were to be heard in hundreds of thousands of beery cellars and back rooms. In Wall Street, where even the important private clubs remained open all that night, the discussions may have been more technical and erudite, but they were no less noisy or confused or laced with anger and frustration.

So passed the hours of darkness.

It was a brief period of frenzied deceleration, a respite during which there was a mass frantic effort to slow down, to return to normal.

A half-hour or so after the sun rose bright and fiery, presaging a fairer and warmer day for New York and vicinity, tens of thousands of Wall Street–bound workers and investors arose with hurting heads, scratchy eyes or queasy stomachs, in some cases all three maladies, and commenced to do some second thinking about it all. They thought about it as they made their way to the world's financial capital from the great circumference of their commuting zone—from Danbury to Poughkeepsie to Far Hills to Staten Island to Huntington to Westport, and from all points inside the circle.

Beyond all doubt it had been the biggest market crash in history, either in this country or abroad, but what, after all, did it mean?

Was the nation en route to bankruptcy?

Was the economy ruined?

Would the factories and mills close down?

Would those consumers stop consuming? Would wheat and corn stop growing? Would the rich iron ore of the Mesabi disappear? Would the swift power-producing rivers of America stop flowing? Would the nation's deep-water ports silt in and become too shallow for navigation, simply because the market had crashed?

Maybe stock prices had been too high. Maybe the old formulas shouldn't have been junked and forgotten the way they had been, such as, for instance, a stock's price being roughly ten times its earnings per share. Maybe the overeager investors had, as Max Winkler observed, discounted not only the future but the hereafter.

Even so, what about the economy itself—that solid, rock-foundationed Coolidge (now Hoover) economy? The

Gross National Product for 1929 had already topped the $100 billion mark, setting an all-time record, and it was predicted that it might reach $105 billion before year's end. (It attained $103,800,000,000.)

Who or what could possibly hold back the automobile industry? The nation had, as W. C. Durant said, entered the automotive age on all cylinders. New highways, bridges and connecting roads were encouraging every American to own an automobile. Indeed, in three million American homes there were already two cars per family. Car sales for 1929 were the highest in history and there was every indication the record would be broken again for the 1930 models. (The 1929 record was not to be equaled until the mid-1950s.)

Many new industries were coming along, some of them only freshly formed but boding great promise. Aviation, for instance. Only two years before, Charles A. Lindbergh had flown his *Spirit of St. Louis* across the Atlantic to Paris in the world's first transoceanic solo flight.

Less than a month ago, Lieutenant James H. Doolittle, said to be the army's best pilot, had grumpily climbed into a biplane at Mitchell Field near Uniondale, just east of the village of Hempstead on Long Island, and had pulled a sight-obscuring piece of duck cloth over his head and successfully conducted the world's first "blind" all-instrument flight.

He had lifted the Consolidated plane from the Mitchell runway, circled in a fourteen-mile climbing arc over Long Island, and brought the craft back to a perfect three-point landing at Mitchell, right down the white stripe in the center of the runway, without once looking at sky, horizon, sea or land.

Watching from the ground was the sponsor of the event, Harry F. Guggenheim, president of the Guggenheim

Fund. (Fifteen years later he and his wife, Alicia Patter-
son, were to publish one of the nation's most successful
newspapers, *Newsday*, about a mile away from the site of
the flight, though by then it was to be renamed Roosevelt
Field as a result of Billy Mitchell's court martial.)

As an aviation enthusiast and pioneer, Guggenheim,
foundation-backed and copper-rich, had funded the experiment. He, probably more than any other, recognized
that the Doolittle flight opened wide the doors to year-
around all-weather commercial aviation. Lieutenant
Doolittle's uncharacteristic sullenness on that occasion
had resulted from Colonel Guggenheim's insistence that
a copilot accompany him. Doolittle had wanted to do it
solo, as mail pilots did. But the sponsor had been adamant
and the copilot had gone along, ready at any moment to
take over the controls. His services had been unneeded,
his reward an uneventful air ride.

Until Jimmy Doolittle flew "blind" for the first time, a
pilot who could not see the horizon could not fly, else he
would be lost. He also might be flying sidewise, losing his
"lift." He could not cope with fog, snow, heavy rain or low
clouds.

Now he could.

Doolittle carried three new instruments, all of them
still in use, all still basic and ranking in importance with
modern sophisticated instrumentation. They were: the
VRDF (the Visual Radio Direction Finder), which
showed him the direct path to the center strip of Mitchell's runway; an altimeter, which, being barometric and
adjustable, showed him his exact altitude at any height
from the ground; and a horizon indicator, which showed
him whether he was flying level or tilted.

Other gut-tightening jobs were to befall Jimmy Doolittle in years to come. He was destined to become a coura-

geous and inspiring general of the Air Corps in Europe
and North Africa during World War II, and then to go on
to lead the "impossible" first American air attack against
attackproof Tokyo.

The rich men of Wall Street had watched aviation bud-
ding on several branches, and the Guggenheim-Doolittle
achievement at Mitchell Field had attracted much notice.
Also investing heavily in experimental aircraft and instrumentation were the Vanderbilts, the Rockefellers, the
Schiffs, the Kahns and, among many other individuals,
Morgan partner Dwight W. Morrow, new father-in-law of
Charles A. Lindbergh, who had stated he never wanted to
become rich, but who, finding himself in that luckless
condition, was attracted first to aviation development,
then to international diplomacy.

Aviation was "hot." It was destined to grow and prosper,
decided many Friday-morning analysts the day after the
market crash. All, indeed, was not bleak.

Others thought of the movie industry. It had, in 1929,
just about completed the transition from silent to sound
films, and now almost every theater in the nation was
wired for sound. You could even discount the stars. Bing
Crosby, a special kind of person, was earning a million a
year, and many other stars were up in those stratospheric
brackets.

The "talkies" had brought sensationalism, sentiment
and sex to the screen and all were selling well. The last
was symbolized by a bouncy, shining girl named Clara
Bow, who was known as the "It Girl" because she had "it."
She possessed "it" in abundance, and much money
passed through many cashiers' cages when her films
were shown.

Her fashions in 1929 were like those of the late 1960s
and early 1970s. The skirts she wore were a cross between

the mini and the micro. The pantie girdle hadn't yet been popularized, however, and press agents let it be known that beneath the abbreviated garments, Miss Bow sometimes wore her teddy and sometimes not.

This intelligence sent many more millions of leering hopefuls, many in plastered-down hair, turtleneck sweaters and bellbottoms, through the box-office barriers and into the darkened theaters. They persisted in forgetting or ignoring the fact that czar Will Hays insisted that any little slips on Miss Bow's part be edited out. Many were.

(There was, in fact, a rather brisk business at that time in reprints of film clips taken from the cutting-room floor, involving, it was said, female stars. The reprints were reduced by one-half size from the 35-millimeter movie film and some say that those 16-millimeter reprints gave rise to the hand-cranked home movie projector.)

Playing in the downtown movie palaces on the day the market crashed were some examples of high box-office earners.

At the Roxy, Fox's film *They Had to See Paris,* with Will Rogers, was concluding its second week, and starting Friday was Lenore Ulric in *Frozen Justice,* with Louis Wolheim and Robert Frazer.

The Gold Diggers of Broadway, with a host of hit tunes scheduled to endure for two or three decades, was playing at the famed Winter Garden Theatre at Broadway and 50th Street.

At the Astor, right at Times Square, was M-G-M's all-talking *Hollywood Revue,* starring a newcomer to movies, one Jack Benny, who had clung to vaudeville to its last gasp and then made the transition to films just as sound techniques had been perfected sufficiently to take delighted advantage of his nasal Illinois drawl.

The George M. Cohan Theatre was featuring Lila Lee,

Jack Holt and Ralph Graves in *Flight.* At the Capitol, the envied and mysterious Marion Davies was drawing crowds with *Mariana.*

Warner Bros. Theatre at Broadway and 52nd had a smash hit: George Arliss in *Disraeli.* Right up there, too, with box-office returns was Richard Barthelmess in *Young Nowheres* at the Central.

The first of the new tear-jerkers, which were to be so popular in the early thirties, was playing in, of all places, the Gaiety Theatre—*Sunny Side Up,* starring Janet Gaynor and Charles Farrell.

Harold Lloyd had his first talkie in *Welcome Danger,* playing simultaneously at the Paramount, Rialto and Rivoli. Sharing the screen with him in a co-feature named *Why Bring That Up?* was a pair considered to be the funniest of men, two men who were so advanced in their professional planning that they had left successful careers in radio, then an aging toddler, to enter into the infant talking-picture business. They were Moran and Mack, the "Two Black Crows," who had set audience records in radio. Eddie Moran and Johnny Mack are credited with having set the stage for the vastly popular "Amos 'n' Andy Show" that followed them on the airwaves.

The biggest thing playing the neighborhoods was the incomparable *Madame X,* starring Ruth Chatterton, Lewis Stone and Raymond Hackett. It was playing at the giant Kings Theatre in Brooklyn and at the even larger, grander (world's largest Wurlitzer) Loew's Paradise in the Bronx, as well as in several other locations.

The boom in the moving-picture business coupled with the demise of vaudeville left a void on stage. Theater managers either had to plan for a co-feature, not always available, or had to fill in with acts that were getting worse as the headliners deserted the boards.

This gap in scheduling gave rise to the stage appearance of "Name Bands," due to reach their heyday in the decade and a half to follow.

On Thursday, October 24, 1929, Rudy Vallee and his Connecticut Yankees were on stage at Brooklyn's Paramount, and Horace Heidt and his Californians (later to become his Musical Knights) were at New York's Hippodrome at Sixth Avenue and 43rd Street.

Wall Street's movie-industry watchers noted with satisfaction that every show in town was a talkie of one kind or another. The transition was complete. A delightful innovation had been introduced with the *Gold Diggers of Broadway*. It was called Technicolor, and it had received tremendous critical acclaim.

Oh, yes, the Friday-morning reappraisers said, the movie industry was one of those that couldn't be stopped by a mere market collapse that was no doubt going to be of brief duration.

There were in Hollywood mighty big names who wouldn't be slowed by a faulty market. These stars had made highly successful pictures in 1929—people like Gary Cooper in *The Virginian,* Ronald Colman in *Bulldog Drummond,* Mary Pickford and her dashing husband Douglas Fairbanks in *The Taming of the Shrew,* to say nothing of Maurice Chevalier, Lon Chaney, Walter Huston, Loretta Young, Boris Karloff, Norma Shearer, William Powell, Tyrone Power, Gloria Swanson, Adolphe Menjou, Charles Boyer and others. These mighty performers couldn't be stopped.

Radio was another unbeatable industry, many thought, sharing the views of Eddie Gallant, Eddie Cantor, Fred Allen, Jimmy Durante and others who were burned in the crash.

More than ten million American homes were equipped to receive radio broadcasts in 1929. All-electric sets had replaced battery-operated ones in the appliance stores, and homes with alternating current could merely plug in their receivers. A smaller vacuum tube had been introduced; capacitors were replacing some condensers; modular circuitry had been installed in the better equipment; the superheterodyne speaker was bringing in static-free reception.

National Broadcasting Company owned ten stations and was affiliated with 221. Columbia Broadcasting Systems, only a year old, owned eight stations and was affiliated with 121; and with the inclusion of the independent stations around the country, more than one thousand broadcasting outlets were available, most of them prospering.

The Katz Agency had been formed to represent broadcasters to the advertisers, and now orderly advertising schedules were being set up, bringing increased prosperity to the industry. Time purchases (sales) in the radio industry by October had amounted to nearly $40 million and, said the analysts, no one could look at the industry without realizing it was destined to grow. (Sales would be more than a billion dollars annually before a quarter century had passed.)

Other Wall Street appraisers thought about the railroads and how the country was served now by the most modern, complex and sophisticated network of rails ever devised by man.

Self-generating electric locomotives were replacing some of the larger steam engines (forerunner of the diesel engines), but at Baldwin and American Locomotive Works bigger and more powerful steam engines were being produced to haul long trains at high speeds over greater distances.

Luxury passenger trains included hot showers, private dressing rooms and lavish appointments. Their dining cars served gourmet meals. Even "luxury freights" were being devised, those with high-speed delivery for perishables, or extra-strength springs for fragile loads. All-refrigerator freights had been put into service in some of the market garden areas.

The bounty of this "land of plenty," its agricultural wealth, was of great importance to Wall Street and to many of the corporations whose stocks were listed there, so that many assessors, that Friday morning, thought of the enormous harvest that had been completed only weeks before, bringing in a genuine bumper crop year.

The 355¼ million acres of land under cultivation in 1929 set a record (one that remains unchallenged). The cultivated land yielded 2½ billion bushels of corn and 825 million bushels of wheat.

The most significant thing about the harvest, though, was the fact that over eight hundred thousand mechanical tractors had been used in the process. The scientific age had arrived at the farms. It meant an infusion of prosperity for the tractor and farm-implement industry.

Wall Street's real concern was not with farms and farmers, but with food processors, packagers, distributors, canners and sellers. Thus the outlook was exceedingly bright.

On the farms, however, where the bumper yield had depressed wheat prices to less than a dollar a bushel and corn to something like eighty cents a bushel, the prospect was less hopeful. More than four thousand farms had gone under the bankruptcy auctioneer's hammer in 1929. Net income for a farm family was less than $950 a year, on a national average.

This, the Wall Streeters thought, if they thought of it at all, was of little concern in a consumer's economy. Farmers weren't consumers. If they were, they consumed what they, themselves, produced.

More sophisticated investors in Wall Street also looked to the banks as havens for solid investments in turbulent times. The public banks—those whose stock was available to the public—could be counted on to act as ruthlessly, and with as much self-serving profit-motivated concern, as they had when issuing call loans on vastly inflated stock during the just-ended boom. (And as they would during the boom of the late 1960s and early 1970s.)

There was little in the past performance record of the banking community to indicate that it would not continue to think first of profit before concerning itself with its responsibility either to the "little" customers or to the economic system as a whole.

Subsequent events in the Depression-ravaged 1930s verified that those who had counted on the bankers to be fishy-eyed and flint-hearted were well rewarded, for bank stocks bought after the crash held up remarkably well during the following decade of "bad years." Bankers performed profitably.

Utilities also presented a reassuring picture to those taking a second look the day after the market debacle. How could anyone stop the impending electrification of America? Certainly no market crash could hold back

such a strong demand. Behind the electrical utilities were
water utilities, gas utilities, and that new giant, American
Telephone and Telegraph Company, which, in 1928, had
earned a net profit of $143 million.

With an announced emphasis on "research," AT&T
was offering to do something that smart investors felt was
necessary and worthwhile. Operating a government-con-
trolled near monopoly, AT&T was bound to be embar-
rassed by its riches and castigated at the slightest letdown
in service, unless—unless it could lead in private industrial research. Since that was what AT&T was already
doing (as it would continue to do through the years), there
was no reason to believe it was not a surefire investment
for the future, the reasoning went.

And right here in New York, ground had already been
broken for the Chrysler Building and the Empire State
Building, one of which (it hadn't been determined yet)
would be the world's tallest. Rockefeller Center was being
planned for fourteen ultramodern office skyscrapers. The
papers had been signed.

Early Friday morning, New Yorkers and suburbanites
had rushed to get their morning newspapers. The first
thing most wanted to check was the identities of the suicides of the day before. There had been rumors of as
many as seventeen in the Wall Street district alone, and
certainly ambulance and police sirens had been heard to
wail throughout the area most of the day.

They looked through the papers, then looked again.

There had been none. There were to be a few suicides
here and there around the country in the months to come,
and the market crash would be blamed, but none was
directly attributable to the collapse of the stock market on

the day it occurred or in the weeks immediately afterward.

Strangely, however, the notion that it was almost dangerous to walk in the canyons of Wall Street because so many people were taking high dives off the tall skyscrapers, persists to this day, even in some accepted literature.

Thus it came about that on Friday the stock market held its own and displayed a mild rally. The recovery seemed to continue a bit during the brief session on Saturday morning. Wall Streeters went home to enjoy their abbreviated weekend fairly relaxed, and most of them were confident that the worst had been seen in the market.

Monday, however, a huge backlog of sell orders had accumulated, and prices trended downward all day. News of this hung gloomily over the entire land that night, and radio broadcasts played it up.

Fearing national despair, leaders in every position, from the White House to the college campus to the business office, rushed to microphones and press conferences to reassure the people, as shall be seen in the following chapter, but the memory of Black Thursday still lay on the land.

On Tuesday, October 29, even as the statements were being issued by the reassurers, sell orders tumbled into the market faster than it could absorb them. It did not come as a surprise as had the crash of Black Thursday, but the weight of the selling was so great that even the most optimistic leaders realized there was no way to bring meaningful support to the market.

Prices, already lowered by the tumultuous selling of the previous Wednesday and Thursday, tumbled through the

bottom as speculators, investors, amateurs and professionals, the experts and the clods alike, stood by and
watched helplessly.

When it was over at three o'clock that afternoon, the
greatest depression in mankind's recorded history was
under way.

CHAPTER 19

The Gray Days

The weekend after Black Thursday was a time for reassurances from high places. From the White House, Herbert Hoover issued a statement saying that "the fundamental business of the country—that is, production and distribution of commodities—is on a sound and prosperous basis." It was the hymn of the New Era, and it sounded good.

Charles M. Schwab, head of United States Steel, said he could see nothing to justify any "nervousness."

Eugene M. Stevens, president of the mighty Consolidated Illinois Bank, declared that the business situation looked good to him.

Some newspapers, appraising these statements, felt inspired to point out that the stock list was now loaded with bargains, and that the key to successful investing was to "buy them when they're low." By this time, however, millions of Americans realized that you never can tell, unless you're a genius or endowed with psychic powers, when a stock has reached its low. Once burned, twice warned, said Americans that weekend.

During the weekend only the top bosses of the brokerage houses had time to contemplate the statements or to speculate on their effectiveness. Other employees of Wall Street's firms were struggling to catch up on their paperwork, to match orders, to send stock to transfer, and to post their records in readiness for Monday's trading session.

Rumors swept the Street, and persisted, that some prominent brokerage houses were insolvent and would be ordered by the Exchange to suspend and liquidate. This led to a syndrome later to be called "back-room nervousness." Errors were compounded by clerks and workers because, already tired to the point of exhaustion, they became apprehensive and began to worry about their own futures.

For many the worry was justified, though they were not to know it for certain until a few more weeks had passed.

For those who had time to analyze the figures, there was one ominous note: Toward the close of the brief Saturday session, prices had begun to slide again and the entire list had seemed to turn soft. But hope was in the air. Recovery seemed certain. After so many years of boom, it all couldn't be ended so quickly.

Or could it? Monday might tell the story.

Monday dealt the first of two *coups de grâce.* The losses were earth-shaking. General Electric lost 47½, for instance, and Allied Chemical, 36.

The bankers' pool of Black Thursday, which might have been brought in again under the aegis of hero Richard Whitney, was too busy plugging "air holes" in the list, that is, buying stocks and setting a price for issues that were offered and for which there were no bids at all. Someone had to "make the market" (for there can be no sellers if there are no buyers), and it was deemed wisest to use the banks' "rescue money" to provide the stability of matching offers to sell with at least one bid to buy.

It was a defensive ploy, born of desperation. The bankers' consortium, instead of buying stocks to set higher
prices, was buying shares at lower prices solely to prevent
them from dropping through the floor.

Again the ticker dropped so far behind that it was useless as a measurement of what was happening. Liquidation orders poured in from all over the country—and the
rest of the world.

The closing gong sounded with a great backlog of unex-
ecuted orders.

Throughout that night Western Union and Postal Telegraph delivered tens of thousands of additional margin
calls and demands on loans.

Tuesday morning, October 29, the residue of unex-
ecuted orders was dwarfed by the sell orders of thousands
of additional early liquidators. With the striking of the
gong, the pentup storm burst and unleashed a fury never
witnessed before or since.

Blocks of stock in ten-thousand share lots, then in
twenty-thousand share lots were tossed into the market
with no thought of a sales price.

People who only a week before had described themselves as millionaires were wiped out in minutes as they
offered their securities "at market," and no market could
be made because no buyers could be found. With no way
to match up their orders with bids, prices cascaded. Every
specialist on the floor was surrounded by a small army of
brokers screaming and fighting to sell stock—to buyers
who were nonexistent.

Stark, frenzied panic took over and reigned.

A story recounted by Frederick Lewis Allen credits a
clever messenger clerk in the stock exchange with what
was probably the most noteworthy financial coup of that
dreadful day. The young man put in an order to buy

White Sewing Machine stock at $1 a share, and got it. Sewing Machine had been selling at 48 earlier in the year and on Monday had closed at 11¼. In the complete absence of other bids, he got his stock for a dollar a share.

By twelve, noon, more than eight million shares had been traded, most of them at losses to the sellers. In the next hour and a half, the volume had jumped to twelve million shares. At the close, the all-time record of 16,-410,030 shares had been set.

There had been a rally toward the end of the session, but it had no effect on the general attitude or on the broad market psychology. It was too late. It was too little. Gloom had taken over. It was to settle in and establish a long tenancy.

Losses for the day ranged to forty points, and were added atop the losses that had been accumulating since the preceding Wednesday.

At the most tumultuous point of the selling frenzy, at high noon, Richard Whitney called a secret meeting of the board of governors of the Exchange to discuss whether or not to suspend all trading. So incendiary was the state of panic, so deep the despair, that he asked the governors to meet, not in the president's office, but in the office of the head of the Stock Clearing Corporation, one story beneath the trading floor.

He requested the governors to appear in twos and threes, "strolling casually," so as not to arouse suspicions or excite fears. There were forty of them, plus at least two guests.

In an address made months later, Whitney said,

> The office they met in was never designed for large meetings of this sort, with the result that most of the governors were compelled to stand or to sit on tables. As the meeting progressed, panic was raging overhead on the Floor [the trading floor].

The feeling of those present was revealed by their habit of continually lighting cigarettes, taking a puff or two, putting them out, and lighting new ones—a practice which soon made the narrow room blue with smoke.

Whitney also reported that two Morgan partners who had been invited to the meeting were refused admittance by one of the guards who caught them trying to sneak into the stock-exchange building without attracting notice, per their instructions from Whitney. Ultimately they were rescued by a member of the governing committee who had been dispatched to see what was delaying their arrival.

The governors decided to keep the Exchange open for the balance of the day because they were fearful that to close it abruptly, would fuel rather than allay the panic.

They did make tentative plans for alternative measures, however, to be used the next day and subsequent days, if conditions warranted, and gave Whitney power to act on those alternatives on the exercise of his own judgment.

On Wednesday, October 30, more of the nation's business leaders stepped into the breach, trying desperately to reinforce confidence, to bulwark the bastions of the marketing system.

Some of the oil poured thus onto the troubled waters came from the largest and most prosperous refineries. Standard Oil Company of New Jersey announced that it would lend forty-three dollars a share, or eleven dollars above the market, to employees who had borrowed on their company's stock.

John D. Rockefeller, Sr., Standard Oil's principal stockholder, issued a rare statement:

"Believing that fundamental conditions of the country are sound and that there is nothing in the business situation to warrant the destruction of values that has taken place on the exchanges during the past week, my son and I have for some days been purchasing common stocks."

Assistant Secretary of Commerce Julius Klein issued a press statement, reading it over the air, that described the nation's economy in nothing short of exalted poetic terms. It all but guaranteed continued prosperity. Only four percent of the nation's families were affected by the crash, he said. He might have added that twice as many had never in their lives received as much as $1,000 a year to live on.

John J. Raskob, the Democratic national chairman, and the financial head of both Du Pont and General Motors, announced that stocks were at bargain prices and that he and his friends were buying.

On that same day, Wednesday, United States Steel declared an extra dividend.

Hardly was that news on the ticker than American Can Company not only declared an extra dividend but raised the regular dividend.

American Tobacco soon followed with the declaration of a two-dollar extra dividend not only on the common but also on the Common "B" shares.

The president of Sun Life Insurance Company of Canada announced that his company, one of the largest institutional purchasers of stocks, was not selling, but buying.

William Wrigley, Jr. announced that he, too, was buying stocks. You could make millions of dollars from nickel packs of gum, but the millions had to be invested in stocks.

In Chicago, Julius Rosenwald, chairman of Sears, Roebuck & Company, expressed himself so confident of the economy that he offered to cover the margin accounts of all employees.

Eddie Cantor, who had been wiped out by the Black Thursday fiasco, reported later that as soon as he heard of Rosenwald's offer he sent him off a telegram—collect. The wire, according to Eddie, read:

I UNDERSTAND YOU ARE PROTECTING YOUR EMPLOYEES ON THEIR MARGIN ACCOUNTS STOP. CAN YOU USE A BRIGHT INDUSTRIOUS BOY IN YOUR OFFICE STOP. I AM READY TO START AT THE BOTTOM STOP.

EDDIE CANTOR

Almost immediately, Eddie said, he received Mr. Rosenwald's reply:

PLEASE COME AT ONCE STOP. HAVE JOB WAITING FOR YOU STOP. WIRE TIME OF ARRIVAL AND WILL MEET YOU AT TRAIN STOP.

JULIUS ROSENWALD

The only reason he didn't accept the job offer, Eddie reported, was that he was unable to borrow the fare to take a train to Chicago.

(Cantor, who suffered extremely severe financial losses in the crash, became America's Number One comedy star by spoofing the crash and making fun, somewhat defiantly, of the subsequent Depression. He told of a man who had accumulated a huge estate to leave to his family, but because it shrank so much, he postponed dying until better times. In his own case, Cantor said, before the crash he had a million dollars, a house, three cars and four daughters. Now, he said, all he had left was *five* daughters.)

On Wednesday, in the wake of so many bullish comments, plus the irrefutable evidence of prosperity displayed by United States Steel, American Can and American Tobacco (irrefutable, if one overlooked the fact that the dividends were based on earnings enjoyed in the preceding quarter), prices rose on the stock exchange.

The whole stock structure looked firmer. By all assessments, Richard Whitney decided, the panic was ended and the time had come to relieve the pressure on the Exchange, whose employees had been working practically around the clock and had taken to sleeping in relays on cots in the corridors.

Thus, at 1:40 P.M., Whitney stepped to the rostrum and announced that the Exchange would not open until noon on Thursday, would be closed on Friday and Saturday, would open on Monday, and would close on Tuesday, Election Day.

He said it, then held his breath. Panic might ensue.

Instead there were cheers.

The crisis seemed to be past.

It was true, of course, that the worst of the stock-market panic was past, but the effects of the crash were merely beginning. The severity had not yet even been imagined.

Prices wobbled all over the field on Thursday, but managed, during the brief session, to extend the recovery somewhat. It was impossible, traders found, to reach a reasonably specific base for a true price. The big waves of sell orders had dried up, leaving stocks hanging in midair, so to speak, without a firm bid-price underpinning. For men who had just put in several years of judging the value of a stock on the basis of its previous quote, it was unnerving to trade in stocks on which there had been no recent quotes.

As brokers gradually caught up with their bookkeeping, following the long preelection weekend for resting up, great numbers of liquidations were forced on investors, large and small. House accounts were closed out.

Millionaires, whose very liquid assets had induced brokers to extend uncommonly high margin, were forced to surrender title to their properties, sell their cars and put their yachts on the block. In small homes throughout the nation, absolute bankruptcies were forced.

The same brokers who had, themselves, been spared bankruptcy by the kindness of the bankers on Thursday, October 24, and again on Tuesday, October 29, seemed to be powerless to forestall or to ease the demand on margin calls and other loans among their customers.

On Tuesday, the 29th, the corporations that had so willingly loaned money to the brokers through the banks in order to get their high call-money interest rates, demanded that the loans be called as the bottom dropped out of the market for the securities that collateralized the loans. Banks, faced with the prospect of either making good the loans themselves by picking them up, or forcing the brokers to liquidate, chose to protect the system by paying off the corporations and accepting the loans themselves.

On that one day, through their "good-faith response" with hard cash, the bankers paid the piper for the free and profitable dancing they had been doing in the call-money market for five years. It made many banks virtually insolvent until they, too, could rearrange their affairs. But it preserved the nation's economic system.

A dozen bank presidents and chairmen could have been sent to jail on October 29 for accepting loans from brokers without possessing adequate reserves to warrant such massive lending. In addition, of course, they could have been brought to task for issuing loans to such shaky credit risks. The brokers, if secured at all, were collateralized with stock that had not only dubious value but ever-changing value.

During the next week, in short sessions, stock prices created jerky chartlines as they sought new levels. Around the country, accounts continued to be liquidated in wholesale lots. Customers who a few weeks before had been planning European trips over the year-end holidays suddenly began to wonder whether they would have a roof over their heads by Christmas.

Each day the price level of stocks was just a bit lower than on preceding days.

Finally, on November 13, the bottom was reached and prices were at the lowest point for 1929.

No one knew that the downward thrust was ended, however, for confidence not only had flown from the stock market, but also seemed to have deserted the entire nation.

Gloom had settled over America in a polluting cloud-bank that stretched from border to border and sea to sea. Nowhere could be seen even the faintest light of hope.

The Big Bull Market was dead. Not a breath of life remained in it.

Three billion dollars' worth of brokers' loans had been liquidated.

Thousand of families were destitute.

Thousands more, by November 13, had joined the ranks of the unemployed.

Billions of dollars' worth of profits, as well as paper profits (as real as gold to most speculators), had disappeared in the auction marketplace.

Remaining as a residual memento was record-setting indebtedness, including hundreds of millions of dollars' worth of installment debt—monthly payments that had to be met by people who had lost their savings and who would soon lose their jobs and possibly their homes.

Suicides, rumored since October 24, became tragic facts.

Suddenly the newspapers were carrying sad, too brief stories of men who had found the situation intolerable and life unworthy of the struggle.

In New York, James J. Riordan, president of the New York County Trust Company, took his own life. In Chicago, Herman L. Felgenhauer, prominent grain broker, turned on the gas and let it put him to sleep forever. Philadelphia broker Frank S. Palfrey shot himself, as did his business neighbor and fellow broker, W. Paul Brown.

The market had crashed. All was in shambles and the perspective was bleak and desolate.

CHAPTER 20

Sing out the Old . . .

~~~~~~~~~~~~~~~~~~~~~~~~~~~~~~~~~~~~

In 1776, America had fired the shot heard round the world, and in October 1929 it produced the crash felt round the world. Forever after, the word *crash* was to mean 1929, and the year itself would stand as a symbol of something special to the nation and to the world, as do 1492, 1620 and 1914.

Though reverberations of the crash were felt as far away as Cairo or Shanghai, most Americans, in November and December of 1929, did not know exactly what had happened. Indeed, four decades later they still didn't know for certain what it was that had taken place, and why; great and learned economists were to discuss it for many years to come.

Immediate analysis of the disaster by New Era economist Irving Fisher of Yale produced a new expression that would roll off tongues in countless homes: "Mob Psychology." That was what hit the investors and speculators, he said. It remains a valid partial analysis of what actually happened, unchallenged through the years.

Later, many economists were to say that high production had outrun the needs and wants of the consumers, causing a backup, and for years thereafter people were to blame overproduction or underconsumption as the contributing cause of the crash.

Then, in the mid-1950s, Harvard professor J. Kenneth Galbraith, having subjected the crash to remorseless inspection through the microscope of time and distance, decided that overproduction was less the culprit than the fragility of the business structure. It was vulnerable to the kind of blow it received from Wall Street, he said.

Upon completion of the extensive research required for this book, the writer has reached the view that most of the analysts have been correct—as far as they went.

Too widely neglected has been consideration of the role of the Federal Reserve Board. It has played but a small part in the postmortems on the crash. I cannot dismiss the sincere hope that some serious student one day will delve into the musty files and records to assess the old postures and attitudes of the Reserve Board and to view them against the backdrop of the wild speculative orgy that was transforming Wall Street into a vast gambling casino. From a doctoral thesis, such a study could be expanded into a notable contribution as a book.

It was more or less an amateurish Reserve Board in those days, composed of political appointees and small-town bankers who relied overstrongly on the one solid professional in their number, Ben Strong, president of the New York Federal Reserve Bank. Not only was he an honest-to-goodness banker, a Morgan protégé, and exceedingly knowledgeable, but also he presided over the Reserve Bank that domiciled the New York Stock Exchange and the Curb Exchange, and had jurisdiction over the key banks that serviced the exchanges.

Ben Strong's preoccupation with the foreign economies, the British pound and reparations, seems to have diverted the attention of the Reserve Board from the festering problems on Wall Street until it was too late for the board to do much to help, even though, belatedly, it tried.

Thus it was culpable, in the view of this reporter.

Others must have thought so, too, for in the revisions of the Banking Law in the early 1930s, the Federal Reserve Board was given greater control over Wall Street and much more responsibility for the functions of the stock market and all of its working parts.

Snow fell early in many parts of America in 1929, staging the background for the blizzard of valueless securities that fluttered down on Wall Street. As the drab, chilled days dragged into December, the accumulating snow and descending securities blanketed and muted the end of the Roaring Twenties, one of the most spectacular decades in the history of the Republic, if not in the world.

Wall Street returned to work, but on a diminishing scale. Richard Whitney resumed his normal daily activities at the New York Stock Exchange, soon to be joined by the president, Edward H. H. Simmons, who returned from his Hawaii honeymoon after the cleanup squads had finished their work and a degree of tranquility had descended over Number Eleven Wall Street.

Chesterfield coats and homburgs reappeared along the street, and for awhile, at least, chauffeur-driven Rolls Royces, Cadillacs, Packards, Pierce-Arrows, Graham-Paiges and Franklins lined the curbs at five o'clock so that their owners might be conveyed in warmth and comfort to the illegal but not-too-illicit martinis awaiting them uptown in less-Spartan surroundings.

The cutback in back-room operations began almost immediately after the Thanksgiving holiday. Layoff bulletins were posted.

The volume of business, it was said, simply did not warrant so much help in the clerical departments of brokerage firms.

Help-wanted ads for commission salesmen increased, however. Brokers were seen to snap at each other over the piracy of a securities salesman with an impressive record.

Commission earnings began to drop and profits in the front offices of the brokerages showed a decline.

It snowed.

As the first flakes fell on Washington, Herbert Hoover convened a meeting of the nation's business and economic leaders for the purpose of dealing with the mounting crisis. Unemployment was beginning to capture headlines. It fretted the Chief.

Again, Mr. Hoover seemed to think that what was needed most was a simple explanation, a definition, of what had happened, though he implied the opposite as he opened the session.

"Words are not of great importance in times of economic disturbance," he said. "It is action that counts."

"IT IS ACTION THAT COUNTS!" was the headline that reached many of the newspapers, and those who read no further were cheered.

For those who required clarification, he summarized the market crash in this manner:

"The long upward trend of fundamental progress gave rise to overoptimism as to profits, which translated itself into a wave of uncontrolled speculation in securities, resulting in the diversion of capital from business to the stock market, and the inevitable crash."

This was as his engineer's mind saw it. It was logical. The diversion of capital from business left business weakened, vulnerable.

In 1955 that is how John Kenneth Galbraith also saw it —business was "fragile"; it was "vulnerable" because of thin capital.

It is amusing in the 1970s to remember that Galbraith

was called a liberal and a leftist, when what he was doing was following to a conclusion the logic started by Herbert Hoover. Conversely, it is amusing to consider that history records Hoover as an archconservative, while Galbraith is considered a progressive. There must be a lesson in there somewhere for people who have a penchant for labeling thinkers because of their thoughts.

Henry Ford, who attended the conference at the White House, agreed with the President, basically, but his summary was pointedly caustic: The collapse of the market, he said, was "due to a serious withdrawal of brains from business."

The notion lingers that not only were President Hoover and Mr. Galbraith correct, but so was Mr. Ford.

As far as Mr. Ford's disappointment is concerned, it must be remembered that it was a time of Big Men—men of great stature and recognized individuality. The times may suddenly have become too big for the men caught up in them. Perhaps, by the time the speculative juggernaut got rolling, no one industrialist or single group of business leaders could have done much to stop it.

Ford was accustomed to putting his money where his mouth was. He backed his statement with the recommendation that "prices be reduced to the level of actual value," and that wages be increased. America would soon recover from the economic doldrums, he said, if this formula were invoked, for people would buy more goods and services and they would have more money to buy them with.

Lacking was a definition of "actual value." Ford had meant that everyone would produce at cost, distribute at cost and sell at cost. The members of the "economy," however, purported to be confused. They asked who was to go without profit—the prime producer? the manufacturer?

the distributor? the wholesaler? the retailer? Apparently the structure was too complex for the business minds.

Undaunted, and believing himself confirmed in his assessment of business brains, Ford went ahead, anyway, and increased wages. He also dropped prices on his cars, though his new Model A was exceedingly popular and would likely have sold at a higher price than he put on it.

Other industrial leaders, put in the spot where they had to do *something*, announced that they would not cut wages, nor would they increase prices on anything, if unions would agree to cooperate and refrain from making new demands. This "sacrifice" was accepted graciously by the White House, though it would have been interesting to hear what Henry Ford had to say about it in private.

Soon it became apparent why Mr. Hoover was being most agreeable in his relationships with the industrialists.

The President had plans. He intended to ask for a special emergency fund to be raised from the private sector of the economy. This, the President reasoned, would eliminate the need for taxing the people to help themselves. The private sector of the economy meant—Big Business.

Thus it was that thirty-five public utility officials, led by Owen D. Young, board chairman of General Electric, pledged almost two billion dollars to the President's program for stimulating industrial activity aimed, primarily, at expansion and new construction. The Chief explained that in his opinion, prosperity started with capital investment (or expansion) and resulted in higher employment and higher wages, and this, in turn, caused greater consumption, which, in the end, utilized the facilities that were built with the capital infusion or expansion. He called it the trickle system. "Trickling" came back to plague him three years later in the steamroller campaign of Franklin D. Roosevelt for the Presidency.

Owen Young was to go on to a major role as perhaps the most helpful American of the time, working closely with Hoover during the next three years in raising many billions for the relief and rehabilitation of those affected by the Depression.

He headed the Committee on Mobilization of Relief Resources of the President's Organization for Unemployment Relief, and in October and November of 1931 he activated the greatest charitable event in modern history.

In so doing, he brought about the greatest collaboration of the mass communications media, including radio and movies, ever achieved, before or since.

The idea was to have everyone donate small amounts of money—pennies, nickels, dimes—to be pooled to help feed and clothe the destitute during the winter months. In New York City alone, $1,300,000 was collected in house-to-house calls. People pledged a dime a week for twenty weeks, and faithful collectors plodded their rounds for five months, making sure pledges were kept.

Owen Young supervised the kickoff with a gigantic rally at Madison Square Garden, addressed by the most impressive leaders of the times. Movie houses, under the direction of Hollywood czar Will Hayes, proclaimed National Motion-Picture Week, when every dime above costs was turned over to the fund. Newspapers promoted the movies and the corollary drives with black-headlined campaigns. Former President Coolidge came off his retirement farm with a letter to be read over the radio. J. P. Morgan, heretofore the most publicity-shy of the prominent Americans, made a personal appeal for gifts over a nationwide network of radio stations.

In time, of course, the private money gave out, and the states and cities had to take care of the needy. Then, within a year, states found themselves broke and many cities were bankrupt, or nearly so; only the federal government remained as a barrier to imminent wide-scale starvation in the land.

Private funds, in time, simply could not cope with a situation of such magnitude. But while they could, Owen Young dug them out and channeled them in the proper avenues.

Shortly after the crash, Mr. Hoover started to get government involved in the problem.

Just after his meeting with the industrialists, Mr. Hoover sent telegrams to the governors of all states urging them to inaugurate "energetic yet prudent" public-works programs to relieve unemployment. As the last of the prudent (many called him overprudent) money managers in the White House, Hoover arranged to keep in touch with these programs via monthly report and cautious use of the long-distance telephone.

One day, a week or so before Christmas, President Hoover heard some singing on Pennsylvania Avenue. Peering out the window at what he thought at first were carolers, he saw three dozen young men and women carrying placards. The song they were singing was not a yuletide hymn; it was the Communist's "Internationale."

Their signs bore no Christmas message. They proclaimed:

"HOOVER WARS ON WORKERS"

"DOWN WITH HOOVER"

"HOOVER BUSINESS CONFERENCE IS A DECLARATION OF WAR ON THE WORKING MASSES"

The young people were from Pennsylvania, some from the industrial areas, some from the coal fields. District police led them off to the stationhouse, but when Hoover heard that they had been arrested, he requested their release, saying that he did not believe that their "discourtesy seriously injured the Republic."

In December, another Communist issued a statement for the world. He was Joseph V. Stalin, dictator of Russia.

Stalin had been gravely ill, a fact that had been concealed from his people, but as the year waned he returned to the Kremlin to vast ovations. He was well pleased with himself, for despite his incapacitation he had caused to be banished from Russia his old enemy, Leon Trotsky, and had caused a purge of the few lingering Trotskyites. As he beheld the snowy plains beyond Moscow from the towers of the Kremlin, the world looked good to him.

It looked particularly good to him as he gazed westward and contemplated the devastation left in the wake of the Great Market Crash in America. "It is a year of Mighty Change," Stalin declared.

"We are attacking capitalism all along the line and are defeating it," he went on. "Without foreign capital we are accomplishing the unprecedented feat of building up heavy industry in a backward country.

"When we have industrialized the Soviet Union and set the peasants to driving tractors, we shall see which country can be called backward and which the vanguard of human progress. . . ."

Stalin had cause to be proud. Huge industrial complexes had been built and there was concentrated activity at such centers as Moscow, Vladivostok, Sevastopol, Leningrad and Stalingrad. Big hydroelectric systems had been built or were under way. A merchant marine was abuilding as well as a navy.

It had been achieved, as Wall Street was well aware, with internal capital only. Bankers at that time were beginning to look to the "New Russia" as a potential for good investments, but the Russians didn't want outside capital, and wouldn't, in fact, until World War II, when Stalin discovered the need for importing it.

Even as Stalin chortled over America's capitalistic market crash, something strange was happening. Recovery seemed to be on the way. As the year drew toward its close, activity picked up all over the country. Mills went back to full schedules. Holiday shoppers thronged the main streets of most cities and retailers chalked up the highest Christmas sales volume on record.

Many new radio sets were sold—the Fada, the American Bosch, the Murad, the Silver-Marshall, the Stromberg-Carlson, the Atwater Kent, the Majestic, the Philco, the Sparton, the General Electric, the R.C.A. Victor, the Zenith.

The stock market, catching a second breath, tacked twenty points onto the leading averages between November 13's low and Christmas.

Technologically America still led the world, as confirmed by the fact that a couple of weeks before the holiday, Commodore Richard E. Byrd and his crew of three had flown the trimotored plane *Floyd Bennett* over the exact South Pole, claiming it and its continental territory in the name of the United States.

Along their once-again sunny streets, Americans hummed or sang a gay and stimulating new song: "Happy Days Are Here Again!"*

November had been drab. December days were bright, crisp, gay, hopeful. The holiday loomed. So did the challenging third decade of the twentieth century. New Era —pshaw! It was only just beginning!

*"Happy Days Are Here Again!" from the film, *Chasing Rainbows,* words by Jack Yellen, music by Milton Ager. Copyright 1929 by Ager, Yellen & Bornstein, Inc.

There wasn't much profit-taking in the stock market as
the year drew to its close, nor was there much tax-selling.
Bigger market investors had sustained sufficient losses
between October 23 and November 13 to make adequate
adjustments in their tax returns. Those with incomes under $25,000 didn't have to worry about paying much, any-
way, under the mild regulations.

At the stock exchange, a fresh painting program for the
halls and corridors was being completed and the entire
building seemed brighter and abuzz with efficient business.

Richard Whitney, the hero of Black Thursday, found
himself much sought after as a public speaker, but because of the heavy year-end schedule and workload, he
postponed many of the speaking engagements until after
the New Year. He found himself "booked" right up
through March—destined to be a horribly significant
month in his life.

(It wasn't until nine years had passed, until March
1938, that Whitney would be brought to the bar for numerous irregularities. He was accused of embezzlement,
misappropriation of customers' funds and securities, and
other offenses. After a short but spectacular trial, prose-
cuted by Thomas E. Dewey, he was sentenced to from five
to ten years in Sing Sing Prison.

Among other things, he was accused of using for his
own or his firm's purposes over a million dollars' worth
of bonds and cash of the Stock Exchange Gratuity Fund,
which was a special fund set aside for the welfare of
wives and families of the members of the Exchange, and
of which he served as trustee.

He returned the bonds and cash by borrowing the
money from J. P. Morgan and Company, secured by his
brother George, a Morgan partner, who played a major

role in patiently and uncomplainingly bailing his brother
out of seemingly innumerable financial scrapes, many of
them coming when he was president of the New York
Stock Exchange.

At the time of his downfall in March 1938, Richard
Whitney had compiled an impressive record as a borrower in the circles of high finance. Since Thanksgiving
1937, a scant four months, he had negotiated 111 loans
totaling $27 million! In addition he owed, unsecured,
nearly $3 million to his brother George, $474,000 to J. P.
Morgan and Company and a little less than a million
dollars to others.

His financial downfall was occasioned by his unsuc-
cessful efforts to bail out a liquor company that he owned
and controlled—Distilled Liquors Corporation, which
owned a half-million gallons of spirits never destined to
become very popular, "Jersey Lightning," or applejack,
made from apple cider.

At Sing Sing, Dick Whitney was hailed as a model pris-
oner, played a good game of baseball [surprising, for a
man of fifty] and was accorded the respect of being called
"Mr. Whitney" by all of his fellow convicts and even by
the toughest prison guards. He was paroled on the earliest
possible date, August 1941.

During his incarceration, his brother George paid off
every debt that Richard Whitney owed. Richard returned
to a quiet and highly respectable life in New Jersey. His
wife, Gertrude Sheldon Whitney, had stuck by him and
was awaiting him when he came home.)

The year and the decade wore to their close amidst
great hustle and bustle, to all appearances en route to a
rapid return of prosperity. The stock market was still far
below the September highs, of course, but it seemed to be
undergoing a wholesome convalescence.

In December, the New York State Tax Department in
Albany, catching up on its figuring, announced that because of the wild selling on the stock exchanges in October, the state netted $4,884,427 for the month from its
two-cents-per-share tax on stock sales.

Reflecting the attitude and atmosphere of the times,
Time magazine said that the money thus could be used to
build better roads and broader bridges to bear the increasing traffic of U.S. prosperity.

That this was the calm eye of the storm, no one even
suspected. None guessed that the new decade, though
wildly hailed, would be, like the decade of the sixties,
thirty years later, shelved into history as one of the more
unpleasant periods in mankind's progress.

Americans danced and sang and shopped their way
toward the year's end, and even those who had been
wiped out by the crash came to accept their fate and to
talk about making a comeback. Jobs were tightening up
and unemployment was mounting, it was true, but for the
ones willing to look around and search just a little bit
harder, there was work to be found and there were wages
to be earned.

The shadows of gloom were being contained in their
corners.

Around Wall Street there were "leaks" about corporate
earnings, and from every indication, it seemed that
profits for 1929 were going to break all records. (They
did.) General Motors' profits would be more than a *billion
dollars,* the rumors said. (They were.)

In Washington it was announced that there was a federal budgetary surplus of $700,000,000.

Secretary of the Treasury Andrew Mellon recom-
mended an income-tax reduction.

Because of the market crash, liquor prices tumbled,

making life pleasanter for imbibers. It cost only about $10 for a bottle of Scotch that had been only slightly cut with water. Genuine French or German champagne in a speakeasy was down to only $75 a bottle from its previous price of $100.

Many pressing things occupied the ladies of the land.

The mini skirt had given way to the midi. Lengths fell to about two inches below the knee, and last year's dresses, which had exposed the rolled stocking and bare thigh, now had to be discarded. The new silhouette was different, too, showing hips *and* busts. Then there was a new bridge game that seemed to have been mastered by a husband-and-wife team—the Eli Culbertsons of Chicago—and it was becoming popular throughout the country. It was called the "forcing system."

Newspaper forecasts for 1930 were bright. Universally, good times, sans speculative inflation, were predicted.

On the last trading day of the year, celebrating at the New York Stock Exchange started at 1:30, an hour and a half before closing, with the arrival of the 396th Infantry Band, a smart squad of thirty Negro musicians.

With trading going on at some posts, confetti began to shower over the trading floor. Noisemakers were handed out. Singing erupted at post after post. Champagne, Scotch, rye and even some Jersey Lightning mysteriously sprang into existence in various spots around the trading floor.

A little ceremony was held when one trader, to the chanting and jeering of many, burned a copy of the newspaper carrying the account of Black Thursday and its 16-million share day. It was a symbolic gesture that was much appreciated by the traders.

The news tickers also carried a symbolic story. Bankruptcy was filed that day by the Stutz Motor Car Company, manufacturers of the Stutz Bearcats that had carried the flappers, the gin flasks, the porkpie-hatted, raccoon-coated funsters of the Roaring Twenties to their pranks and frolics.

At precisely 3:00, the Exchange's president, Edward H. H. Simmons, himself, sounded the gong.

Immediately, a great cheer broke out, a roar that could be heard as far away as Broadway.

Up by Trinity Church, passersby thought it sounded just as loud as the noise that emanated from the Exchange on Black Thursday, October 24, 1929.

Bibliography

Allen, Frederick Lewis. *Only Yesterday.* New York: Harper Brothers, 1931.

Angoff, Charles. *The Tone of the Twenties.* South Brunswick, N.J.: A. S. Barnes & Company, Inc., 1966.

Bird, Caroline. *The Invisible Scar.* New York: David McKay, 1967.

Boardman, Fon W., Jr. *America and the Jazz Age.* New York: Henry Z. Walck, Inc., 1968.

Brooks, John. *Once in Golconda.* New York: Harper & Row, 1969.

Burton, Theodore. *Crises and Depressions.* New York: D. Appleton & Company, 1931.

Cantor, Eddie. *Caught Short.* New York: Simon & Schuster, Inc., 1929.

———. *Yoo-Hoo Prosperity.* New York: Simon & Schuster, Inc., 1931.

Caroso, Vincent P. *Investment Banking in America.* Cambridge, Mass.: Harvard University Press, 1970.

Colvin, Fred H., and Duffin, D. J. *Sixty Years with Men and Machines.* New York: Whittlesly House, McGraw-Hill, Inc., 1947.

Daniels, Jonathan. *The Time Between the Wars.* New York: Doubleday & Company, Inc., 1966.

Dulles, Foster Rhea. *The Twentieth Century American.* Boston: Houghton Mifflin Company, 1945.

Ford, Corey. *Time of Laughter.* Boston: Little, Brown and Company, 1967.

Mattfeld, Julius. *Variety Music Cavalcade.* Englewood Cliffs, N.J.: Prentice-Hall, 1966.

Morris, Joe Alex. *What a Year!* New York: Harper & Brothers, 1956.

Neill, Humphrey B. *Inside Story of the New York Stock Exchange.* New York: B. C. Forbes & Sons, 1950.

Nevins, Allan, and Hill, Frank Ernest. *Ford—Expansion and Challenge.* New York: Charles Scribner's Sons, 1957.

Paradis, Adrian A. *The Hungry Years.* Philadelphia: Chilton Book Company, 1967.

Phillips, Cabell. *From Crash to Blitz.* New York: The Macmillan Company, 1969.

Ross, Walter S. *The Last Hero: Charles A. Lindbergh.* New York: Harper & Row, 1964.

Sloan, Alfred P., Jr. *My Years with General Motors.* New York: Doubleday & Company, Inc., 1964.

Slosson, Preston W. *The Great Crusade.* New York: The Macmillan Company, 1969.

Snowman, Daniel. *America Since 1920.* New York: Harper & Row, 1968.

Stevenson, Elizabeth. *Babbitts and Bohemians.* New York: The Macmillan Company, 1967.

Stigler, George J. *Essays in the History of Economics.* Chicago: University of Chicago Press, 1965.

Sullivan, Mark. *Our Times VI (The Twenties).* New York: Charles Scribner's Sons, 1935.

Tanner, Louise. *All the Things We Were.* New York: Doubleday & Company, Inc., 1968.

This Fabulous Century. By the editors of *Time* and *Life.* New York: Time, Inc., 1969.

Time Capsule, 1927; Time Capsule 1928; Time Capsule, 1929. By the editors of *Time.* New York: Time, Inc.

Tugendhat, Christopher. *Oil, the Biggest Business.* New York: G. P. Putnam's Sons, 1968.

MAGAZINES

Liberty, issues of 1929.

Literary Digest, issues of 1929.

World's Work, issues of 1929. New York: Doubleday Doran & Company.

NEWSPAPERS

Hartford Courant, Hartford, Conn.

New York Herald Tribune, New York, N.Y.

New York Post, New York, N.Y.

New York Times, New York, N.Y.

Providence Journal and the *Evening Bulletin,* Providence, R.I.

Springfield Republican, Springfield, Mass.

Winsted Evening Citizen, Winsted, Conn.

Worcester Telegram and the *Evening Gazette,* Worcester, Mass.

Index